By the same author:

Kate Gallagher and the Bexus Prophecy
Kate Gallagher and the Hornshurst Talisman

Kate Gallagher AND THE ZIMMERMANITE QUEST

ALAN CUMMING

PARTRIDGE
A Penguin Random House Company

To order additional copies of this book, contact
Toll Free 800 101 2657 (Singapore)
Toll Free 1 800 81 7340 (Malaysia)
orders.singapore@partridgepublishing.com

www.partridgepublishing.com/singapore

For Sue

CONTENTS

PROLOGUE

Marcus Augustus Zimmerman's hands were shaking as he dropped his hammer and bent to pick up the chunk of rock he'd chipped from the overhanging pipe of igneous rock jutting out from the wall of the canyon. Zimmerman had spotted something in the rock formation that his geologist eye was trained to notice. The rock was streaked a darker grey as if it were permanently damp—impossible out here in the famed, parched Anakie Sapphire fields, located in the barren northeast hinterland of Queensland, Australia.

The rock had been buried deep within the earth's crust and subjected to enormous forces of change by the intense heat and pressure at that sort of depth. Gradually, over millions of years, the magma had cooled slowly and crystals had begun to form, caused by minerals dissolved in water becoming trapped within the surrounding rock. This is nothing unusual, it's the way quartz is formed: long and angular, with sharply defined edges, cloudy white, or pink, arrayed like pipes on a miniature pipe organ.

Except, quartz wouldn't have caused Zimmerman's hands to tremble. He could flog off large crystals of the stuff to rock shops and novelty stores, which catered to the needs of New Agers along with cut geodes containing amethysts, but the money he made from these sales barely dented his expenses. Quartz was the mineral form of the Earth's discarded trash.

Corundum was, however, a different story. Formed primarily from aluminium oxide, its peculiar molecular structure makes it the second-hardest natural substance on earth after diamond. As the surrounding rock forms slowly metamorphose, other impurities gather, and it is these impurities that give the corundum minerals their characteristic colours: from violet and deep indigo through the colours of the rainbow to the orange and red ends of the colour spectrum. Less common are the greys and browns, but the rarest of them all is black. Another name for red corundum is ruby; all other colours are called sapphires.

Another feature of sapphires is asterism, also called the star effect. This is due to microscopic inclusions of titanium dioxide, folded in such a way that light passing through a cut stone will be reflected back in a star pattern with six radiating arms. Asterism within a sapphire gem will vastly increase its value to buyers and collectors, movie stars and spouses of powerful businessmen.

Given these criteria, it stands to reason that the most valuable sapphire would be a large, black, star-producing sapphire. Black sapphires were unknown before 1938 until a young boy named Roy Spencer found one by accident when he was messing about in his father's claim within the Anakie fields. It was discarded by his father and used to prop open the front door of the house so that the fickle breeze could blow through when it made an occasional appearance. It remained a doorstop until Roy's miner father learned that sapphires could exist in black form, and he took a closer interest in it. It weighed an immense 1156 carats, and despite its star-reflecting qualities being unknown, Mr Spencer was able to sell it in 1947 for the princely sum of $18,000. An American jeweller named Harry Kazangian had heard rumours about the stone from his home in Los Angeles, and he flew out to Australia to negotiate the deal himself.

Kazangian knew his precious stones. After he'd returned to Los Angeles, he took a calculated gamble and cut away more than a third of the stone to reveal the brilliant star radiating out of the carved dome. By 1949, its value was estimated at more than one million dollars.

Around the same time, the Kazangian family jewellery business expanded to the point where they became one of the world's leading gemstone dealers, and Harry attributed all the good fortune to his possession of the black sapphire. It remained within the family for a further fifty-three years until an offer too good to refuse was made and the gem changed hands to an anonymous buyer for a reputed one hundred million dollars. The gem became known as the Black Star of Queensland, and since its discovery in 1938, it has continued to attract operators, both large and small, to the area in search of another fabled find.

Operators like Marcus Zimmerman, an unemployed geologist fresh from the opal mines. There was money to be had in the mining boom, and Marcus had received his fair share of it through a generous contract package rolled over for nearly a decade. He owned a beach house on the Gold Coast, an apartment in Denver, Colorado, and a small studio apartment in New York City, though nothing in Canada, the country of his birth. He wasn't married, although he could count a string of ex-girlfriends on the fingers of both hands and a few extra toes. He was footloose and free, and he was more than happy with that.

He was a member of that rare breed of geologists who were not content with analysing dirt and rock for others to exploit. His heroes were unsung outside of the cloistered world of geology: men like the mineralogist Pavel Jeremejev who discovered the precious pale-coloured Jeremejevite in 1883, now fetching two thousand dollars per carat; or Arthur C.D. Pain, after whom Painite was named. Painite was once thought to be the world's rarest mineral, and was currently fetching close to sixty thousand dollars per carat. He wanted to be one of heralded few with his name in lights; wanted to have a rare, new mineral species named after him—Zimmermanite had the right ring to it, he thought.

The problem was, Zimmermanite was never going to be discovered while he worked for a company. Anything he found belonged to them. So Marcus packed his bags, handed in his notice, applied for an exploration licence with the Department of Mines and Energy, and set off for the Anakie Sapphire fields with all his worldly goods and a few tools of the trade stored in the back of his Toyota Hilux 4x4.

In the three months he'd been working the site, he'd found a steady supply of small, aqua-coloured sapphires, particularly among the boulders along the alluvial beds of dried-out rivers. He wasn't going to be rich or famous with those, but the good news was that they covered his cost of living. He made the journey twice a month into the town of Emerald, where he was able to convert his stones into cash and buy in more supplies.

The blue sapphires were almost incidental. The elusive main prize was uppermost in his mind, and this drove him to search for detail among the rock strata that he might otherwise overlook on a salary.

The extruded pillar caught his eye since it closely resembled an old igneous lava pipe that had finally been exposed through weathering. It was one-of-a-kind, surrounded by layers of folded sedimentary rock. The column looked as if it had been rapidly squeezed up through the crumbling sediment like a giant pimple. Generally, extrusive rocks do not hold large crystals, but this one called for closer investigation.

Zimmerman had hammered away at the column with no reward for his effort until he spied the small patch of damp-looking rock almost hidden in shadow. Its surface was streaked, and this was usually a surface sign that crystallization had occurred somewhere inside. It also swelled outwards slightly; another good sign.

He slipped a stone chisel from his belt, one with a wide, flat blade and angled the cutting edge just above the bulge. He drew his club hammer back and brought it swinging down in a swift arc. There was a hollow, metallic *clang!* immediately followed by a sharp crack as the skull-sized rock fragment sheared and rolled in the red dust at his feet.

Zimmerman realised he was staring down at a single, black crystal of corundum tightly encased within a chunk of bedrock. This was what caused his hands to shake uncontrollably. He picked up the rock, but then sank to the ground, and slumped against the canyon wall in the shadow of the overhanging pillar, not trusting his legs to hold his own weight.

Marcus couldn't believe what he was holding. The stone gleamed back at him, crisp and black like the surface of a deep, dark pool, exposed to light for the exact first time in the billion or so years it had taken to form. He estimated its size to be at least eighteen hundred carats, perhaps as high as two thousand, which would make the Black Sapphire of Queensland seem puny by comparison. He still hadn't discovered Zimmermanite, but this was going to be one of *the* historic geological finds of the twenty-first century.

He tilted his head back and laughed, all the while embracing the rock tightly against his chest. He'd just won the lottery!

"Hahahahahahahahahaha!" The sound echoed off the opposite wall and reverberated around him, and he laughed even harder.

Marcus had discovered the single, largest source of black sapphire hidden within the rock, but much of the rest of the stone column was riddled with veins of the mineral; stubby, short crystals or slippery sheets that were a millimetre or so thick. They were encased by the rock, but acted like little fault lines, slippery gaps where the sections of rock could slide past each other.

When Marcus had slammed the hammer down on the blunt end of the chisel, enough of the shock of the impact passed through the rock, using the mineral veins as an alternate route through the dense Andesite. The net effect was to weaken the whole structure so that it was like wet paste trying to hold a heavy sheet of wallpaper that had begun to peel away from the wall. Collapse was inevitable; it was simply a question of when.

A slab the size of a small horse dropped without warning and landed on top of Zimmerman's outstretched legs. It crushed them to pulp and pinned him where he sat. His laughter was transformed into a high-pitched scream, and he promptly passed out from the pain.

He continued to pass in and out of consciousness for some hours until he lost all feeling in his legs and the intensity of the pain subsided. Once he stabilised, he had to confront the odds against surviving. He recalled the story of Aron Ralston, the American climber trapped in a slot canyon in Utah, who had to amputate his right arm using a dull, two-inch knife blade in order to escape and live to tell the tale.

The best he could do was to try and slice through both thighs using his hammer and stone chisel, and he knew for certain he wasn't up for that. He wept throughout the night.

It was a combination of shock and dehydration that killed him within twenty-four hours Towards the very end, he hallucinated, and the black crystal rose out of the rock in the shape of a dark demon and hovered above him, leering down until his chest rattled once and refused to rise again.

Zimmerman's mouth was dry, and his tongue felt like sandpaper as it rolled around inside his mouth. His eyelids were crusted and gummed together, and his head spun and throbbed in the usual way after he'd consumed far too much gin. He sat up, resting his head in one hand while he rubbed the grit away from his eyes with the other.

He discovered to his surprise that he was sitting stark naked in a grassy field. He was confused and embarrassed. Where was he, and how did he get here? As the cobwebs slowly cleared from his addled brain, he was horrified to discover that his body glowed with a soft, green aura a couple of inches thick that enveloped him like a layer of fog.

He tried to stand, but an immediate, sharp pain shot through both legs, and he rolled back on the grass and pulled his thighs up to his chest. He lay in the grass, panting and staring up at the clear morning sky until the pain passed and he could struggle into the sitting position once again.

He heard a sudden noise and spun his head to the left. He saw a trio of red deer, munching the grass while staring back at him. At least, they looked like deer, except they all had a single horn, maybe a foot and a half long, protruding from their heads where the antlers ought to be. He immediately thought: *Unicorn!* but just as quickly dismissed the idea, since unicorns were mythical creatures—he remembered that much.

Two of the animals were large and the coats of all three were thick with glossy, long red hair, golden-tipped at the end. The fur gleamed, backlit by the sun, and rippled like wind through a wheat field whenever buzzing insects disturbed the animals. The third was smaller, younger, and more nervous of Zimmerman's head poking through the tall grass.

The two adults each took a protective step forward and continued to stare back at Zimmerman. Neither of them seemed afraid of him, which led him to believe they were domesticated animals. They certainly posed no threat to him.

He tried to stand again. His legs ached as if they had been run through with red-hot needles. He bent and massaged them, hoping to revive his circulation and relieve the stinging sensation. This seemed to work.

He took a couple of tentative steps towards the watching animals, and saw their short tails stand erect in alarm.

"Oi! I wouldn't do that if I were you!"

Two men, one much older than the other, came striding through the grass towards him, each carrying some kind of harness in his hands. Zimmerman dropped to his knees, and his hands flew down to cover himself.

"They're not much used to strangers," said the older man as they approached. He spoke in the kind of lilting, difficult-to-understand dialect of a Cornish farmer, and smiled broadly as he noticed Zimmerman's obvious discomfort.

"Just arrived, have we?" he asked, but before Marcus could say anything, he had turned to the younger man and said, "Guillaume, nip back to the house and bring back some clothes for this 'ere gentleman."

The younger man barely suppressed his own smile as he turned and jogged back through the field in the direction he'd just come.

"You're lucky you didn't spook them, lad," said the farmer, nodding towards the animals still bunched tightly together. "Them there horns ain't just for decoration."

Zimmerman was astounded. The man appeared to be oblivious to the fact that he was naked. He'd bent and plucked a grass stem and was chewing it thoughtfully as he watched the animals.

"Wha—what are they?" Zimmerman stammered.

"They're *Hon'chai,* is what they are. Beau'iful specimens too, I might add. You can always tell by looking at their coats."

"Where am I? What happened to me? How did I get here?"

The farmer tore his gaze from his animals and grinned at Zimmerman. He pulled the grass stem from between his teeth and held it like a pipe as he answered.

"You're dead, is what you are, son. You're the second one we've come across this week."

Zimmerman felt as if he'd just been slugged with a shovel, and his head swam with a mass of swirling, dark images. He had vague recollections of holding a piece of rock in his hands, of hearing a dull, sickly thump of something falling, of intense pain and panic. Fragments of memory were being stitched together slowly, and Zimmerman suddenly felt a sense of dread settle about him.

"*Dead?* What do you mean—dead? I . . . uh . . ."

"You're not on Earth any more, laddie. Welcome to Bexus." The farmer raised one arm and gestured as if to say: look about you; it's not such a crummy place.

More memories coalesced.

"I remember . . . I remember being trapped by falling rock. I couldn't move."

"Well, since you've turned up here, quite obviously, you didn't make it."

"I still don't understand."

"You're nothing more than a ball of energy, son. Don't ask me how it all works. This is where we end up, is all." The farmer shrugged and began chewing on his stalk again.

"How did you get here?" Zimmerman asked.

The farmer looked a little sheepish. "I slipped and fell into a hay baler. Put me right off wantin' to make any more of the stuff, I can tell you. Grass is all they're gonna get 'ere." He nodded toward the *Hon'chai*.

It was all too much for Zimmerman, who sat with his head in his hands until he heard the farmer say, "Look lively, lad. Here's Guillaume back with some kit for you to wear."

Guillaume arrived, panting from the exertion, and handed Marcus a long-sleeved, white linen shirt, a pair of supple leather breeches, some woollen socks and a pair of black, calf-length boots that laced up the middle. The pants were loose around his waist, and the shirt a little long in the sleeve, but Zimmerman wasn't about to complain. He dressed while the other two men casually approached the horned deer and slipped the harnesses about their heads.

They walked back to where he stood, the two animals trailing meekly behind them, and the young animal nuzzling the haunches of the older female.

"You're welcome to stay with us a day or two until you sort your head out if you like," the farmer offered. "Usually takes most folks a couple of weeks to get their heads around things here."

"Thanks, but you've already been too kind. I don't want to intrude further."

"Suit yerself, lad." He pointed towards a stand of trees at the far edge of the paddock. "Head through those trees over there, and you'll pick up a road. Well, it's more of a footpath, really. Turn left along it and keep going, and it'll bring you out at Hogarth. That's the nearest big city in these parts. Someone'll look after you there."

They shook hands, and Marcus headed for the belt of trees. He found the path and spent the next couple of hours ambling along it. His memory returned in short bursts of startling clarity. He remembered who he was, where he'd come from, what he was doing, and how he'd died. There were many things he couldn't explain: chief amongst them was the fact that he felt so real, so physical, despite the farmer's assurance that he was a gob of plasma in an unexpected and distant part of the universe. He wondered if he was invincible.

The path descended in a winding track, and he caught his first glimpse of Hogarth through the trees. It looked like a packed, sprawling collection of buildings, chimneys and spires, surrounded by a massive stone block wall.

Up close, the fortifications were even more massive than he'd imagined. They towered above him, crenellated like the walls of a medieval castle and every bit as imposing. He was caught up in a steady trickle of humanity headed across an arched stone bridge leading to a pair of giant iron gates, which were open to permit the flow of traffic into and out of the city. The bridge spanned a near vertical ravine.

Most of his fellow travellers were headed inwards; very few passed by the other way. Zimmerman quickly became aware of a level of quiet intensity. People had their heads down and marched with purpose. It was as if they were seeking sanctuary behind the walls, for many of them humped their belongings with them.

He saw soldiers in uniform, milling about at the entrance. They carried long, carved wooden staffs; a few had blades dangling from their belts, but there wasn't a gun in sight. The soldiers watched him pass. None made any move to stop him from entering.

He spent the afternoon wandering through the city centre, and traipsed back along the base of the mighty wall, searching out somewhere to stay. He had the dazed look of the recently departed about him, and received a degree of sympathy from the townsfolk, though not quite enough to warrant free board. Zimmerman had no currency, and he had no idea how to go about getting some.

"The army barracks," someone suggested. "They're signing on as many as they can get up there. You'll get a new uniform, somewhere to stay, and someone to look after you."

After two days of sleeping in doorways, huddled against the cold and soaked by a passing storm, Zimmerman gave in and became a newly drafted private in the army of Hogarth. He was handed a staff and given a crash course on how to use it.

About the time he could clamber up a rope netting, swing from a vine from one side of a mud-filled trench to the other, and fire bolts of white hot plasma from the end of his staff, the invading army of Cherath, with Lord Varak at its head, arrived on the other side of the deep ravine.

CHAPTER 1

Private Marcus Augustus Zimmerman gripped his staff so tightly that his knuckles turned white. His helmet was a size too large and kept slipping over his eyes, obstructing his view. He pushed it back, then cautiously peered between the battlements at the events unfolding on the bridge out to his right.

There was a gaping hole in the top of the wall further along, where a savage bolt of energy had recently obliterated a section of stone and the soldiers who had hunkered behind it. Fragments of stone had rained down around him. Zimmerman pressed himself tight against the wall until the smoke cleared. He knew the walls had been carved from monumental blocks of granite, and he quietly marvelled at the power that caused them to blow apart with such ease.

He observed the powerful, obese figure of Varak raise his staff, about to fire another blast at the wall. He squeezed his eyes shut, and waited for the explosion, which never eventuated. When he opened his eyes again, another person—this one small and slight by comparison—had been dragged out onto the bridge and hurled at Varak's feet. The tiny figure stood slowly and removed a helmet to reveal a cascade of flowing, black hair that caught the light as she shook it free.

"It's *her!*" a soldier named Carruthers exclaimed.

"Who?" Zimmerman had only heard of Varak.

"The girl—the one in the prophecy! The Gallagher girl!"

A low murmur buzzed around the top of the fortified wall as more of Hogarth's citizens reached the same conclusion. The noise died away altogether as they watched the girl struggle, encased inside a large, gelatinous bubble of plasma.

"He's got her!"

"She's done for! *We're* done for!"

Zimmerman silently cursed his luck for having landed on the wrong side in an impending battle, then watched amazed and transfixed as events unfolded, the tide suddenly turned, and the victor became the vanquished. He could hear Varak's muffled screams from where he squatted, and when the screams died away, he couldn't tear his eyes from the red rope of plasma that was being drawn back up inside her staff. Varak had disappeared.

He was still staring when she raised her staff and launched another bolt of energy over the heads of the opposing army. The ensuing shockwave from the thunderclap slammed against the city wall, and Zimmerman's helmet was wrenched from his head. He would have toppled backwards off the top wall walk if Carruthers hadn't grabbed his tunic and held on. His ears were ringing, and he was deafened by the blast as he struggled safely back onto the cobbled pathway.

The girl was still standing on the bridge, unaffected by the blast, which seemed to have bypassed her completely. Then, the unexpected happened as—one by one at first—the opposing army knelt in obeisance before her, and a tumultuous roar erupted from the walls.

The spell had been broken. Soldiers packed their arms and turned in groups for home while the gates of the city opened and people poured out to surround the girl in celebration. Carruthers slapped Zimmerman on the back and shouted gleefully, "That's my kind of war! Over before it started!"

Marcus leaned against the wall and blew out a sigh. He watched the masses of black-suited soldiers disband and considered that they'd all had one lucky escape. This was no sort of life for a geologist.

His life of respite was short-lived. He was stood down and returned to barracks along with most of Hogarth's army. The soldiers were jubilant because they'd survived possible oblivion and certain enslavement, and the Gallagher girl was the topic of praise on everyone's lips. Zimmerman learned of the Bexus Prophecy—that a golden girl would defeat Varak as foretold by a set of mysterious cave etchings. Few had known of it; even fewer had dared believe in it. Zimmerman didn't think she looked all that golden down on the bridge, but she'd done the job, and had become an instant hit: the Heroine of Hogarth.

Ten days later, it was a different story altogether. The army was on the march, passing through the dreaded Great Forest on its way to Cherath. Rumour and gossip scour a city faster than a flash flood, and the word on the street was that this was the girl's doing. Somehow, she had coerced the city fathers to dispatch the army as a peacekeeping force, to act as a buffer in a probable conflict between the cities of Cherath to the east, and Hornshurst to the north and west.

The mood was one of resentment, and it infected the troops like a virulent flu bug. Marcus Zimmerman was not immune, and he muttered along with the rest of his pals, and cursed the stiff footwear that would have caused blisters back on Earth and continued to cause a similar pain here. He caught glimpses of the Gallagher girl, riding one of those weird, pronged deer at the head of the column, and he wished she'd been made to march alongside the men. Maybe after a few dozen miles, she wouldn't have been quite so keen to whisk them off to war.

Zimmerman's heart sank when they finally reached the vast plain that circled the city of Cherath. It must have been a fertile grassy prairie once upon a time, but after years of neglect it reflected the barren waste of Varak's rule: starved, thirsty, and trampled upon. There was nothing left but dust.

The walls of the city appeared impregnable, even from that distance, but that was the least of Zimmerman's concerns. Another army was encamped in front of the city, and flanks extended out and around to encircle it fully. Zimmerman suddenly felt small and insignificant. All eyes were turned towards them as the soldiers of Hogarth pushed on like eager spectators drawn to a schoolyard brawl.

Commander-in Chief Carter galloped past on his *Hon'chai*, urging the men forward with the promise of a swift, decisive victory. The Gallagher girl had inherited Varak's throne, and she was about to dispense another thunderbolt and take control. *Or so he hopes!* thought Zimmerman. He wasn't nearly as confident about that as Carter appeared to be. He was watching the flanks of the Hornshurst army unfurl and curve around towards them like the horns on the head of a colossal bull. It was a standard flanking manoeuvre, opening like the jaws on a steel trap, inviting the unwary to step inside.

The commanders of Hogarth's army weren't that stupid, and the column was halted about five hundred yards out and ordered to form up in a protective wedge that had been an effective defensive strategy since the days of the Roman Empire. Zimmerman stood shoulder-to-shoulder, dripping under the midday heat, and packed in like a sardine with his staff pointing outwards. He waited; he expected something to happen.

He watched the girl peel away from the tip of the wedge, followed by the warrior they called Hawklight. She rode towards the opposing army as if she hadn't a care in the world, and

Zimmerman was amazed to see the Hornshurst troops part either side to let her through. They closed ranks again after she'd passed and he lost sight of her.

He continued to wait anxiously for the flash in the sky that would signal the thunderbolt, and he reached subconsciously for his helmet strap and secured it under his chin. There was some sort of commotion along the top of the city wall just above the gates, and something caught his eye as it had flashed briefly in the sunlight before it was gone. Zimmerman could hear raised shouts, and then the girl's clear voice cut through the desert air. Something about a crystal!

He strained to catch the gist of what she was saying and had to piece the fragments of words carried by the wind. The men beside him shuffled nervously; they'd come to the same conclusion that she was surrounded by two hostile armies and totally powerless to prevent anything from happening. Back at Hogarth, they'd had the walls to hunker behind, at least; out here, they were vulnerable and exposed. He heard the stern commands of the NCOs restore order and the disquiet subsided.

And then, to the amazement of all, the imposing gates of the city swung outwards.

Just before sunset, the Hogarth army was roused, and organised into a loose column five abreast to begin filing through a gap in the Hornshurst lines and take up position on the field in the no-man's land between the two opposing sides.

Zimmerman was now a peacekeeper, made official by the round of complicated negotiations, which Elward Carter oversaw. As with any peacekeeping force, his army was reviled by both sides, each thinking the force favoured the other in any dispute. The men were threatened as they passed between the ranks of

Hornshurst soldiers, but the officers on both sides managed to maintain order, and the transition was made without incident.

Zimmerman was just a cog within a cog within the many wheels that made up the army of Hogarth; all he ever did was follow orders. He was part of a group of six troopers, including Carruthers, who were organised to share one tent for the duration of the siege. The men spent the remainder of the dwindling daylight having to erect the tent and sort out their equipment. Zimmerman knew all five of his tent mates; four of them snored. It was going to be a lengthy stay!

He lay awake under his bedroll until the snoring drove him outside. Carruthers had pulled the first watch, but Zimmerman offered to relieve him; he wasn't tired, and he wanted some 'quiet' time, made difficult by the fact that almost all the soldiers slept on their backs while their jaws gaped slackly.

He gazed upwards at the stars, but the ambient light from the many campfires had tempered their intense twinkling. He stirred the embers of their own meagre fire with a broken branch, then added it to the coals, and watched the sparks rise and the smoke swirl before the branch burst into flame. He heard the muffled thump as one of Carruthers' boots was thrown across at a sleeping form, and he smiled to himself as the snoring dropped to a different level of intensity.

He yawned and sat in the dust beside the fire, and drew his collar up against his neck to ward away the chill. He sat like this for some time, hunched forward and staring into the red and black coals until his back grew stiff and sore. He leaned backwards and stretched, placing one palm on the sand for support.

He felt something hard and sharp beneath his hand, and twisted around to investigate. He discovered a couple of stones half-buried in the dirt. He prised them loose and was about to toss them aside when one of them captured the weak firelight and glinted as if the fire were trapped inside it. Zimmerman frowned, and tried to examine the stones more carefully, but the glow from the embers was too dull to see anything clearly. He debated whether he ought to build up the fire and provide more light, but they'd lugged their own firewood across the desolate plains, and he was loathed to use up their precious store on a whim. He pocketed the stones and huddled in the lee of the tent, away from the drifting winds.

Marcus awoke the following morning, stiff from lying on the hard ground with only a blanket as a mattress. His hip was sore where he'd lain on his side, and something hard had dug into him. He remembered the pebbles from the previous evening's watch, and cursed himself for not removing them from his pocket before he'd settled down to sleep. He turned on his back and stretched before he crawled from his bed and laced up his boots once more.

Outside the tent, the day had begun to shunt forward reluctantly. The air was blue with wood smoke and made even hazier by the diffuse light of the early morning sun. Soldiers sat around in clusters, rubbing the sleep from their eyes, splashing their faces with cold water, or soaking up the sun stripped to their undershirts while chatting and laughing. This was the period of grace before the NCOs came stomping through the camp to inflict the latest exercise regime.

Zimmerman sat to one side away from the others and pulled the stones from his pocket. Only, they weren't stones. They weren't like anything he'd seen before. They were two halves of a perfect crystal that had snapped cleanly in two. One of the ends had a gold clasp attached to it, so a chain could be threaded through and the whole thing worn as a pendant about the neck.

In shadow, the crystal was a clear cobalt blue, but when he held it against the light, the colour changed, seeming to pulse with yellows and greens. It remained cold to the touch, despite the warmth his hand generated, and the broken edges had remained razor sharp.

He examined one of the broken faces carefully, and it appeared to his unaided eye that he was looking at a cross section of tiny tubes, much like looking at a tight bunch of straws end on.

However, when he turned the crystal section on to its side, he could see clear through the stone, with no sign of the microtubules he would have expected to find. He was mystified, and longed for a jeweller's eyepiece to examine the surface more intricately.

He was so engrossed with the stone's features, he was unaware of anyone nearby until a shadow fell across his lap and blocked out the sun. He glanced up, annoyed by the intrusion, and found himself face to face with Elward Carter and members of his entourage. He hid the stones in his fist, but by then it was too late—Carter had seen what he had been holding.

"Atten—*chun!*" shouted one of the adjutants, and everyone, Zimmerman included, immediately leapt to their feet and stood ramrod still.

"What's your name, soldier!" Carter barked.

"Private Zimmerman! Sir!"

"You have something in your hand, Zimmerman?"

"Sir! Yes sir!"

"And what is it?"

"Two halves of a crystal, sir. Possibly some form of calcite, due to the observable birefringence, but unlikely because of its hardness and the fact that it's insoluble. It looks orthorhombic, which means it could be related to the olivine or aragonite families, but without closer examination I—"

"I don't need to be bored to death, soldier. I'm searching for a broken crystal left lying in the dirt somewhere around here. You seem to have found it. I want it!" Carter held his hand out, and Zimmerman was left with little choice but to hand it over.

"Thank you." Carter's eyes never left Marcus's as he slipped the stones into the top pocket of his tunic. "Dismissed."

"Sir! Thank you, sir!" Marcus slapped his forearm across his chest, fist closed, by way of an official Hogarth army salute. Carter nodded fractionally, turned on his heels and left, with his coterie of advisers flapping in his wake. Zimmerman watched them leave.

"Why didn't you tell us that you'd found the crystal?" Carruthers demanded as he sidled up to Marcus.

"I don't know what you mean."

"You drongo! That was Varak's crystal, the source of all his power. The girl dropped it in the sand yesterday. She broke it. She never had it the whole time we were marching along behind her, thinking we were invincible."

"So, what's the big deal?"

Carruthers shook his head and gave Zimmerman a *What were you thinking?* kind of look. "It might have been broken, but it still would have been worth something. Now Carter's got the bloody thing!"

"Tell me about it."

"When Varak killed people, he used the crystal to suck their souls up. It trapped them inside; it trapped their energy. He was able to live off that energy somehow for hundreds of years. She broke the crystal. Why would she want to do that? Now it doesn't work."

Carruthers gave Marcus a queer, rather sly look.

"Saa . . . ay! You seemed to know a lot about it." It wasn't quite a question, and Carruthers' tone implied that he suspected Zimmerman knew more than he was letting on.

Zimmerman shrugged. "I used to be a geologist. I find rocks fascinating."

Carruthers yawned in reply and said nothing. He didn't want to risk getting Marcus fired up again about the intricacies of mineral impurities.

Throughout the following nine weeks, camp life proved to be a monotonous series of patrols, watches and training exercises. Towards the end, the tensions between the two camps escalated, and Marcus was involved as part of a policing team in a running pitched battle in which four people were killed, and numerous ringleaders intent on upsetting the delicate balance of power were arrested.

His tunic had been singed, and he was sitting with a medic who was patching up an open wound in his arm, attempting to staunch the energy leaking away in a steady stream of tiny sparks.

"Ouch!"

The medic glanced at him and pursed her lips, and continued to apply a sticky poultice to stem the bleeding. He still couldn't reconcile the fact that he felt pain, despite having no flesh or nerves beneath his skin. On the other hand, he'd always been squeamish at the sight of blood; this fountain of sparks was more like a fireworks display and it fascinated him.

"Ouch!"

"Sit still! It's just a scratch. Here, press down on this while I prepare a bandage." The medic took his other wrist and planted his hand on the dressing covering the goo that had begun to trickle slowly down his arm. She reached across him for a roll of gauze, snipped the end, and wound it expertly around his arm, applying enough pressure to stem the sparks completely.

She was in the process of tying it off when the curtains were drawn back, and two soldiers dressed in the uniform of the Hogarth palace guards stepped in.

"Are you Zimmerman?" one of them addressed him.

Marcus nodded, and winced as the medic pulled the final knot tight.

"You're to come with us!"

Marcus was perplexed. "What's this about?"

"Orders, son," replied the older, gruff sergeant. "Step lively."

Zimmerman stood and gingerly slipped his tunic over his head, taking care as he threaded his injured arm through the sleeve. The soldiers stepped either side of him and escorted him from the hospital tent. They turned right and directed him along the paths between the rows of tents until they hit the road leading directly to the gates of Cherath.

Marcus wondered what this was all about. Perhaps he was about to be awarded a commendation for his role in the skirmish. After all, hadn't he been wounded in the line of duty? He was certain it had to be something like that.

There were sentries on the gates, although they stepped aside and allowed the trio to enter the city. They passed patrols of Cherath's soldiers who policed the streets and alleys, but again they weren't challenged.

They climbed the stone steps leading up to the broken gates of the palace that the dictator Varak had called home. The guards seemed to know where to go for they moved through the inner courtyard and headed towards the grand entrance to the Chamber, once Varak's assembly hall and now the site of constant negotiations involving parties from each of the three cities. Zimmerman started to feel nervous—he wasn't going to get a medal here this late in the day. His arm was throbbing, and his mouth was dry.

The sergeant pushed against the imposing, carved wooden doors without knocking, and they entered the dimly lit Chamber. Zimmerman saw a solitary figure at the far end of the room, hunched over a table as he shuffled through a pile of papers. He recognised Carter, who didn't even bother to look up as they approached.

They snapped to attention in front of him, and the sergeant bellowed, "Sir! Private Zimmerman, as requested!"

Carter slowly raised his head. He was wearing a pair of half-moon spectacles that had slipped to the end of his nose. He removed them and rubbed his eyes as if to relieve eyestrain.

"Thank you, Sergeant. See that we're not disturbed. Dismissed."

The two soldiers saluted and turned on their heels. The sound of their heels clacking against the stone floor echoed hollowly around the empty room.

"Come with me!" Carter ordered, and Zimmerman followed him through a side door into a small, adjoining room. It held a table with two chairs either side, and an oil lamp turned low. Carter indicated one of the chairs and moved around the other side of the table. He sat and reached across and turned up the glow on the lamp.

Sitting on the table was a soft white cloth; on it lay the two halves of the crystal that Zimmerman had handed over two months before.

"I never asked what it was you did before you arrived here," Carter began. He had placed his elbows on the edge of the table and clasped his hands together and was flapping his fingers up and down like a slow flying bird. He watched Zimmerman and waited for a response.

Zimmerman cleared his throat.

"Ahem. Er, well, I was a geologist, working out in the sapphire fields of Australia."

"And were you a good geologist?"

Zimmerman smiled at the memory and nodded.

Carter unclasped his hands briefly and gestured towards the broken crystal. "Would you like another look at these?" he asked.

Zimmerman's hands trembled once again. What was a medal compared to this?

"You wanted one of these?" Carter slid a drawer open and removed a stubby magnifying glass with a thick elliptical lens. "Take your time," he added encouragingly as he handed the lens over and settled back in his chair to observe Zimmerman at work.

Marcus picked up one of the crystal halves and immediately bent and scraped one edge against the flagstones in the floor. It left a clear, sharply defined scratch in the stone. He pulled his knife from its sheath and tried to scratch the flagstone with its point. The mark was faint and indistinct, almost invisible.

"It appears to be as hard as diamond," he muttered to himself. "I'm surprised it shattered; it shouldn't have."

He pulled the lamp closer and raised the magnifying glass to his eye. He examined the broken face closely.

This time, he noticed the detail in the honeycombed appearance. The stone was solid, but there were clearly defined circles. Each tiny circumference was edged in dark-grey, and many were blurred as if a line of wet ink had been smudged. The light was reflected in different hues about the surface as he rotated the crystal. A slight smile flitted across his lips.

"What?" Carter asked.

"I've never seen a crystalline structure like it. It is translucent when viewed through any of the carved facets. You can see clear through it. But if you look closely at either of the broken faces, you see thousands—millions—of solid tubes, all running in parallel lines. There is some kind of impurity around the edge of each microscopic tubule. I'd hazard a guess and say iron, but it's just a guess. However, this means the crystal ought to be opaque, which clearly, it's not. And on the surface, the lines are smudged and the refractive index changes completely. It suggests to me that there was some sort of intense heat that radiated laterally and created a shear-plane or fracture. It's the only reason it could have split in two like this. Even that seems impossible as it would require a huge amount of energy."

The sentence hung in the air, and Zimmerman looked slyly at Carter.

"You know about the crystal." It was not a question.

Zimmerman nodded.

"If the impurities prove to be iron in origin, then the tubules will be lines of force trapped during the formation of the crystal. It would have been spectacular; an event on a scale equivalent to this planet being totally engulfed by a solar flare, possibly a billion or more years ago. That scale of ionisation was also focussed, similar to the way you can use a magnifying glass like this to burn a hole in a piece of paper just using sunlight. What you have left is a unique crystal, with truly unique properties."

"Why doesn't it still work?"

"I'm not sure. I'd say it must be a certain size; it needs to be bigger. And if the energy it had stored then created the fracture, I'd say it was just about worn out, like an old battery you can no longer recharge."

Carter grimaced and leaned his jaw against his clenched fist as he considered this information.

"Thank you, Zimmerman. You can go."

Marcus remained seated and watched the Commander, lost in thought, rubbing the bridge of his nose with his finger. Moments later, Carter stirred and realised the geologist was still seated across from him.

"Dismissed, solder!" he barked.

"What you need is another crystal," Marcus whispered.

Carter's eyes narrowed suspiciously. "What do you mean?"

Marcus shrugged. "Leave the stones with me and let me have access to a chemical laboratory. I might be able to tell you where you could find more. Of course, I'd have to resign from the army first . . ."

Carter nodded. "Take the stones. Leave the rest to me. Just get on with it!"

Zimmerman barely contained his excitement. He quickly swept the stones into his pocket. He paused at the doorway. "One more thing, Commander. This is a completely new geological find. I'd like to call it Zimmermanite."

Carter dismissed him with a wave.

"Call it what you like."

—⁊⁊⁊—

A week later, all patience had worn thin, and the prospect of war seemed inevitable. Carter and other members of the Hogarth

War Council had withdrawn a safe distance—a strategic ploy, according to Carter—but he had remembered to take Zimmerman with him.

The rest of the army of Hogarth remained trapped between the two sides. Carruthers was back there somewhere, nervously clutching his staff and facing down the soldiers of Hornshurst. The troops were marshalled and directed by the woman called Mirayam, the mentor of the Gallagher girl who, by now, had been given up as lost.

Nobody was fooled by Carter's cowardice, but nobody wanted to be sent back to the front lines, so everyone remained tight-lipped.

The arcing thunderbolt took them all by surprise, and the shock wave blew Carter from his mount. No one was sure of its source, but everybody recognised the signature of the Gallagher girl. Half an hour later, the first outrider arrived with news that the talisman had been returned, and battle had been averted once again. The girl's timing was impeccable, according to Zimmerman.

This time there was no celebration: no cheering and flag waving from the top of the city's ramparts and no tossing of helmets into the air. The whole atmosphere was subdued by grief from Hornshurst, and by trepidation and resentment from Cherath, as the armies began the tiresome chore of breaking camp and preparing for the long journey home.

Four days later, a solid remnant of the peacekeeping force was still in the final throes of departing. Zimmerman was seated at a table in one corner of Carter's tent, going over figures from his initial findings when the warrior Hawklight pushed through the tent flaps. He was dusty and dishevelled, and his aura was subdued in shadow. His eyes were hollow and distant, and he seemed weary and resigned like a man who had lost his way.

"You sent for me."

There was no salute, no standing rigidly at attention in the presence of the Commander-in-Chief of the Hogarth army.

Zimmerman could tell Carter was rankled by the apparent insubordination, but that he was also intimidated by the presence of Hawklight.

"At ease," Carter replied.

Hawklight didn't respond, so Carter got straight to the point.

"You have a new assignment, starting immediately." He tossed the two halves of the broken crystal onto the table in front of him. "Do you recognise these?"

Hawklight nodded once and said nothing.

"Varak's crystal. Used wisely, it could have been a powerful tool for peace and prosperity." He glanced up at Hawklight who returned him a blank stare; he was fooling no one with this speech. He pressed on. "Captain Hawklight, this is Marcus Zimmerman. Mr Zimmerman is a trained geologist who believes he can locate the source of this crystal."

Hawklight turned his head and scrutinised Zimmerman. Marcus nodded and gave a hesitant wave, but he felt cold disdain wash over him in return, so he dropped his hand and looked away.

"You are to liaise with Mr Zimmerman. Meanwhile, I intend to assemble a protective expeditionary force which you will lead immediately after we return to Hogarth. It will take about two weeks to get back, and I want the whole expedition kitted and ready to leave within a month after that. You'll take your orders from Mr Zimmerman from that point onwards. Is that clear?"

Hawklight didn't react.

Zimmerman coughed politely. "Do you have any questions, Captain?"

Hawklight spoke for the second time.

"Where are we going?"

Zimmerman paused. "For the moment, let's just say south."

Hawklight kept staring at him, and Marcus started to feel unnerved and uncomfortable.

"Will there be anything else?" Carter saved him from further embarrassment as Hawklight returned his gaze to his commander.

"In that case, you are dismissed. You can arrange to meet with Mr Zimmerman on our return to Hogarth, and he will outline the project in more detail then."

Hawklight gave Marcus another chilly appraisal as he left the tent.

"Are you sure he's up to it?" Zimmerman asked. "He looks as if he's suffering from a case of post traumatic stress disorder. I don't want him to turn loose halfway through this."

"He's the best we've got," Carter replied. "You worry about your end; he'll do the rest."

Zimmerman stared at the swaying flaps of the exit. *I hope you're right!* he thought to himself.

He wasn't the only one staring after Hawklight. Crouching down outside in the shadows, the hunched figure of Copely watched as Hawklight stalked away into the gloom. His dark eyes burned with intensity and desire as he slipped away into the darkness, careful to avoid the sentries who were less than vigilant.

CHAPTER 2

Three months later

Kate Gallagher felt physically ill. Her stomach heaved, and she felt the bile rise in the back of her throat, all of which was, of course, impossible. She had no stomach, nothing to vomit, but the physical memories embedded in her soul were too strong to ignore.

Ethan's words had hit her like a brick.

"Kate, Hawklight was in command of the platoon. He's been killed, and we don't even know who did it!"

Her legs gave way, and she collapsed into Kareem's arms. He picked her up and carried her back out into the sunlight and set her down against the side of the stall.

When her mother had sacrificed herself in order to save the contents of the talisman, the loss had been too keen to bear. Hawklight had restrained Kate and had instead colluded with her mother. Siobhan had known that her daughter would try to stop her and so prevent her from taking the only option available: to save the ancients housed within the talisman by acting as the vessel herself, knowing she would never survive the event.

18

Kate had reacted with fury, and Hawklight bore the brunt of her grievous anger. He had been her saviour on Bexus, and they had formed a relationship that went deeper than friendship. In that moment, he had betrayed her, so she cut him off, pushed him away. She had seen the hurt cloud his eyes before he withdrew back into the stoic shell of a man he'd been when she'd first met him. Now she knew him better; she knew that every pointed barb she fired at him found its mark although he gave no outward sign of it, and she took every opportunity to continue to wound him with every sentence she uttered.

He never once fought back. He carried Siobhan's withered, feeble form all the way back to Cherath. He stood by as Kate handed her across to the druids who waited to collect her and begin the final preparations that would see her join the company of the ancients within a new talisman. And then he was gone. He led his mount from the field and walked out of Kate's life.

Kareem's arrival in Hogarth had presented her with a new path. He had been sent to accompany her back to Hornshurst, to attend the ceremony and to farewell her mother. A new *Toki-Moai* had been fashioned to house Siobhan and the ancients. The advice her mother had offered during their last moments together had begun the healing process.

She'd been hardest on herself. She blamed herself because she was the one who had broken the statue in the first place. In accepting her mother's guidance, she had taken the first steps to forgive herself, and the edifice of hate and blame and anger that she'd built finally began to crumble. She had cried on Kareem's shoulders as the realisation of all she had done hit her. He was gentle with compassion and made no judgements. He was just . . . there for her.

He filled the vacuum Kate had created when she'd forced Hawklight from her life. Kareem became her silent protector. He was her solid rock when the ground beneath her feet shifted. They would sit together, nestled beneath a tree or would lie on the grassy banks beside a stream, and he would hold her in his arms without speaking while she struggled with grief and sorrow.

She broke through to the other side. Life is nothing if not a series of compromises, accepting events that you cannot expect to change, and changing those that you can. Her psyche was battle-scarred from too many direct hits—the losses of Jaime and her mother—but she survived and grew stronger in the process.

The ground shifted less often, and the need to seek solace beneath the tree disappeared. It was time to make the return journey to Hogarth. Kate was unable to disguise her joy in learning that Kareem would come with her, and she laughed and flung herself into his embrace, which now felt so familiar to her.

Throughout the return journey, Kate had one person on her mind—Hawklight! His loss was an event she could change. She was plagued with doubt, nonetheless; she had been intentionally cruel beyond belief to him, raking him with hatred at every opportunity. She knew him well enough to know he would avoid her now; knew him well enough to know he would fend off her apologies, and keep himself aloof and beyond the temptation to repair the relationship and risk getting hurt again.

She had to try. She had no idea what she would say to him. Still, she had to try.

"Kate, Hawklight was in command of the platoon. He's been killed, and we don't even know who did it!"

Ethan's words had pummelled her senseless. Whatever was left unsaid between Hawklight and her would remain unsaid forever. She closed her eyes, and all she could see was his hulking, dejected frame walking away from her and disappearing through the crowd on the field at Cherath.

There was a commotion—the sound of running footsteps slapping against the dirt floor of the stall—and Kate heard the sound of familiar voices. She opened her eyes as her friends came bursting through the doorway. Kate was back, and they had torn themselves from the grilles through which they were eavesdropping and had hurried to the exit.

Kate looked anxiously up at Jackson and Sigrid, who would have been the ones with their ears tuned to the conversations of the councillors.

"Is it true?" she whispered.

Sigrid bit her lip and closed her eyes, and both she and Jackson nodded.

"When? How?"

"Two, three weeks ago. He was leading an expedition south, apparently ordered by Carter, who won't come clean on its purpose. They're up there arguing about it at the moment. It was turning into a real bun fight. Carter's saying it was a top-secret mission and the Council members don't have the proper clearance, and the councillors are howling that the Council never sanctioned the mission; also, it had already failed. He's just stormed out."

"How did they find out about it?"

"There were a couple of survivors who managed to make it back. They've just been interviewed by the Council."

"What did they say?"

"They don't know anything, apart from the fact that they were headed south and had packed a whole heap of cold weather equipment."

"Sounds as if they were headed *way* south," quipped Olivia.

They were sprawled about the courtyard when the door opened, and Mirayam stepped through. She gave them a tired smile, but her face lit up as she spied Kate. The students leapt to their feet and made room for Mirayam on her favourite couch beneath one of the trees thick with golden fruit.

Mirayam was their mentor, the one they turned to for advice and direction. She was one of only two women on the War

Council; the second had only been a most recent appointment. She was also one of the remarkably few people willing and able to withstand the bluster and bullying of Elward Carter. Somehow, this frail, delightful woman intimidated him with her wisdom and her courage to speak up for what she felt was right, often in the face of antagonism from the other members of the Council.

She took Kate's hand and kissed her cheek before lowering herself into a comfortable position on the couch.

"Kate, it's so good to see you," she smiled, although her eyes scanned Kate's face searching for any hidden signs about her wellbeing. More than anybody else, she knew the toll the planet had taken on Kate's soul. She had witnessed the decay of Kate's once-golden aura to the point where now it was patchy and dimmed through violence. She had also engineered Kate's death on Earth, and was deeply indebted to the girl for all that she had done on her behalf.

"Kareem, welcome to our home." She also acknowledged the young man who had been seated at Kate's side. She had noticed the change in Kate: suddenly a young woman, no longer a girl.

Kate knelt in front of her.

"Then it's true? Hawklight is dead?"

Mirayam gazed into Kate's eyes, and Kate found the answer there.

"Why? What was he doing that was so important? And who would have killed him?"

Mirayam shook her head. "I can't answer your questions. Elward is very tight-lipped. I've got to think it was something illegal, or something that would be very embarrassing to him if it ever became public."

"Didn't Hawklight say anything to you before he left?"

"I never saw him again after Cherath. He avoided us all. The only thing I can remember is Elward fuming about him because he'd missed some deadline preparing for his assignment. When I asked Elward what the trouble was, he didn't answer and changed the subject. I didn't think anything more about it at the time."

Kate looked at the others. "Did anyone else talk with him?"

They shook their heads.

"We saw him occasionally up on the training field," Mia said, "but he avoided us. He'd walk away if we came near."

They grew silent.

"Carter has the answers," Kareem said quietly.

Kate glanced across at him. Kareem recognised the look; he'd been on the receiving end of it a few times. It was business time!

"Then let's go ask him, shall we?" she grinned.

"Kate, be careful!" Mirayam warned. "Elward can be a devious foe. Do not underestimate him. Having said that, I think you'll find that, if you hurry, you might catch him. He generally heads home from the Ministry around this time."

Carter checked his office for the last time before he shut and locked the door. He'd arrived back after storming out of the meeting, and had spent the afternoon locked away, sorting through his piles of memos and files and destroying any evidence he found of the botched mission. His public, highly political life would be over in an instant if anyone were to discover its true purpose.

When he was finally satisfied with his efforts, he relaxed. He could deny everything, demand any incriminating evidence be produced, and rail about the loss of due process of law. He was enough of a bully to know that few would even dare accuse him in the first place.

He whistled as he cut diagonally across the main square outside the entrance to the Great Council Chambers that sprawled for a city block at the base of the immense, fortified wall. The far corner of the square emptied onto one of the main thoroughfares that sprouted numerous, smaller streets and alleys. These narrow, twisting lanes were often little more than a footpath in width, lined with terraced buildings two and three storeys high.

Carter had to cut through this clutter on his way home. He lived further away from the city's bustling centre, in more spacious accommodation. The narrow alleys provided a variety of shortcuts, but Carter was a man accustomed to routine and that proved to be a mistake.

He rounded a corner and was confronted by Kate Gallagher who was leaning against one of the buildings waiting for him. The whistle died away.

"You're late!" she said.

"You! What are you doing here? I thought you'd dried up and blown away," he sneered.

"I want to know what happened to Hawklight."

He smiled. "It's a bit late for that, don't you think? Last time I looked, you two weren't exactly bosom buddies."

"I want to know what was so important that it got him killed."

"How did you fi—?" He stopped abruptly as the answer dawned on him. "Mirayam!"

Kate shrugged. Their secret was still safe.

"You didn't answer my question."

"And I'm not about to, either. Get out of my way!"

Kate moved away from the wall. She stepped out into the middle of the lane, blocking his way. Carter noticed she was unarmed. He leered at her and casually pointed his staff in her direction.

"You think you can threaten me?" he asked. "You're not so tough without your big, brawny bodyguard behind you." He paused. "In fact, suppose there was an accident; suppose you leapt out at me, and I reacted in self defence, and realised too late what had happened. Naturally, I'd be too distraught at first, but I think I could rally to deliver your eulogy in time. Or suppose—"

The tip of a staff touched his lower jaw just beneath his ear, and Kareem stepped out of the shadow.

"Suppose you were mugged on your way home from work, and all they found was a pile of clothing and a few loose papers," he whispered in Carter's ear. Carter's staff clattered to the pavement, and a bead of perspiration appeared beneath his hairline.

"Do not give me any excuse. Do not believe that snuffing out your miserable existence is beyond my capability," Kareem whispered so quietly that Kate could not hear him.

"I am going to ask you one more time," Kate said. "If you don't answer my question, I am going to turn around and walk away. I will not look behind me. I will not see a thing."

Carter tried to stare her down, but he couldn't meet those ice-blue eyes. He had looked for the lie. It wasn't there.

"Where was Hawklight going, and why?"

Carter's eyes darted as he struggled to compose a plausible half-truth. He opened his mouth to speak, but it was as if the girl had already caught him out. She turned and stepped away.

"No, wait!" he cried.

Kareem took a step back from him. Kate paused. She could hear the sound of running footsteps pounding along the alley down which Carter had come.

An armed soldier dressed in regimental colours burst around the corner, closely followed by the rest of his troop. He slid to a stop, surprised by the apparent face off, but he was quick to acknowledge his supreme commander.

Carter recovered quickly. "Arrest these two!" he barked. "They are trying to kidnap me!"

Kareem had stepped back beside Kate and had lowered his staff moments before. The trooper in charge tried to make sense of the scene. All he saw was an unarmed woman and a young man standing in front of his boss. They didn't look the least bit threatening, and he hesitated.

"*Arrest them, dammit!*" Carter was almost apoplectic.

The troopers formed a semicircle in front of Kate and Kareem and pointed their staffs at them.

"Let's not be too hasty here," said a voice as three more young people emerged from the shadow behind the troopers with their staffs also levelled. Two more appeared over the balcony of the building above them.

The trooper in charge recognised them. He remembered Kate. He'd witnessed her courage; he'd watched her defeat the villain Varak. He was thoroughly confused.

Kate spoke softly.

"I think there has been a misunderstanding, Corporal," she said. "I think if you ask Commander Carter once again, he'll explain he was mistaken. Naturally, it would be a wise move to accompany the commander and make sure he gets home safely. Isn't that correct, Commander?"

Carter was outnumbered, and he'd noticed that the boy's eyes never left him throughout. The Gallagher girl had known he was hiding something, but she was offering him a way out.

He coughed. "Yes. I'm sorry. My mistake, it would seem." He glanced at Kate who returned the look with a crooked grin of amusement across her lips. "Good evening, Miss Gallagher. I'm sure we'll meet again sometime soon."

He nodded curtly at the corporal.

"Take me home."

The students lowered their staffs and stepped away to allow Carter and his bemused bodyguards to pass through. They watched the party hurry to catch up with Carter before they all disappeared around the corner at the end of the street.

"We blew that one," sighed Jackson.

"He's going to be more careful in future. We won't likely get another crack at him," Ethan agreed.

"It doesn't matter," Kate said. "He wasn't going to tell us the truth in any case, and he wasn't worth another stain on your soul." She glanced at Kareem, who just grinned back at her.

"We'll never know what happened," sighed Sigrid.

"Maybe," replied Kate, "but we haven't run out of options just yet. We need to find the two survivors. Perhaps they can tell us something."

"The Council didn't seem to think so," replied Sigrid. "From what I heard, it was a dead end."

Carruthers lay on his bunk trying to sleep, but the events of the past two weeks kept intruding on his thoughts. He and Gonzales had thrashed their way down the mountain, losing the track numerous times, and had almost plummeted off a sheer precipice. They'd been tracked by a pack of wild *Abyssi*, monstrous dog-like creatures the size of a lioness. The creatures had the two of them cornered up a tree and out of reach for three days until they lost interest and slunk away into the undergrowth. Carruthers relived each terrifying moment when one of the animals would lunge for the lower branches. He could still hear the gashing, tearing sounds as their curved claws ripped the bark apart in feeble attempts to scale the trunk. He could still see the long snouts peeling back to reveal twin rows of curved teeth as gaping jaws snapped shut on empty air.

Often, these images would be shunted aside by the recurring nightmare of battle. His recollection was confused, but he remembered that the expedition had halted for the night. Hawklight had been wary and pushed them onward until the scout encountered a circular clearing, naturally fortified by the massive buttressed roots of a grove of towering trees. Even so, the captain had doubled the guard detail, which had included Carruthers.

It was a mistake. The first explosion hit the waist-high buttress he'd been leaning against. The blast blew him head-over-heels and into the undergrowth where he lay unconscious and bleeding in a steady fizzle of spluttering sparks.

When he eventually came to, the silence was overpowering, and fear gripped his insides. He rose unsteadily to his feet and stumbled into the clearing. His worst fear had been realised; there was no one left alive. Uniforms lay in disarray, smoking and charred; many were burned beyond recognition. He found the helmet that Hawklight had been wearing, but it had been blown in two, the metal twisted and punched outwards. He kicked it aside and sank to his knees in utter despair.

He was lost and alone in a place seething with intimidation and the likelihood of a grisly end seemed inevitable. He couldn't even remember the path he'd trodden to get here. He wanted to scream, to wail, and to beat his fists on the ground, but a groan off to his right made him paralytic with fear, and the scream caught in his throat. He swivelled his head slowly, and a wave of relief surged through him when he saw the haggard form of Gonzales crawl into the clearing.

He had no idea how they had survived the journey back. They ought to have perished a hundred times, and it was nothing more than dogged luck that dumped them, incoherent and deranged, at a distant farmhouse door where they were rescued and returned to Hogarth.

A voice cut through the swirling images in his brain.

"Are you Private Carruthers?"

He kept his eyes squeezed shut as if in doing so, he could shut out the world.

"Who wants to know?"

"I do!"

It was a woman's voice. Carruthers opened his eyes. His bunk was surrounded by a group of young people. He knew them from the training fields. In front of them, standing over him, was a young woman with jet-black hair and ice-blue eyes. He recognised her too.

"I know who you are!" he stated, and pushed himself onto his elbows as if he were trying to edge away from her.

"We just want to talk to you," she said and sat down on the edge of the bunk.

"I've told the Council everything I know."

"Then perhaps you can repeat it for us."

"I've already told them, and I'll tell you—I don't remember anything."

"Did you see who attacked you?"

"No."

"Do you know why they attacked you?"

"No."

"What were you doing? Where were you going?"

"I don't know. Nobody told us anything. All we did was follow orders. The only thing we knew for sure was that we were headed south. We went prepared for extreme cold weather."

Kate frowned. What could Carter hope to gain by sending a party towards one of the polar ice caps of the planet?

"You were certain there were no other survivors?"

"Believe me, Gonzales and I were the only ones moving up there."

"What about Captain Hawklight?"

Carruthers knew about Hawklight and the girl. For a while there, they had been inseparable. He wondered if this was the reason she was here. He shook his head.

"All I found was his helmet—well, half of his helmet. I'm sorry." She paled at his words. He looked at her quizzically.

"What?" she asked.

"Something strange just occurred to me. You two were friends, right?" She paused but nodded. "Well, I guess you could say that you were the topic of conversation more than once on the trip, what with Varak and the Hornshurst thing. Well, I noticed the Captain never joined in; he just used to move away, sit by himself. I thought that was weird, you know what I mean?"

Kate bit her lip. He'd pushed her away, right to the end. It was exactly the way she had treated him. What else could she *expect*?

29

"I've served under the Captain before. He was always—" Carruthers searched for the word, "—considerate, for an officer. We got the feeling he'd never order us to do what he wouldn't do himself, you know? All the lads would breathe a sigh of relief when they were assigned to his command.

This time was different; he wasn't like that at all. He kept himself apart from the rest of us. If you asked me, I'd put it down to the fact that he couldn't stand taking his orders from Zimmerman, the arrogant little—"

"Zimmerman?"

"Oh! Don't get me started!" moaned Carruthers.

"Who is Zimmerman?"

"A jumped-up nobody, is who," Carruthers spat. He saw Kate's frown of confusion, and he hastened to fill in the gaps. "Private Marcus Zimmerman, at least, that's who he used to be. We served together in the same company. You think you know a man when you go to war alongside him; turns out you don't, really. Mind you, he was a sneaky little bugger."

"Sneaky? How?"

"Well—when he found those stones is a good example. He nev—"

"Stones?"

"Yeah, you know!" Carruthers' face lit up, and he snapped his fingers and pointed at Kate. "The crystal! The one you had! You must have had the two pieces of it in your hand, and you dropped them. Zimmerman found them in the dirt. He was going to keep them for himself, not share them with the rest of us. They'd have been worth something, yeah? I thought so."

"Zimmerman found the broken crystal? What did he do with it?"

"Nothing. Carter—uh, Commander Carter—came along and took them off him. Zimmerman started blathering on about them. I couldn't understand a word he was saying, and neither did Car—uh—the Commander. Turns out he was a trained geologist, which was just as well because he was certainly no soldier, I can tell you!"

Kate wondered if Carruthers knew the meaning of the word, irony. She had already heard the story of his escape down the mountain. Also, she had a bad feeling about the direction the conversation was headed.

"Are you telling me that Carter has the crystal?"

"Yes. Well, no. A couple months later, Zimmerman doesn't show. I thought he'd gone AWOL, but he was decommissioned as it turned out. Next thing I know, he's got the stones back in his pocket, and he's barking orders at Captain Hawklight, who was none too impressed about it either!"

"Zimmerman was leading this expedition?"

Carruthers nodded. "I went up to him and said hello; the little jerk looked right through me! You think you know some people!"

"Was Zimmerman one of the casualties?"

"Yeah. I mean, he must've been, right? There was no one but me and Gonzales left up there."

They learned little more from Gonzales, save that there had been no sign of the supplies and the pack animals. Gonzales thought the *Urguts* had scattered during the ambush. These were solid creatures, like a cross between a water buffalo and a llama: long-necked, bulky with muscle, and a head bearing long curving horns. Gonzales had noted the muddied tracks they'd left behind when they bolted after the one-sided battle had begun.

He also had a better idea as to where the ambush had taken place, and was able to indicate it roughly on a map that Sigrid produced. He pointed to a region that was mostly uncharted, and there were no obvious paths or trails. The party had been headed through a mountainous wilderness, guided by Hawklight.

"They were looking for the source of the crystal, weren't they?" Kate said, once they had returned home.

Mirayam nodded. "It's the only thing that makes any sense," she replied.

"Do you think Hawklight was in on it?" Jackson asked the one question that hung on everyone's lips.

"No, I don't," Mirayam stated firmly, "and yet he would have guessed the purpose of the expedition. I can't explain his reasons for agreeing to lead it, and I guess we'll never know."

"Whoever ambushed them must have known the purpose also," Kate said. "That means someone else is after the crystal!"

"Or someone else was trying to stop them," Olivia observed dryly.

"But if others were after the source of the crystal, they'd have to know where to look for it," said Kareem. "They could only do that if—"

"—If Zimmerman wasn't dead after all," Kate completed his sentence. "Whoever is behind this organised the ambush and kidnapped him, I'd bet on it!"

"If they succeed, we'll have another Varak at our gates again," Sigrid murmured.

Kate thought about Carter and the initial expedition. *We may have had one even closer than that!* she thought.

The students turned to Mirayam for guidance. The old woman sat silently, unhurried and pensive. For a time, the only sound was that of the water splashing across the stones at the base of the fountain in the courtyard.

Finally, she said, "We have to stop them. There is no alternative. And, we can't afford to let Elward find out what we plan to do. He'd surely stop us. We need to get ourselves organised as quickly as possible; speed is essential, so take only what you will need. Start with the ambush. Kareem, can you find it?"

Kareem grinned at her.

Jackson burst out laughing. "Finally, we all get to go!"

"Whoever they are, don't underestimate them!" Mirayam warned. "Remember that they killed Captain Hawklight."

The mention of his name again was like a fist around Kate's heart. According to Carruthers, Hawklight had been broody and preoccupied, and that had made him careless, and had led to his murder. She wondered what his last thoughts were, and if they were of her. She had to begin to make amends for the sorrow she had caused. She knew she couldn't live with herself if she didn't try.

CHAPTER 3

*T*his was going to be the beginning of Copely's redemption.

Things had gone wrong from the moment he'd first met the Gallagher girl when he was working as a security guard in Westfield Mall. Both their journeys to Bexus were interconnected and had happened within days of each other. The girl had pulled away from his outstretched hands and toppled from the platform into the path of an oncoming train.

Then Copely woke up on Bexus on the wrong side of all the events that had followed. He'd been one of Varak's pawns, used to track the girl and deliver her up for execution. He had not succeeded, and the rest was now history. Copely himself had barely managed to survive. He had locked eyes with the girl as she stood on the bridge at Hogarth with Varak's crystal firmly in her grip. He'd been trapped like a deer mesmerized by the headlights of an oncoming car. He'd watched the tip of her staff point towards him, singling him out, but then the moment of madness passed and she'd spared his life.

It was nothing to be grateful about. He was a traitor to one side, a wheedling pariah to the other side. Nobody liked him; nobody wanted him. He was shunned and outcast. His fall from grace was epitomized by the fact that he had found Varak's crystal that the girl has tossed into the ravine, only to discover it had split in two on impact. It was as powerless and worthless as he was.

Or was he? He alone knew the secret that the girl had discarded the stone. He had the advantage. Somehow, he hoped to turn that information to his advantage.

He thought he'd succeeded when he saw her ride through the battle lines of Hornshurst that had encircled Cherath. No one made a move against her. They still believed she was the guardian of the crystal. This was his opportunity to expose her as a fraud. Copely was certain she would be cut down by both sides, and he had the prime viewing platform on top of the city walls to witness and enjoy the spectacle. Hawklight's presence beside the girl was a bonus; it was going to be two for the price of one.

That was the plan. It backfired. Copely was like the poker player with a nervous tic that signalled his intentions: he was bound to lose.

He leapt on the opportunity when the girl threatened to blow the gates apart.

"Let's see what she can do," he had cried. "Go ahead! Blow the gates apart! You ought to be able to manage that!" He couldn't hide his smirk when he saw her astonished look as she recognised him.

His general had other ideas. "Seize that man!"

It was Copely's turn to be astonished as a cohort of soldiers charged in his direction.

That idiot! he thought as he crawled up on to one of the battlements and reached into his pockets.

"The girl is bluffing! She has no power. If she had, she wouldn't need *this!*" and he'd tossed the broken crystal out in a high arc. The pieces flashed once in the sunlight before Copely was buried beneath a mound of volatile soldiers, and was dragged from the parapet screaming and laughing maniacally.

He continued to struggle and kick, all the while waiting for the sound of explosions. They never eventuated, and he was hauled down into the cellars that reeked of the stench of fear and the threat of relentless pain.

Copely was tossed into a large holding cell, and the gate clanged shut behind him. He picked himself up from the greasy, wet stone floor and wiped his palms against his uniform.

All eyes were turned towards the newcomer, assessing whether he was a potential threat or a hapless victim. Most of the prisoners were too shocked to care, but there were a few predatory stares among them, and Copely felt extremely vulnerable once more. They all had one thing in common: they wore the unique insignia on their tattered uniforms, which marked them as Varak's favoured few.

Rough hands grabbed him from behind, and he was shoved hard into the brick wall which lined the cell, and pinned by a forearm against his throat.

"You're standing in my spot!"

Copely's eyes swivelled in his head, and he caught a whiff of rancid breath as the arm crushed against his larynx.

"I'm waiting for an apology!"

He tried to speak; instead, he choked. He tugged at the arm, but he couldn't budge it.

"Maybe you need to be taught some manners!" the voice rasped. "And then, I'm gonna want those boots!"

Something moved in Copely's peripheral vision, and he heard a sickly, crunching sound. His attacker grunted in surprise and collapsed in a heap at his feet.

Copely began massaging his neck with his hands. It hurt when he swallowed. He was gasping for breath and staring at a squat silhouette standing in front of him in the gloom.

"Don't mind Miggs," said the figure. "He's claustrophobic."

The voice was high-pitched, and Copely realised the person in front of him holding a brick was a woman. She came up to his shoulder, and was almost as wide as she was tall. Her grey hair hung in a tangled, greasy mat, and her head sat low as if she had little or no neck. Her arms strained against the cotton sleeves of her shirt. Copely saw that, although she was short and stout, she wasn't fat.

She moved from the shadow into a band of light, which lit her face. He noticed her cheeks were pockmarked. She'd clearly had overzealous oil glands during adolescence, which would have been three decades earlier, at least. Her eyes were a jaundiced shade of hazel, and a lazy eye meant Copely had to flick from one eye to the other to see which one was staring back at him.

"I'm Griselda Chisholm," she said. "I know who you are. You're Copely, the spy."

'Spy' sounded much better than 'traitor'.

"Thanks." Copely's voice rasped, and he tried to smile. Griselda returned the smile, and Copely cringed inwardly. He'd seen the same kind of smile on Varak, and already knew he was gathering debt with the woman. *Great!* he thought. He wondered if Miggs had been paying off another favour with that act. He was still out for the count.

Griselda took him by the arm and led him to the other side of the expansive cell.

"You'll be safer on this side of the room," she said.

Copely remained locked up for two weeks before some guards came down to collect him and toss him back out on the street. During that time, he fell under Griselda's protection, and no one bothered him further. He was never quite sure about Miggs, who accosted every new prisoner hurled through the door. Griselda clocked him twice more with the brick if she saw any value in the new inmates; otherwise, Miggs had his way and was left alone to bully and harass those on the other side of the cell.

It turned out that Griselda had been Varak's spymaster during the old regime. She had seen the need to recruit Copely since he'd already met the girl, and would recognise her again, and had arranged to have him crushed beneath a taxi. She resembled a Russian peasant, but she had a mind like a steel trap. Copely quickly learned to keep his mouth shut and listen.

Griselda had already perceived Copely's near pathological cunning linked to his ability to survive tight situations. Such talents were rare for a spymaster to encounter, and Griselda was delighted by the opportunity to rehabilitate one of her own. She had plans for the two of them.

Once Copely had been released from gaol, he set about rescuing Griselda Chisholm. He tailed the gaoler for two weeks, and learned where he lived, and then targeted his family. His wife was kidnapped, and that guaranteed the gaoler's cooperation.

Around the same time, Madame Dubkiss disappeared. Madame Dubkiss was a woman who was as generous with her soul as she was in girth. One of the regular stallholders in the markets off the main square of Cherath, she was last seen in the company of a lean, dark-haired man, and it set tongues wagging, for Mrs Dubkiss had never lost a day through ill health, nor had she ever been seen arm-in-arm with a man.

Copely waited another three weeks until the tensions between Cherath and the besieging army of Hornshurst threatened to spill over into outright battle and the peacekeepers of Hogarth were thinly stretched before he made his move. With the aid of the gaoler, he smuggled a heavy and stupefied bundle down to the cellar in the dead of night.

The gaoler unlocked the cell door and the somnolent form of Madame Dubkiss was swapped for Griselda Chisholm. Miggs tried to escape as well, but Griselda laid him out for the last time using her brick. This wasn't a gaol break, after all.

The gaoler's wife was dumped in front of the prison doors the moment Copely and Chisholm disappeared. She was no longer required, now that they had something more secure to hold above the gaoler's head if the circumstances changed. If news got out that he was involved with a prisoner escaping, he'd be joining his charges, and that was a prospect no gaoler willingly invited.

By now, Copely feared a massacre. He and Chisholm badly needed an escape route through the lines, and so they spent the next two weeks plotting and reconnoitring.

He would pass through the gates and wander freely around the encampments of Hogarth and Hornshurst. He cut such an isolated, insignificant figure that no one gave him more than a brief, passing glance. Nonetheless, he took considerable care when passing by the tents of the peacekeeping force. The woman Mirayam had arrived in the camp, and she and her fawning group of students would have identified him in an instant if they'd clapped eyes on him.

Copely was surprised by how much of Griselda's network was still active. Word leaked back that Carter and his War Council had withdrawn from the battlefield. They had cut their losses and had run for safety. This meant that war was inevitable and also impending. They had to make their own break.

Griselda's army of recruits had grown to twelve. There were thugs, thieves, mercenaries and black marketeers among their number, but they were all ruthless and without mercy. Copely couldn't imagine a plan that would successfully sneak all of them through enemy lines at night, but he hadn't factored in Griselda Chisholm.

"Where better to hide a tree than in a forest?" she had asked as she handed around uniforms of the Hogarth peacekeepers. They looked and felt authentic, and Copely didn't dare ask how she had come upon them.

They waited until mid-morning before they left the safe house, when the sun was still low but bright, and there was a swarming mass of humanity flowing through the streets. Then, like any agitated patrol, they lined up two abreast and pushed their way through the city and out the gates. They were hissed at and jeered, but allowed to pass by without further incident. They stormed past the sentries at the gates and veered left, away from the bulk of the Hogarth buffer zone and towards the Hornshurst soldiers who appeared to be lining up in battle formation.

The sound of iron chains rattling behind them caused Copely to glance backwards. The huge portcullis, an enormous grate of thick iron bars, was dropping into place as the great gates of the city swung closed. They'd just managed to escape the city, but there was no turning back now, nowhere to hide.

The group came to a halt scant feet from the fortified line of Hornshurst soldiers, bristling with staffs all pointed towards them.

"Get back where you belong! Your time here is through!" someone snarled at them.

Griselda was undeterred. She stepped forward and brandished a rolled parchment.

"Who is in command here?" she demanded. "This guarantees us safe passage through your lines to deliver a message to Commander Elward Carter!"

A young man in a lieutenant's uniform said, "Let me see that!"

Griselda leaned forward and whispered in his ear. "Look around you, you fool! This may be our last chance to avoid a battle, and you're holding us up? Time is of the essence!"

The lieutenant peered about him. All along the line, soldiers were clamouring in full battle dress as sergeants marched up and down screaming battle cries. Were these peacekeepers indeed carrying the conditions for a negotiated surrender? What harm could they do?

"Let them through!" he barked and a path opened up wide enough to allow the group to pass by in single file. But before any of them could take the final steps through, a scattered cry of alarm arose along the line of troops.

Copely glanced skywards and saw the three converging plumes of vapour, and he knew immediately what was coming next. He dropped to the ground and covered his ears just as the thunderclap tore the air apart, and the shockwave blew outwards. Bodies were bowled like ninepins. Several of the group toppled on to him and shielded him from the rushing air and the flying stones and grit.

By the time he'd pushed them away and struggled to his knees, he'd seen the mounted rider and the wagon. He spat the sand from his mouth and watched as the wagon circled and pulled to a stop in the barren ground between the opposing armies of Hornshurst and Hogarth. Copely felt the chilly ice of hatred run along his back as a black-haired girl tossed a shiny object towards one of the druids of Hornshurst and then sank back down inside the wagon. It was the Gallagher girl, alive and well, and who'd once again helped sideline another imminent massacre.

A hand reached out and gripped his shirt.

"Get going!" Griselda barked. "No one is watching us any more!"

Copely shook his head.

"No! Go without me! I have some unfinished business here!" He turned and glared at the girl once more.

Griselda paused. Copely had an unspoken reputation for saving his own skin first. He was a survivor, and Griselda had trusted his instincts to save them all. Suddenly, he was waving away the chance to escape scot-free for some other purpose. Whatever it was, perhaps it was worth waiting around for. Where Copely was the survivor, Chisholm was the opportunist.

She pulled the group around her in a tight huddle.

"Spread out! Get lost! We're not leaving! Find your own way back into the city! Meet up back at the house! Now, go!"

The group disbanded; they melted away in the confused crowd of soldiers, discarding the Hogarth uniforms as they went. Only Copely remained rooted to the spot, watching the events on the field unfold.

He noted with satisfaction the way Hawklight led his mount morosely from the scene, never once looking back at the girl. She, in turn, had ignored the warrior, and had sat weeping with her head buried between her hands.

There had been a falling out between the two, a situation Copely could only have dreamed about previously. He would never have been able to get close to the girl with Hawklight hovering in the background. Suddenly, things were different. He was going to need the help of Griselda Chisholm and the others. Chisholm was shrewd enough to have sniffed out an opportunity already, and Copely could not afford to underestimate her, nor to deceive her. It wouldn't matter to her if the Gallagher girl lived or died. Copely had to come up with something else to sweeten the pot.

———m———

That was the deal. *Make it worth my while!* she had said. *Do that, and the girl is yours!*

There had to be something!

Copely had hoped to shadow Kate, but she had become reclusive. He spotted her twice the following day, but then only at a distance as she was constantly surrounded by her friends in public. He learned a day later that she had already left the city en route to Hogarth, and he cursed himself for not uncovering that titbit earlier.

Madame Dubkiss was also back on the streets, albeit a shadow of her former self, and arrest warrants had been posted and rewards offered for any sightings of Griselda Chisholm.

As a result, Griselda had quickly grown impatient. She cornered Copely with a brick in her hand.

"This has been a complete waste of my time!" she harped, and then her voice dropped to a growling threat. "Find me something within the week, or so help me, I'll use this on you!"

He changed tactics. The threat of grievous bodily harm helped direct his attention to Hawklight, something he'd resisted up until that point. And then, he struck the mother lode while eavesdropping outside Carter's tent.

Copely slipped back into the shadows and melted away in the darkness. His black cape wrapped around him made him almost invisible. Twice, sentries passed within a few feet of him, but none saw him rooted to the spot as he waited for them to pass by. He had learned the hard way not to underestimate Hawklight, and had taken a considerable risk in following him to Carter's headquarters, although Hawklight did appear tired and drawn, and Copely had correctly suspected that his defences would be down.

He'd pulled Griselda out of earshot of others, and had recounted everything he'd overheard. He watched as her eyes turned glassy, and he knew she was in a private world of her own with a glowing crystal hanging from her neck.

The plot was hatched.

—m—

The group split into twos and threes and departed for Hogarth separately. Chisholm and Copely tagged on to the back end of the retreating army, always keeping within sight of Zimmerman riding at the head of the column with Carter, and of Hawklight, who rode alone.

Once they had rendezvoused in Hogarth, the plan was thrown into action. Copely and a couple of the others were assigned to keep tabs on the geologist: watch him, follow him, report everything back no matter how trivial it seemed. The rest of the gang set about organising weapons and supplies they would need.

Copely's main concern was Hawklight. Out there in the wilderness, he'd be back on his game. He'd know if he were being followed. If they got ahead of him on the trail, he'd know that too. He voiced his concerns to Griselda, who until now had been preoccupied with the geologist Zimmerman.

Griselda leaned back in her chair and smiled at him—a knowing smile—and said, "Bribery and corruption: never underestimate their power to oil the squeaking wheel."

"What do you know?" Copely squinted suspiciously at her.

She laughed.

"We have Timmins in our pocket."

"Timmins? Who is Timmins?"

"Corporal Timmins is a scout—one of two on this expedition. We made it very worth his while to give us this—" and she pointed to a map spread out in front of her. Copely followed the line of her finger and saw a spidery red line inked across the surface of the map, pointing south.

"They leave in three days' time," Griselda continued. "There's an alternative, little-known track here—" she pointed towards another black line of ink, "—which *we* will use. The tracks converge at this point, which is where we'll be waiting for them. Timmins is taking them the long way round to give us plenty of time to get into position."

"Can you trust him?" Copely asked.

Chisholm flashed him her knowing smile again.

"The Gallagher girl left for Hornshurst last week," Copely mumbled.

"I know."

"You *knew?*" Copely replied incredulously. "Why didn't you tell me?"

"Priorities, Mr Copely," Griselda said evenly. "She'll be here when we return. You'll get your chance then."

But you promised—!"

She silenced him with a grim stare.

"You'd better get ready to leave with the rest of us."

They stole away from Hogarth in the dead of night. It took them the better part of a week to reach the point where the two tracks converged. Much of that time was spent endlessly hacking at the undergrowth that had spread across the slim trail and all but hidden it from view.

Copely was reminded of his first brush with nature, following innocuous markers that had been left behind by soldiers of Varak's raiding parties through the Great Forest. He had led Kate and two of her fellow students into a trap. There had been times when he didn't think he'd survive the deception. The Great Forest was filled with any number of deadly animals and plants; a single, inattentive moment was all that was needed to disappear.

At night, surrounded by the screams, wails and calls from creatures hidden well above them in the canopy layer, Copely could discern the unmistakable low growling of an *Abyssi* pack that appeared to be tracking them. The animals were hesitant and unsure, and the party was well armed, but they took the added precaution nonetheless of weaving protective gel bubbles around themselves before they settled into sleep.

Each morning, Copely would wake to find a slew of different animal tracks that had circled their sleeping forms during the night. This was no place for the unwary.

The party reached the base of the mountain range part way through the fourth day. They rested for an hour, after which they started the long, slow ascent. They cut across rocky streams and followed one upriver through a series of tumbling water races and short waterfalls. The air was cooler, and the clouds of midge-like insects that had plagued them on the lower slopes disappeared.

No one spoke. They were all intent on putting one foot in front of the other, and trying to maintain an even, slow rhythm as they gradually wound their way up the side of the mountain. They camped near the top that evening, but the following morning, they dropped into a valley, and had to begin the seemingly endless process once again.

The party had relied on the skills of a slightly-built lock picker named Khushk who had also proved to be adept at tracking. He'd been a goat herder once, and he'd retained his skills in locating his lost animals in the wadis north of Quetta, Pakistan.

When Copely trudged around another blind bend on the trail, he was relieved to see those who'd gone ahead now stalled at the side of the track. He dropped the load from his shoulders and rested until the rest of the party including Griselda caught up. Khushk had been leaning against a tree waiting for the group to arrive. He didn't want them to go any further.

"This trail meets the other just beyond the ridge," he said. "We must be careful not to taint the ground where they come together."

He drew a rough sketch in the dirt, using a pointed stick. He showed a small clearing where the two tracks joined. On either side, the ground rose forming a natural basin enclosing the clearing. It was a prime spot for an ambush, with clear lines of fire on each side. They would be firing down into the bowl, eliminating the risk of cross fire. The only problem might be the thick undergrowth encroaching on to the clearing, but they couldn't risk clearing it back. Huge trees anchored by spreading buttresses sat at each end of the clearing, as well.

"What about other possibilities?" Copely asked.

Khushk shook his head. He had crept parallel to the other trail each side of the clearing for three hundred yards. Any ambush might take out a couple of soldiers, but there was plenty of cover, and they'd be strung out along the trail, not closed up in the clearing. No, the clearing was a natural place to stop and rest. It was a straightforward choice to make.

They split the party in two, and Khushk led one group uphill through the bush to a point where they could cross the track safely and work their way back down the other side. They took up their positions that Riegel had designated. Riegel was one of the few members of the band of cutthroats with any real military experience, and he seemed to have an eye for attacking the unsuspecting.

Once everyone was in place, Khushk slipped like a wraith into the bush to follow the trail downhill. He was the sentry; he would warn them when to expect company. Copely leaned against his pack, and glanced across at Griselda who still looked beetroot red despite her pale green aura. The only thing to do now was wait.

Copely was snoozing lightly with his head drooped between his legs when Khushk gently shook him awake. Khushk placed a finger across his lips to signal silence before moving on. Copely reached for his staff, and then risked poking his head above the undergrowth to look around.

He was impressed. They had lain in wait a day and a half, and he'd expected the motley crew to be careless and impatient. He saw nothing to indicate that the clearing was bristling with killers waiting to strike, and he smiled to himself. He lowered his head, and pressed his face into a space between some ferns, which afforded him a reasonable view of the clearing without being seen.

They had been warned about Zimmerman. He was to be left untouched. Anyone else was a hindrance to be removed.

Timmins was the first to arrive at the clearing. He raised one arm in a gesture signalling a halt to the march. Others straggled in one-by-one behind him, and dropped their packs in the dirt out of the paths of the lumbering *Urguts,* also heavily laden with equipment.

Copely saw Hawklight. The warrior was alert and suspicious, and he stood to one side and carefully surveyed the surrounding bush. Copely slowly lowered his head and buried his face in the ground cover. He imagined Hawklight's gaze sweeping above him like a searchlight as he lay still.

The plan was to wait, in order to allow the party time to relax and feel secure. It was late in the afternoon, and Khushk had assured everyone that the expedition was unlikely to press on.

When Copely risked raising his head again, he saw that the expedition members were setting up camp for the night. He recognised Zimmerman and watched where he dropped his bedroll. He hoped others had done the same. He searched for Hawklight and saw him sitting apart from the others. His staff was lying across his lap. This unsettled Copely and he was determined that his first shot would head in Hawklight's direction.

He shifted his gaze to Timmins. The corporal was moving among the men, barking orders. In between, he kept glancing around nervously at the underbrush. *The fool!* thought Copely. His eyes flicked back to Hawklight, but the captain seemed preoccupied with Zimmerman.

The attack was timed to coincide with the last light of day. Night-time in the forest kept men on edge; it was the playground of predators then. Most of the soldiers were gathered around a solitary campfire in the middle of the clearing, wrapped in cloaks as they quietly chatted amongst themselves. A pair of sentries had been posted at each end of the clearing where the path led off into the bush between the buttressed stands of trees. Zimmerman was leaning against a fallen log trying to read by using a weak light emanating from the tip of his staff. Hawklight had already retired into his bedroll, and Copely could make out his hulking horizontal form through the gloom—just.

The first explosion ripped into the base of the trees at one end, and two bodies were tossed beyond and into the undergrowth.

"Exstinguere!" Copely yelled. A fizzing ball of blue energy rocketed from his staff, and Hawklight's sleeping form erupted in a brilliant orange wall of flame. Copely screamed with elation as he turned his staff towards the gathering at the middle.

The mayhem lasted no more than thirty seconds. The attackers were merciless. Timmins had scampered for cover, but Griselda

Chisholm caught him with a blast between the shoulders, and when the smoke cleared, he had vanished.

The attack ceased as suddenly as it had begun. The air, which had been torn apart by loud explosions, was starkly silent; all the forest chatter had ceased.

Shapes slowly materialised out of the gloom as the attackers stepped from their positions and moved cautiously into the flickering firelight. The area was littered with the remains of smouldering uniforms as the clearing was searched for any signs of survivors. Three men were dispatched to head up the trail and retrieve the lumbering *Urguts*, which had fled as soon as the fight had started.

Copely wandered over to where Hawklight had been sleeping. His cloak and blanket had been turned to grey ash, and his helmet had been split apart. He had kicked at the ash mound before a whimpering sound made him turn.

Zimmerman was curled like a foetus, with his hands cradling his ears.

"Please! Don't hurt me, please!"

Griselda Chisholm bent over him and extended her hand.

"Get up, Mr Zimmerman. We're not here to hurt you."

Zimmerman opened one eye fearfully, and the whining stopped.

"Who are you? How do you know my name?"

"Do you have the stones with you, Mr Zimmerman?"

"Wha—? What stones?"

Griselda cocked her head at him as though she were peering over a set of pince-nez. This time, there was an unmistakable steeliness in her voice.

"Come now, Mr Zimmerman, we haven't travelled all this way just to be polite. The stones?"

Marcus reached into his top pocket and extracted the broken halves of the crystal.

"You're wasting your time," he said. "They no longer work."

She smiled at him. "But you know where to get more."

Marcus corrected her. "I *think* I know."

"Let's hope so," she replied, "because your life depends on it!" She watched his Adam's apple bob up and down as he swallowed. "Try to get some rest," she advised him. "We'll be leaving early in the morning. Meanwhile, Mr Copely, here, would like to be reunited with the crystal."

She passed the broken shards across to Copely as they turned back towards the fire.

Marcus watched them leave. "It's called Zimmermanite," he uttered feebly.

Khushk led the way once more. Zimmerman was sandwiched between Copely and Chisholm in the middle of the strung-out column. Riegel brought up the rear, pausing often to check that they were not being followed.

Just before midday, Carruthers stumbled from the thicket of ferns, dazed and bleeding. His first thought had been that his party had gone ahead without him until he spied the piles of blackened uniforms. He was alive, but alone and decidedly lost in the wilderness.

He nearly wept with relief when Gonzales appeared. His arm throbbed constantly, and he had a blinding headache, and Gonzales didn't appear to be in much better shape. Yet, when the forest fell silent, and they heard the distant howl of the hunting *Abyssi*, they immediately found the strength to begin the harrowing journey home.

CHAPTER 4

he pounding on the door was brutal in its intensity. Mirayam appeared from the house and hurried to unlock the front gate. As she tapped out the code in the shape of a pentangle, it flew open, and she was knocked backwards against the wall.

A squad of soldiers burst through the opening and flowed into the courtyard. Two of them grabbed Mirayam by the arms and manhandled her along between them.

"You're hurting me! Stop it this instant!" she insisted, and although she was old and outwardly frail, she commanded such a presence that the two burly guards instantly did what they were told.

"How dare you burst in here like that!" Her eyes flashed with righteous anger. "On whose authority are you acting?"

"Mine, Mirayam!"

Mirayam wheeled about as Elward Carter strode through the entrance. She redirected her anger at him.

"Get out of my house now! I warn you, Elward, I will take this to the Council!"

Carter ignored her. He stepped into the courtyard and looked about as if he were a prospective buyer for the property.

"Kate Gallagher. Where is she?"

"She's out!"

"That's not an answer!"

"It's the only civil one you're likely to get, Elward."

He turned to his soldiers.

"Search all the rooms!"

Mirayam quickly reined in her anger. She needed a cool head. She pointedly ignored Carter and found a seat on one of the couches, and watched him pace back and forth. The sound of doors slamming shut punctuated the silence between them. Eventually, the soldiers returned.

"There's no one else here, sir," the squad sergeant reported.

Mirayam smiled and said nothing.

"Wait outside, Sergeant!"

"Yes sir."

The sergeant cocked his head towards the gate, and the squad filed out. Carter followed them, and shut the gate as the last soldier left. He stalked back to where Mirayam was sitting.

"We had a 'chance' meeting four days ago, your wonder girl and me. Did she happen to mention that?"

Mirayam said nothing. She ignored his glare, and concentrated on outwardly controlling her own emotions, which were heaving inside her.

"She already knew about Hawklight." His eyes narrowed. It was an accusation.

"You know me better than that," Mirayam admonished him. "Yes, she knew about Hawklight."

"She threatened me!"

Mirayam smiled. "She didn't do a very good job, Elward. You're still standing."

Carter bristled and his ears burned red.

"She can't hide for long. The moment she turns up, I'm arresting her, her 'boyfriend', all of them! They're all in on it!"

"Then what? Are you going to drag them before the Council? Before the Court?"

"Damn right!"

Carter was seething. Mirayam paused; she allowed him to stew for a minute, and watched as his jaw muscles clenched and unclenched. He finally checked his rage, but his hands were still shaking.

"She knows about the crystal. She knows about the geologist. What will you do when she brings that up at the Council?"

Her words startled Carter and an expression of guilt and fear flickered across his face.

"How did she—? Wha—? When did—?" He stopped himself. It was an admission, and now he'd confirmed to Mirayam what she'd only suspected.

He leapt to his feet and glowered over her. For a moment, Mirayam feared he would strike her. Instead, he turned and stormed towards the gate. As he was reaching for the handle, he stopped suddenly, and then turned slowly to face her once more. His face had changed as if he had finally remembered the answer to a question that had been puzzling him for days.

"She couldn't let it go," he whispered. "She's gone looking for the site of the massacre. They've all gone!" He strode back and bent his face close to Mirayam's. "It's more than that, though. There's something else! She suspects something else!"

Mirayam fought to keep her face impassive, but a tiny twitch beneath her left eye betrayed her. Carter saw it and smiled.

He turned and left without saying another word. Mirayam started to shake and she had to grip the arm of the couch to steady herself. She was seized by a sudden misgiving and hurried to the gate. She twisted the handle quietly and eased it open a fraction.

"—has the map coordinates. Make sure you get them. And send someone to fetch Captain Streikker. He's to meet with me within the hour. Dismissed!"

"Sir!"

The hollow sound of boots on cobblestones echoed off the walls as the squad of soldiers jogged away. Mirayam kept her ear to the gap in the doorway. She could still hear the sound of Carter's harsh breathing, and the heavy slap of his palm against the plastered brick wall as he grunted in frustration and stormed away into the night.

She pressed the door shut and slid an iron bar through metal brackets to lock it. She leaned against the gate and closed her eyes and sighed.

Hans Streikker was a formidable foe indeed. He was equal to Hawklight in strength and courage although he lacked Hawklight's finesse and military instincts. He was a fighting machine who followed orders without question, and he was fiercely loyal to serving the needs of Hogarth. Mirayam feared for the safety of her charges if Streikker were sent in pursuit. He would be as single-minded as a pitbull terrier, and Carter had his ear. She was under no illusion as to what his orders would be.

She needed to expose Carter to the Council to rein him in, and the sooner, the better.

Early the following morning, she gathered her staff and wrapped herself in a warm woollen cloak. She slid the bar back from its housing, entered the code to unlock the front gate, and twisted the handle. As she stepped across the threshold, she was stopped by two armed guards posted outside her door.

"I'm sorry. Please step back inside the gate. You are not permitted to leave these premises."

"I am a member of the Council, Corporal," she said. "Am I under arrest?"

"Beggin' your pardon, but yes, ma'am," the corporal replied. "Orders from the Council, signed by Commander Carter himself."

He flourished a sheet of paper.

Mirayam quickly scanned the contents and turned pale. She handed the paper back.

"I'm sorry, ma'am," the corporal said. The woman standing in front of him was a living legend, and the corporal treated her with the utmost respect.

Mirayam nodded vaguely, and then stepped back inside the gate. She pushed the gate closed and bowed her head.

The word had leapt from the page at her.

Treason!

———《∭》———

Hans Streikker had pushed the company hard. The coats of the *Hon'chai* glistened with sweat, and the soldiers had needed to dismount and walk beside the animals twice to afford them some rest.

Carter's orders had been particularly specific. The students were to be brought back to face a charge of treason. Naturally, the Court would properly ascertain their guilt and the extent of their crimes. Streikker was puzzled by the girl's behaviour, and he had private misgivings about his assignment. She had almost single-handedly prevented two crucial battles and was hailed as the saviour of Hogarth by its citizens, so it beggared belief that she should turn traitorous suddenly for no apparent reason. He had kept these thoughts to himself because of Hawklight.

Streikker held Hawklight in high regard, and the respect had been mutual. Hawklight had chosen to stand by the girl in the quest for the Hornshurst talisman, and yet he had returned apparently estranged from her. Something had happened. What had Hawklight learned? It was this one prickle of doubt that led Streikker to follow his orders like the obedient servant that he was.

No, the Court would decide the level of her guilt; it was not up to him to sit as judge and jury. However, it had been Carter's final remarks that had continued to unsettle him.

"If you cannot bring them back alive, so be it! Use whatever force is necessary!"

It had been whispered in his ear.

"She is dangerous!"

They'd had a four-day lead. Streikker was confident he'd already cut that by half or more. He had the advantage of surprise.

Streikker held his arm aloft and the column of marching men halted.

"Mount up!" he ordered. He gripped a handful of the thick fur and swung his leg up and over his mount in one fluid movement. A ruffled thump of bodies behind him signalled the company was ready to ride again.

"Move out!"

Kate sat with her back against a tree. She cradled Hawklight's helmet in her lap. She ran her fingers over the sharp, jagged edges. It appeared as if a fireball had entered through the front and blasted a gaping exit at the back. She doubted he would have felt a thing.

She'd found the helmet, tossed aside nonchalantly beside a pile of ashes and blackened sand. Some of the sand had melted and had formed droplets of glass. The clearing itself was strewn with rotting uniforms that were little more than damp nests for pudgy, white larvae.

Sigrid sat down beside Kate and wrapped her arm around Kate's shoulders.

"I'm sorry."

Kate was angry with Hawklight.

"This is all so stupid! How could he have been so stupid to be caught like this? I always thought I'd see him again, and now . . ." Her words trailed away as she bit her lip to fight back the tears.

Sigrid pulled Kate's head onto her shoulder.

"I wish I'd been with you when you were teaching him to swim," she whispered. "I'd've liked to have seen that."

Kate recalled watching Hawklight flounder as he'd tried to keep his head above water. His hair had been plastered against his face, and the tendons along his neck had been stretched taut. He'd been so alarmingly uncoordinated in the water that the image caused her to smile with the memory.

"I just wanted the chance to tell him that I'm sorry," she said.

"I think he knew. I think we all knew you'd come around in the end. It was just a matter of time." Sigrid lifted Kate's head up and looked into her eyes. "I think he knew!"

"Kareem's back!" Jackson's voice broke the moment between them.

Kareem appeared at the far end of the clearing. He came to where Kate was sitting, and the other students joined him.

"They've long gone," he said. "Someone tried to cover their tracks, but there is still plenty of spoor along the trail." He looked at Kate. "I think you're right. There's only one set of tracks up ahead that matches anything coming from behind. I think they belong to Zimmerman. We're looking at a group around fifteen strong. They've got three *Urguts* hauling something, and that's going to slow them down."

"Can you track them?" Kate asked.

Kareem raised his eyebrows.

"Of course. Stupid question, really." She turned to the others. "I guess what I meant to ask was: do we want to continue on with this?"

They raised their eyebrows.

"Stupid question, really," replied Olivia.

Kate's eyes returned to the helmet in her lap. She placed it gently on the ground beside her.

"Then let's get going," she said. Kareem offered her his hand and pulled her to her feet. She picked up her staff, Rhyanon, and glanced about the clearing for the last time.

"Do you think we'll catch up with them?" she asked.

"Depends where they're headed," said Kareem. "Three *Urguts* mean a lot of supplies: I'd say tents, and a lot of cold weather gear, as well as all the geological equipment they'd need. That means they're headed way south so yeah—we could catch them. But we're going to have to find similar stuff ourselves somewhere along the way."

"Let's hope they don't get that far." Mia shivered with the thought of blizzards and endless ice.

"We still don't know who's behind it," said Ethan. "So far, they've outsmarted Carter, and they've killed Hawklight. That makes them very dangerous indeed!"

With that sobering thought in mind, they followed Kareem as he led them from the clearing following the trail that had long since turned cold.

—ɱ—

The map was of no further use. The thin line of the path they had been following had ended abruptly, so Ethan crumpled the map back inside his pack. He figured he could use it later to light a fire.

The track was undulating, but they climbed steadily for two more days. They broke out beyond the treeline, and continued on across terrain that was carpeted in tussock and spongy creeping turf, and mired underfoot where the seasonal snowmelt drained into peat basins. The air was colder at altitude, and the extra blankets and thicker jackets they carried were pulled from their packs. Kareem was right about one thing: they were going to need warmer clothing.

The air was clear, but the sunlight was weak and watery, and the wind blustered across the exposed ridges. The party traversed another plateau and dropped down onto the lee side of the hill. Some of the land had slumped, creating a flat apron beside a vertical wall of loose rock. It was dry and sheltered, and a good place to stop for the night.

They dumped their packs and relaxed, grateful for the opportunity to rest. Kareem had forced the pace, maintaining a steady jog despite the extra gear they carried. No one complained; no one lagged behind.

Kate lay against her pack and stretched and arched her back to ward off any stiffness. She closed her eyes, but was soon shaken awake by Kareem.

"Shhhh!" he whispered.

Kate sat up, startled, but Kareem placed his hand against her shoulder to reassure her.

"What is it?" she whispered.

"Come and look," he replied in a hushed tone.

Jackson, Sigrid, and Mia were already spread-eagled in the dirt at the edge of the platform where the hillside sloped away. Kate crawled to join them on her hands and knees, following Kareem's example. He rolled on to his side to make room for her, and pointed with his thumb.

"Down there."

Kate scanned the lower slopes of the hill, where the tussock merged with a belt of stunted trees. Something was moving down there.

She could make out eight to ten animals milling about in a tight group, some with their noses in the tussock, searching for the succulent young, green stems. Their heads seemed oversized for their bodies. Their elongated snouts were black in the waning light but were topped with two long, magnificent horns. A ridge of black hair that was not quite a mane ran back along their necks and continued between their shoulder blades, to peter out halfway along their backs. Their tails flicked lazily in the air to sweep the biting flies away.

The flanks of one of the beasts flashed silver and caught Kate's eye. It looked as if the animal had been wrapped in shiny plastic, but moments later, the plastic folded outwards in twin sets of translucent wings, and the animal lifted off and hovered about twenty feet above the others. It looked like a gross, mutant cross between a blowfly and a wildebeest, and something clicked in Kate's memory.

"Is that what I think it is?" she whispered.

Kareem grinned. "*Galaptagos*. Looks like a family group."

She watched in awe. She remembered them from the mysterious cave etchings in Hogarth, flying above scattered, panicked crowds, each one bearing a rider armed with a longbow.

"You can ride them?" she asked.

"You have to catch them first," Mia answered.

"How?"

"With difficulty," said Jackson, and they laughed.

They continued to watch the animals in the fading light until the *Galaptagos* finally turned and disappeared into the trees. They crept back from the edge and settled around the fire that Ethan had already lit.

"They won't go too far because of predators," Kareem said. "They'll stick close to the clearing in case they have to take flight."

"Have any of you ever ridden one?" Kate asked. They shook their heads, but Kareem said quietly, "Your mother did."

Kate felt the familiar pang of guilt every time her mother was mentioned. Her friends looked away as if to say, *This is embarrassing;* only Kareem was comfortable enough to meet her gaze.

"Tell me about it." Kate broke the awkwardness of the situation.

"They were like chickens, or crocodiles. If you blindfolded them, they were actually quite docile. You could steer them by using your knees and shifting your body position. Your mother used to say it was no different to riding a motorcycle. Eventually, she could have removed the blindfold, but we never kept them in captivity that long. If Varak's troops had captured them, they'd have used them against us."

The mention of Varak's name reminded them of their current plight. Someone ahead of them had designs on his vacated throne. Kate was determined that person would never succeed, if only to avenge Hawklight's death.

Olivia and Sigrid had opted for the first watch, so the others settled down to sleep. Kate lay alongside Kareem. His presence was now so familiar that she took it for granted. Kareem had stepped into the role of protector that had been Hawklight's before Kate had spurned him. Kareem was like Hawklight in another respect: he wasn't fazed by her mood swings, or by the reputation she'd gained in little more than a year on the planet.

It wasn't that one-sided, either. Kate had felt jealous when Olivia had flirted playfully with Kareem. Kate knew it was just a game between them both, but some tiny part of her hotly resented it. She shifted onto her side and forced her mind to think of other things.

Kareem shook her awake. She thought she'd only just dropped off to sleep. Surely it wasn't her watch already? Something was wrong! Everyone was being stirred from sleep.

A brilliant red hummingbird was hovering in the light to one side of the feeble campfire. It was enveloped by a lemon-yellow aura that Kate recognised as Mirayam's. Yet hummingbirds didn't exist on Bexus; no birds did.

Kate watched as it hovered and darted back and forth as if it were feeding on an invisible bush of flowers. The muted noise of its beating wings droned around the campsite. Suddenly, it exploded in mid air in a shower of feathers that drifted down and disappeared in tiny plumes of red smoke. A scrap of parchment landed in the dirt beneath where the bird had been.

Sigrid rescued the paper as it was about to roll into the embers of the fire. She unfolded it while Mia illuminated it using the glowing tip of her staff.

"It's from Mirayam!" Sigrid exclaimed.

"How did she do that?" Jackson wondered aloud. They were familiar with Mirayam's potent grasp of magic, but none of them had seen anything like it before.

"How did it find us? At night!"

Sigrid held up her hand for quiet.

"She's under house arrest. Carter somehow knows we've gone after Zimmerman, and he's sent Hans Streikker and a company of soldiers to find us and bring us back. Mirayam is worried that he's been given other orders. She thinks that, by the time we get this note, he'll only be a day behind us, maybe less."

"Streikker!" Olivia groaned. "Of all the people . . ."

"You know him?"

"He'd have given Hawklight a run for his money most days of the week," Jackson agreed.

"Can we outrun them?" Kate asked.

"Maybe. Probably not," replied Kareem.

"What about hiding from them? We could lay a false trail, cut back, and try and skirt around them."

Again, Kareem shook his head. "That way, they'd be ahead of us, and we'd risk running into them. If this—Streikker—is as good as you say, then he'd find us."

They stared morosely into the fire. This far out, they would surely wind up as collateral damage. Streikker, the professional soldier, would be pragmatic: there would be no survivors to contradict his account of how things ended.

Kate had a sudden thought.

"What about the *Galaptagos*?"

Ethan laughed. The idea was absurd. The others smiled.

"I think that's our best option," said Kareem, and the laughter died away.

"What are you saying?" asked Sigrid.

"All we have to do is trap them and blindfold them. There are seven of us, and if we doubled up, we'd only need four animals.

We could leave your Streikker far behind us, and close the gap between us and Zimmerman at the same time."

"You couldn't possibly track him from the air?"

"I don't think we need to. If Zimmerman continues to head south, he and whoever is with him will have to pass through Poluostrov, on the shores of Bear Lake. It's the last of the big settlements. Beyond that, there's nothing much more than ice and tundra. We can try and pick up the trail again there."

"He's right!" Jackson agreed. "It won't matter where they've got to if we can't manage to get away from here!"

None of them had any experience with *Galaptagos*. They looked expectantly at Kareem for answers.

"We need a hunter's snare charm," he said. "Grab your staffs and spread out."

They shuffled apart until they were dotted about the edges of the slumped platform.

"The command is: *Abiecit rete piscatoris!* It means: cast a fisherman's net. Tilt your staffs slightly, and altogether on three. One . . . two . . . *three!*"

"*Abiecit rete piscatoris!*"

A string of blue plasma shot from the tip of each wand and converged over their heads above the fire. The air crackled with static, and a sphere of plasma netting expanded outward from the central core. Two of the cords spluttered and disappeared, and the web collapsed inward.

"*Desistere!*"

The broken net disappeared.

Kareem smiled. "Not bad for a first attempt. It'll work better when we coordinate the command."

They practised timing the command to a whistle signal until they'd perfected it and the net hovered and hummed above them.

"Whatever you do, don't let go of your staff," Kareem warned. "The *Galaptagos* are going to kick and thrash about and try to fly away, and we're going to get dragged around and bruised, but with a bit of luck their legs and wings will get tangled and they'll trip over one another, and go down. That's when we need to get the blindfolds on. Stay clear of the horns!"

They all heard the last sentence.

They repacked their gear during the night and sneaked down the slope without a sound. They then left their gear in a pile where the slope flattened out, and slithered forward, spreading out to form a circle around the spot where the animals had disappeared into the trees. They lay silently amongst the tussock, waiting on the first light of dawn.

Kate hugged the ground with Rhyanon lying within easy reach beside her. She knew that Kareem would be watching and waiting for the animals to reappear. Grey light revealed a series of dark forms that were humps of tussock grass, but little else.

She heard a soft snort about twenty yards in front of her, followed by the damp swish of an animal treading warily into the clearing. She lay still, but tensed, ready to spring into action. They only had one chance to make it work. If the animals escaped the trap, all hope was lost.

She sensed the movement ahead of her. She knew the *Galaptagos* would be timid and alert. Then—silence! She wondered if souls held a scent that the beasts had somehow detected. Something had made them pause, had made them edgy. She closed her eyes as if, by closing them, she could shut out her own presence.

She was aware of time stretching, passing infinitesimally slowly. She held her breath. Ten minutes became twenty minutes. The tip of her nose itched, and she yearned to scratch it, or bury it in the mud. Her eyes watered as she battled to remain motionless.

Finally, another snort! The sound of grass being ripped from the ground and the sloppy sound of chewing! The animals had relaxed. Whatever had spooked them had gone. Her hand gripped Rhyanon. She was ready for the signal.

A single, shrill whistle cut the air.

"Abiecit rete piscatoris!"

Kate had pushed up onto her knees and had pointed Rhyanon into the air above the startled animals. The plasma ropes collided, and the network flowed out and down like an exploded skyrocket. Kate jerked the tip of her staff down, flattening the floating balloon shape, cutting off the escape routes.

Two of the *Galaptagos* leaped into the air in fright and immediately got tangled in the webbing created by the plasma streams. Two more twisted and bolted back towards the stunted forest and escaped the trap. Another tried to follow, but its long horns twisted in the net filaments. The momentum caused its head to snap backwards, and it flipped onto its back with legs flailing wildly.

The silence of the morning was shattered by the terrified shrieks of the trapped animals. The net snapped shut just as Kate was dragged violently towards the twisting mass of thrashing, screaming animals.

"Hold tight!" she heard Kareem shout above the noise. "Don't break the net."

Kate was aware of Mia to her left, and Ethan to her right, both being dragged through clumps of tussock as they wrestled for control of their staffs. She heard Sigrid shriek in pain from somewhere on the other side of the tumbling bodies.

The tension in her cord suddenly slackened. She used the respite to struggle to her knees, just as one of the old bulls lowered his head and charged at her. She threw herself sideways and rolled into the mud, holding tight to Rhyanon. She felt the heavy impact beside her shoulder as two massive horns were driven deep into the mud where she'd knelt moments before.

The animal bellowed and tried to free itself, but the sucking mud refused to let go. The bull was rammed from behind by another and toppled onto its side. Kate heard a sudden, sickly *crack!* as its neck snapped, killing it instantly.

Part of the net was pinned beneath the dead weight of the old bull's body, which acted like an anchor against the struggles of the other trapped animals. They bucked and reared, and became more tangled and tripped over each other, all the while screaming like rabbits caught in piano wire snares.

The animals were truly entangled. Their futile struggles had teased more of the plasma from the ends of the staffs to the point where they could barely move about inside the net.

Kareem called to Mia, and the two of them disengaged their staffs. Kate watched their plasma paths within the network dissolve away. Holes now appeared in the net, although none was large enough to create a problem.

Now came the dangerous part.

Kareem had spent time slicing a couple of bedrolls into long strips of thick blanket. He ran back to where the gear had been laid aside to retrieve them. Some trailed behind him as he ran back. He passed a handful to Mia.

Kareem had opted to blindfold the beasts, but he needed help. Mia was the most nimble and was chosen, despite the fact that everyone had volunteered for the job.

"How are we going to get past the net?" Mia asked.

"Don't bother with it. It won't matter if any netting gets caught under the material. When we disengage, it will all disappear anyway. Whatever you do, don't get impaled." Kareem gave her the widest grin, and like the others, she fell for his charm and grinned back, forgetting her fear. Something inside Kate bristled with the exchange.

Kareem looked over the tangle of furry bodies and picked out the other older bull.

"We'll tackle him first." He pointed out the animal to Mia. To the others he said, "Keep the leashes as tight as you can. Don't give him any space to wriggle."

They stepped to one side of the bull. He tilted his head back as far as it would go and eyed them warily. On Kareem's signal, Mia began a slow circle to the front, allowing the strips of blanket to catch the breeze and flutter. Kareem remained motionless, so the bull turned his head and followed Mia.

Mia kept the bull's attention by rocking side-to-side and taking short steps towards him. He snorted and screamed at her, warning her away, and he tried to bring his head down to point his impressive horns at her.

Mia talked to him. She kept her voice soft and soothing, and she stepped further to one side so that Kareem was in his blind spot. His head was cocked slightly, away from Kareem, who made his move.

He leapt forward and wrapped his arms around the base of both horns, drove upwards with his legs to twist the massive head further, and then brought his body down to try and immobilize the animal's head. It immediately bellowed and tried to flick him away, but he was too strong.

Mia darted into the gap beneath his arm and tried to wrap the blindfold in place across the bull's eyes. It slipped off twice because of the plasma netting, but she managed to secure it on the third attempt, binding it tightly around the animal's muzzle.

Kareem had expected her to duck aside the moment she had finished so that he could let go of the head. Instead, she bent forward and whispered in the old bull's ear while her hand slipped down to his snout where he could still sense her presence. She stroked his muzzle and ran her hand up to his forehead and down again.

The bull stopped twisting and sank to his knees. He'd given up the fight and knelt panting and turning his head towards Mia's soothing voice. Kareem loosened his grip slightly, but the bull didn't react. The other animals had also stopped screaming, and were watching warily. Kate felt the tension against her staff ease.

Kareem released the bull's horns and stepped back. Mia remained in place, stroking the bull's head. As long as he was placated, the other animals were less skittish. Kareem decided to gamble and remove Kate from the holding crew.

"Kate, disengage your staff but keep her close, just in case. Then come around and grab the blindfolds. Leave Mia with the bull. Just be steady and slow."

The plasma leash connected to Kate's staff disintegrated, accompanied by a soft, fizzing sound. More holes appeared in the net. A concerted effort by the *Galaptagos* would rip it apart.

She gathered up some of the blanket strips and slowly moved to where Kareem now stood. A young cow turned to face them, keeping her rump protected by backing up to the bull. She tried to lower her head, but the netting was tight across her forehead. Kate and Kareem separated to either side of her, so she had to rock her head to keep both of them in sight.

She snorted nervously, and the muscles in her thighs quivered, but she was no longer panicked. Kate started to croon a soft lullaby she'd remembered; one that her mother had sung to her when she was just an infant.

The *Galaptago* cow followed her, twitching its ears erect, and Kareem moved in and gripped the base of her horns. She snorted again in surprise, and shook her head as if trying to discourage a biting fly, but she tolerated him as she listened to the song.

Kate followed Mia's example. She reached out and stroked the muzzle, and allowed the cow to sense her, and perhaps also sense the fact that Kate meant her no harm.

Kate placed the blindfold gently over her eyes and secured it around her head. Kareem released her horns, and she remained standing quietly huffing and testing the air.

It was mid morning by the time they had successfully secured blindfolds to the remaining three adults inside the net. They'd had trouble with the second—a cow with a calf in tow—when Kate inadvertently stepped between them and the calf had bleated, calling for its mother. The cow had lunged at Kate in an attempt to bite her. Only Kareem's quick actions had saved her. He'd twisted the horns to turn the neck, then used his own body weight and pulled down. He fell, and the cow fell on top of him. She bellowed, and the calf screamed back, and the other animals that had been restrained cried out nervously.

Kareem struggled to hold the head still enough to allow Kate to blindfold the eyes. Mia reassured the bull as the screams died away and the animals calmed down once more. As soon as Kate had completed the task, she edged to one side to allow the calf to nuzzle against its mother.

There was one final task to complete before they could disengage the net. Kareem and Kate disappeared into the band of trees in search of supple vines, which seemed to be an integral part of the tangled undergrowth in the forests of Bexus. They used the vines as tethers anchored into the ground and tied the ends to the animals' legs to prevent them from flying away.

Finally, the net was released.

They now had five animals, but still had no idea how to handle them. As easy as riding a motorcycle, Kate's mother, Siobhan had said.

They'd all ridden *Hon'chai*; no saddles had been necessary, but they had controlled those mounts by using a halter. Kareem sliced apart another bedroll, and he showed the others how to construct a basic bridle that could be slipped over each animal's head and inserted into its mouth without causing discomfort.

Kareem had just finished placing the rolled linen bit snugly in the mouth of the fourth *Galaptago* when he stopped suddenly. He held up his hand for silence as the others looked at him in alarm. He dropped to his hands and knees and placed one ear against the ground to confirm what the others were now hearing faintly. The sounds of hoof beats just beyond the ridge!

"We've got company!" he said. "Quick! We've no time to lose!"

He pointed at three of the animals in turn. "Mia, Jackson, take the bull; Sigrid and Kate, the cow; Ethan and Olivia, that one!"

"What about our gear?" Kate called.

"Leave it! Mount up!"

They clambered onto the *Galaptagos*. Their bodies were more streamlined than the *Hon'chai* they were used to. Their legs slotted between the bony plates of the wing bases. Kate sat behind Sigrid, clutching her waist. Kareem pulled a knife from his belt and systematically sliced through the vine tethers. He raced to where Jackson held a set of reins to the fourth animal and swung his body up in one fluid movement. He snatched the reins from Jackson just as the first riders breasted the high ridge.

"Hii—yaah!" Kareem shouted and dug his heels into the *Galaptago*. It turned left and bumped into the old bull, who roared and twisted his head blindly. The *Galaptagos* were milling about, stumbling in circles and bleating in confusion. Wings were extended, but none of the beasts took to the air.

The company of soldiers streamed over the ridge. One fired a bolt of energy, which fell wide of its mark and blasted a crater out to the left. Mud and clumps of tussock rained down, splattering the *Galaptagos* and their riders.

The soldiers were less than three hundred yards away and closing. Kate could see a fair-haired man in a captain's uniform leading the charge, roaring with the bloodlust of battle. She dug her heels viciously into the side of the animal, and it leapt forward so quickly that she almost lost her balance and tumbled from its back.

More explosions thumped into the ground beside them. Kate had no idea whether this was a deliberate distraction or simply a result of poor marksmanship from the back of a galloping *Hon'chai*. She had no intention of waiting around to find out, either.

She slipped Rhyanon from her sheath and aimed at the *Galaptago* calf.

"*Pungere!*"

A dart of green light shot from the staff and embedded in the calf's flanks. It squealed in pain from the sting and launched itself into the air, still screaming. Its mother immediately followed, calling for her calf. Her cry of alarm brought an immediate response.

One by one, the *Galaptagos* took flight. Their huge transparent wings beat the air so rapidly that they were just a silver blur. Up close, the buzzing noise drowned out everything else, so the blast caught Kate entirely by surprise.

The animal had risen no more than a few feet when something lit the air behind it. It swerved to the right and surged upwards, but the residual blast caught Kate and knocked her sideways off the animal's back. She tumbled through the air and landed heavily in the mud.

For a moment, she lay winded, then rolled to her hands and knees and retrieved her staff, which had landed a few feet from her. She looked back up the hillside.

The soldiers had dismounted and were firing pulses of energy at the escaping students. Kate watched in horror as one devastating blast caught the animal ridden by Olivia and Ethan. It was sixty feet above the ground, and it dropped like a stone and landed at the edge of the trees. Olivia's scream was cut short by a sickening thud.

Kate stood and returned fire, scattering the soldiers, but they turned their attention to her. She ducked and weaved as explosions rocked the ground where she'd been standing. She rolled to her left and scrambled on her hands and knees, keeping low, towards the place where Olivia and Ethan had fallen.

Above her, Sigrid, Kareem, and Jackson and Mia circled and darted across the sky as they brought the animals under control. They rolled and dove, swooping like hawks above the heads of the soldiers and provided some covering fire.

Kate found Olivia and Ethan. Olivia had landed on top of him and had briefly lost consciousness. She was moaning softly as Kate rolled her off Ethan's still form.

"Olivia! Are you okay? Speak to me!" She slapped Olivia's cheeks, which seemed to help bring her around.

"Help me with Ethan. We're going to have to try and make a run—"

Her words dried away in her mouth. Ethan was unconscious, pinned beneath the dead *Galaptago* by one leg. There was a cascade of sparks from the stump where his left arm used to be. The blast that had caught the *Galaptago* through the chest had passed on through and blown it away.

There was no time to lose! Kate tore the blindfold from the head of the dead animal, and wrapped it tightly around the stump that ended just above Ethan's elbow. She was able to staunch the flow of energy to the point where it was a slow trickle of sparks leaking around the edge of the bandage.

"He's going to need a doctor," Kate said. She risked raising her head to check on the soldiers. "Or a medic," she added.

"Ka—aa—ate!" Kareem's voice cut through the air above them.

Olivia gripped Kate's head in her hands as she spoke desperately.

"You can't stay!" she pleaded. "Streikker will have orders not to bring you back, and you know it. Without you, Ethan and I stand a chance. If he killed you, he'd have to kill us as well."

"Get ready! I'm coming!" Kareem called again.

Kate glanced skyward. She watched Kareem circling higher in the updraught above the edge of the ridge behind the soldiers, and saw him peel away and plummet towards the ground in a gut-wrenching dive. Sigrid and Mia provided the cover, which kept the soldiers' heads low.

"Go!" Olivia urged. "I'll make sure he gets looked after! Go! I'll cover you!"

Kate bit her lip, then reached across and gripped Olivia in a tight embrace.

"Take care!" she whispered. She slid Rhyanon into the sheath across her back.

And then she was gone. The next moment, she was upright and was sprinting alongside the treeline. She glimpsed the blond captain as he stood and pointed his staff towards her, and she jinked away as first one, and then another explosion thudded into the ground beside her.

She kept running. She hurdled tussock and was pelted by clods of dirt and stung by the stone shrapnel carried by the blasts. From the corner of her eye, she saw a flash, a blur of movement as Kareem raced down the slope barely feet above the ground. He blew past the captain and knocked him sideways off his feet just as another explosion flung Kate into the air.

She twisted in a somersault as flying debris tore through her clothing. She felt a hammer blow against her shoulder just before she was catapulted into a peat bog. The water closed over her head, and she struggled to her hands and knees, drenched and exhausted.

She heard Kareem call her name once more, and she willed herself to stand, and to struggle from the clutches of the sucking mud that was already ankle deep. He called again, and she turned towards his voice as she stepped unsteadily from the pool.

He hauled the beast through a tight turn at the bottom of the slope and bore down on her like a runaway locomotive. The ground erupted about him, but the *Galaptago* held its course, guided by the reins.

When Kareem was no more than fifty yards from her, he locked his legs about the animal's abdomen and leaned sideways with his arm outstretched, so much so that he was almost horizontal. Kate immediately understood his intention, and she turned and began sprinting in the same direction, holding a straight line as she ran.

She heard the buzzing roar of the *Galaptago's* wings, and she prayed that Kareem had enough control to prevent her being impaled by the enormous horns. Something slammed into her back, and she felt Kareem's arm grip her tightly as she was plucked into the air. He hauled her up so that she could hitch one leg over the animal, and she slipped into place in front of him, and felt his arm wrap tightly about her waist.

Her shoulder ached painfully, and she gripped her wrist to stop her arm falling away limply. She felt Kareem lean left. She leaned with him, and the flying *Galaptago* veered in that direction.

The land flew away beneath her, and her stomach dropped as Kareem guided it through a steep climb. They were hundreds of feet above the hillside, circling slowly as Sigrid and Jackson slid their animals alongside.

Kate glanced down. The soldiers were dark specks, spilling down the hillside towards the spot where Olivia lay huddled cradling Ethan in her lap. There was nothing any of them could do to help.

Kareem circled the spot one last time, then straightened out and steered south, and caught up with Sigrid, Mia and Jackson. Up ahead, Kate could make out the keening wail of the mother and her calf, and soon after, the two of them also drew alongside. The mother was still flying blindfolded, but the animals kept together in a tight formation.

Under different circumstances, the flight would have been exhilarating, but Kate was feeling dizzy. She checked her shoulder and was not surprised to see a steady stream of sparks blown backwards by the onrushing air.

She felt herself falling, tumbling—and then her world turned black.

Hans Streikker watched from the ground as the *Galaptagos* headed south and grew smaller. He swore and lashed out at a clump of tussock with his boot. He'd pushed the *Hon'chai* to the limits of their endurance in the belief that he would catch up with the group before the day was out. He hadn't gambled on *Galaptagos*; even now, he struggled to accept the fact the group had outwitted him through a pure stroke of luck. He cursed once more.

His men were spread out, seated in the dirt, some moaning from battle wounds. He did a quick check; no one was dead or missing. His medic was moving among the wounded, dressing the wounds and applying poultices of *Karyanthus,* or Mother's Glove, which effectively stemmed all bleeding within a matter of minutes.

Satisfied, he gripped his staff and strode towards the small circle of soldiers near the edge of the trees. Not all the group had managed to escape.

He pushed through the ring of men and stared down at the girl cradling the head of the unconscious young man. He recognised her as one of the elite young people who'd won the confidence of Hawklight. He checked over the youth and noted the bleeding stump.

He squatted beside her.

"We're going to need to talk," he said.

"Not until you help him," Olivia replied defiantly. "Until then, I've got nothing to say to you!"

Streikker smiled and glanced idly about him. He had a few options, and he wasn't going to be interrupted this far out if he chose one path in particular. But Streikker was not a vicious man by choice.

"Send for the medic!" he ordered.

Ethan was patched up and sedated. The dead body of the *Galaptago* was lifted and Ethan was slid free. However, Olivia refused to leave his side.

Streikker sat across from her. Dusk was less than an hour away, and the soldiers had bivouacked under the shelter of the trees. He had posted two guards over Olivia, and as he sat down, he waved them away.

"Where have the others gone?" he began softly.

"Carter sent you, didn't he?"

"Just answer my question."

"I'll take that as a yes. Perhaps you can answer mine. And while you're at it, let's go for broke. He didn't tell you about Zimmerman, did he? Didn't tell you what Hawklight was doing that got him killed?"

Streikker's eyes narrowed.

"And that puts you in a bind, doesn't it? It seems to me your orders were pretty specific when you came galloping over the hill, and yet, apparently, you don't have the full picture, do you? What are you going to do with us now? The others have escaped, but they know we were alive when they left."

Streikker knew she suspected what he'd planned to do with her.

"Who is Zimmerman?" he demanded.

"He's the one person who could have handed Varak's crown to Carter on a plate. The only trouble is, the opposition has him now. Carter doesn't realise he's already released the genie from the bottle; the only thing that concerns him is trying to tie up the loose ends."

"I don't believe you!"

"He says that Mirayam is a traitor. You know her, Captain. What do you think?"

Streikker smiled and shook his head.

"Let's begin again, shall we? Where have the others gone?"

CHAPTER 5

opely was exhausted. Even the stout Griselda had more
stamina than him when it came to trekking for mile after
endless mile. Zimmerman, however, was buzzing with
delight. He would stop constantly along the trail to examine
unremarkable looking rock specimens. Most of the time, he'd
spend a few minutes turning the specimen over in his hands before
dropping it back where he'd picked it up.

Copely knew that Griselda was growing impatient with these
interruptions, although he wasn't about to complain; each pause
in the journey was a welcome relief for him. He'd tried to make a
case for riding one of the lumbering *Urguts*, but he was met with
contemptible smiles from the rest of the party.

Occasionally, Zimmerman would open the flap of the leather
bag strapped across his shoulder and would drop a specimen
inside. They were hiking up a dried out riverbed, and he was doing
this regularly enough that Chisholm had finally capitulated, and
called a halt for the day.

Zimmerman leaned against a large boulder and dug around in
his bag. Copely dumped his pack on the ground at Zimmerman's
feet. He dug out a canteen of water and poured a generous amount
down the back of his neck.

"What's that?" he asked by way of conversation.

Zimmerman grinned at him and handed him the stone. It sat neatly in the palm of his hand. It was pale yellow in colour, and seemed to have a silver sheen to it. It wasn't transparent, but then it wasn't entirely opaque either. It looked as if a rock had grown over a lump of glass.

"Breathe on it," Zimmerman suggested.

Copely hesitated, then lifted the stone to his lips and exhaled. He noticed his breath fogged the stone, but it had cleared again within two seconds. He examined the stone. It looked greasy although it was perfectly dry.

Zimmerman bent and picked up a river boulder, worn smooth over the passage of time.

"Here," he said, "take this and rub the two stones together."

Copely took the boulder and scraped the side of it with the stone in his other hand. The stone left a clear, sharp scratch in the surface of the boulder. There was no corresponding mark on the stone.

"It's a diamond," whispered Zimmerman. "The riverbed is littered with them." He grinned again as if this were to be their little secret.

Copely stole a furtive glance at the rest of the party. They were busy setting up a campsite; something that Zimmerman had refused to do from the outset. It had been easier just to pamper him, in exchange for his cooperation.

I want the opportunity to explore the area before we move on," Zimmerman said. He added, "You can keep that if you want. In fact, I'd readily swap it for the broken Zimmermanite that Chisholm gave back to you."

The diamond Copely held was the size of a hen's egg. Copely licked his dry lips and surreptitiously hid the stone in one of his pockets. He slipped the useless crystal halves to Zimmerman in return.

"I'll see what I can do," he muttered.

Chisholm had found a shallow pool bounded by scrub. She had removed her boots, and Copely found her sitting on a rock, bathing her feet in the chilly water.

Chisholm shrugged when Copely asked.

"I don't care what he does. Have Khushk and one of the others trail along behind him. We don't want him to get lost."

Zimmerman had beamed when he heard the answer. Neither Khushk nor one of the mercenaries called Draganov was nearly as ecstatic, once they discovered they had been detailed to tag along beside the geologist. Copely had some sympathy for them as he lowered his body onto his bed mat, grateful for the chance to stretch out and snooze.

Zimmerman steadied the rock sample on a river boulder and gave it a single, sharp blow with his hammer. A corner of the rock sheared away, revealing its clean interior.

Marcus brought his magnifying glass close and examined the granular patterns. The exposed face was striped in alternating bands of yellow and green, but there were irregular pink patches—some the size of his fingernail—and tiny crystals throughout. Although the rock specimen was dense and hard, it had shattered easily enough when he struck it with the hammer. He knew the difference between frangibility, or brittleness, and hardness; he would need to test the rock further, but he was nonetheless excited—more excited than he had been when he'd chanced upon the lode of diamonds.

He suspected the diamonds were of industrial rather than gem quality, a fact he'd 'neglected' to mention to Copely. This was different! This was another discovery! He'd never come across anything remotely like it back on Earth. It would have made an excellent candidate for the term Zimmermanite, but then he'd already labelled a superior mineral with that particular name. *Perhaps this find should be recorded as Marcusite*, he thought.

He dropped the rock into his bag and slipped the hammer through a loop in his belt before continuing up the overgrown dried-up creek. He'd gone no more than twenty yards before he stopped and turned.

Where were Khushk and Draganov? Till now, they'd been no more than a few yards from him, following behind like a bad smell. He thought back to when he'd last seen them. Khushk had been seated on a rotting log, and Draganov had been leaning against an enormous chunk of rock close by.

"Khushk?" he called tentatively. There was no response.

"Khushk? Draganov?" Louder this time. Still no answer.

He backtracked to where he'd discovered his newest find. He spied the broken shard lying in the sand.

"Khushk?"

He moved cautiously towards the fallen log. There was a smear of green moss where Khushk had been sitting as if to confirm Marcus hadn't imagined the whole thing.

"Khushk? If you're trying to scare me, it's not working!"

Yes, it was! Zimmerman still hadn't gotten used to the planet and its wild inhabitants. They made the taipans, the brown snakes, the funnel-web spiders and the saltwater crocodiles of the Australian outback seem positively tame by comparison. Here, the creatures ate you from the inside out!

"Dammit, Khushk! Draganov! This will not go unreported!"

Neither man reappeared.

A new thought occurred to Zimmerman. He was under no illusion that he would outlive his usefulness once the source of Zimmermanite had been located. He'd just been handed his one opportunity to escape!

Then again, this could be some sort of test. Were they watching him from the bushes? Checking to see what he would do in the circumstances? He was paralysed with indecision. Stay or run? Stay or run?

Run!

He buckled his bag shut and turned upstream. He was lost from sight at the first bend, and the bush fell silent behind him.

A hand grasped Copely's shirt roughly and shook him awake. Riegel was looming above him in the half-light.

"Get up!" he hissed. "The geologist's gone!"

"Gone? What do you mean, gone?"

"They should have been back by now. We're getting a party together to look for them. You're included!"

Copely heaved a disgruntled sigh and tugged his boots on. Zimmerman was a prima donna. He would want a few minutes alone with the geologist at the end—that was for sure! He took some satisfaction in knowing that, when it came to deciding Zimmerman's fate, he'd be at the back of the queue.

The footprints in the sand weren't difficult to follow, but Riegel was no Khushk when it came to interpreting spoor. They found the shard of stone and the mossy smear, but were none the wiser as to what had happened.

Riegel discovered Zimmerman's unique boot tread a few yards further upstream. He'd headed in that direction, apparently alone.

"Khushk! Draganov!"

Griselda Chisholm had no more luck than Zimmerman. She had some difficulty holding her fury in check.

"Head upstream!" she instructed.

The others hesitated.

"Well? . . ."

"We're losing light," Riegel admitted. "There's no way we can follow him in the dark. We could walk right past him, and not know he was there."

Griselda clenched her jaw and grimaced. She was seething, but Riegel was right. They would have to head back to their campsite and wait for morning. She consoled herself with the fact that Zimmerman would also have to stay put and wait out the darkness, wherever he was.

He was up a tree. He'd torn the skin from his palms while clawing at the rough bark and had edged his way to within reach of the first branch. He'd managed to haul himself up into the crook where the branch met the main trunk, and rested.

Something skittered across the bed of dry leaves below him, and that was all the impetus he needed to climb higher. When he could go no further through fear of the branch breaking beneath him, he sat astride it with his back to the trunk. He removed his jacket, wrapped it around the trunk behind him, and tied the arms about his waist so that he would not topple out of the tree if he fell asleep.

Suddenly he froze. Something else was sitting on the same branch a couple of yards from him. It looked like a black-haired weasel with long chisel teeth, although it was more the size of an otter. It crouched motionless, moulding its body to the branch as it watched him intently.

Zimmerman panicked. He lashed out, swinging his boot at it. The creature hissed at him, and the hackles along its back rose in anger.

"Hi—yaahh! Geddoudovit!" he roared, and waved his arms while he kicked the branch with his boot.

It worked. The animal dropped from the branch and landed on a lower one. It skittered along to the trunk and ran down it.

Zimmerman breathed a sigh of relief, just as an almighty scream pierced the air below him. He was so startled that he almost fell sideways. He glanced downwards, and then wished he hadn't.

A massive reptile had seized the rodent and broken its back in one sickly, wet crunch. It was still screaming in pain as the predator tossed it in the air and deftly caught it between its jaws again. The second bite silenced the thing, and all that remained were the sucking sounds of the prey being chewed and swallowed whole.

Zimmerman held his breath and watched the lizard from his perch in the treetop. It looked exactly like an extremely large Komodo dragon, down to the long, darting, bright yellow forked tongue and rough, armour-like body. Zimmerman estimated it must have been twelve to fourteen feet long, and maybe a quarter ton in weight.

The tongue flicked out and tasted the air. The lizard must have sensed another meal because it raised its head and peered upwards. It spied Zimmerman in the topmost branches, and circled the base of the tree to get a better look at him. He was horrified and, at the same time, fascinated as he tracked the beast's methodical actions beneath him.

It raised itself on its back haunches and leaned its forelegs against the tree trunk. The long fingers were tipped with black claws that dug into the bark of the tree. It tested the air once more, and then dropped back onto all four limbs, and circled the tree again.

Another lizard crept from the undergrowth. It was wary of the first creature; perhaps attracted by the commotion and the screams of the dying rodent, and now was suddenly faced with a rival, a competitor. The larger lizard turned towards it and hissed a savage warning. The second animal slowly backed into the undergrowth but didn't leave.

The first reptile continued to circle the base of the tree, pausing frequently to leer up through the branches at Zimmerman. Eventually, it stopped circling, and pressed its massive triangular bony head against the trunk, and pushed. The tree creaked in protest as the reptile eased back and pushed again.

Zimmerman felt the tree begin to sway. He prayed that the roots were deep enough to prevent the tree from being flattened.

The tree held despite the animal's exertions. The monstrous lizard gave up in frustration and resumed circling and staring.

Darkness had fallen, but enough moonlight filtered down through the branches for Zimmerman to make out the slinking bulk below him. He checked that the knot in the sleeves of his jacket was secured tightly. The good news was that the reptile would dissuade anything else from trying to get at him.

By the time all three moons were visible above the treetops, Zimmerman had begun to feel drowsy. His head drooped forward until he was jerked awake momentarily; then, his eyelids would grow heavy, and his eyes would roll upward, and his head would loll. He balanced on the verge of slee—

The splintered tearing of timber startled him, and he was jolted awake in an instant. The lizard was standing on its hind legs, reaching up into the tree. It had slashed gouges in the bark with its claws. *It was trying to climb into the tree!*

Its hind legs had left the ground and had found some purchase in the bark. The beast was ungainly, and it strained against the drag of its bulky torso, but its eyes transfixed Zimmerman quivering in the uppermost branches as it inched its way up the tree.

Zimmerman had no weapons, save for the collection of rocks in his bag. He fumbled with the flap and unbuckled it. His collection consisted mostly of pebbles and small rock samples, but there were four samples large enough to wrap his hand around. He wrestled with the knot that tied him to the tree and freed himself. His jacket fluttered to the ground past the lizard, which lunged at it and missed.

He clambered down a couple of feet closer to the reptile, to a point where he could stand balanced on the branch with a clear view of the animal. He withdrew one of the rocks with his right hand while he held tight to the tree with the other. He steadied himself, and then flung the rock at the creature.

The rock hit the broad snout and bounced off the skull and into the darkness beyond. The animal stopped climbing, and raised its head, and the tongue slid from between its jaws and licked up and over the spot where the rock had struck.

Zimmerman pulled a second rock from his bag. He threw it, but it hit the tree first and bounced harmlessly against the animal's armoured back. This time, the lizard hissed vehemently at him.

His fingers closed around the sharp edges of the rock he'd christened Marcusite, and he hesitated. Despite the life-threatening situation, he was reluctant to toss it away. The lizard made the choice for him by slashing another foothold with its claws to pull itself closer to him.

He screamed in fury and fright combined, and launched the rock at the creature. One of the sharp edges sliced a gash along the soft fold of skin surrounding the lizard's left eye, and blood erupted from the wound.

The animal squealed, momentarily blinded, and lost its grip on the tree. It tumbled and crashed heavily on its back against the hard ground. The fall had stunned it, and before it could recover, the second lizard lunged out of the darkness and seized it by the throat.

Zimmerman gripped the tree with both hands, and looked on, horrified, as the two animals tussled in the dirt. They crashed against the tree, almost dislodging him as each battled for survival in a fight to the death.

The smaller creature had been raked open in places along its underbelly, but it had kept a tight grip around its opponent's throat, and the tide of battle turned in its favour as the larger animal's efforts faded. Eventually, the thrashing ceased altogether, although the smaller lizard kept its jaws tightly clenched until it was certain its opponent was well and truly dead. Only then did it release its grip and begin to gorge itself, slowly tearing the victim apart with each savage bite.

The victor waddled away and disappeared back into the undergrowth with the onset of dawn, leaving Zimmerman perched in his tree above the decimated carcass. He was still there midmorning when Riegel led the others into the clearing at the base of the tree.

Chisholm seemed to fix him with the same predatory stare that the giant lizard had used. She didn't say a word; she just waited until he gingerly climbed down. His feet touched solid ground, and as he turned to face the music, she strode up in three short steps and clocked him with a savage punch that laid him out for the count.

When he came to, he was groggy, and his jaw ached as if it had been broken. He tried to sit up, and was jerked backwards by a noose around his neck that tethered him to the tree. The rest of the party were ranged casually around the clearing, waiting for him to regain consciousness.

Griselda Chisholm squatted in front of him.

"Where are Khushk and Draganov?" she asked.

"I . . . I don't know," he stuttered.

She frowned like this was the wrong answer, and he thought she was going to belt him again.

"You've got to believe me!" he implored her. "They just disappeared! I tried calling them, but they didn't answer. I don't *know* where they are!"

"So, you decided to run away instead."

Zimmerman bit his lip. He couldn't face her terrible gaze. He nodded meekly.

"I'm sorry," he whispered.

She scrutinized him silently.

"Why doesn't the crystal work?" she asked.

"The crystal?" He was perplexed by the change in the conversation. He gave her the same explanation he'd given Carter. "There was a blockage in the channels within the crystal. Like a clogged drainpipe, I guess. If . . . when . . . we find another stone with the channels intact . . ." He shrugged, and tried to smile, and wondered if she'd noticed his inclusive use of the pronoun 'we' as he'd hoped.

Apparently not. She stood and gave him one final glance, then gestured to the others. One by one, they filed out of the clearing, back along the way they'd come.

Zimmerman was seized with panic. He was tied to the tree like a sacrificial goat. The torn and bloodied carcass was strewn about the ground at his feet. It was an open invitation to any passing scavenger.

"Wait!" he screamed. "You can't just leave me here!"

Chisholm stopped at the edge of the clearing, next to where Copely stood, and turned to face him.

"You're more trouble than you're worth, Mr Zimmerman," she said.

"You won't be able to find the source of the crystal without me!" he pleaded.

She smiled at him, but her eyes were cold and impassionate.

"We'll see, Mr Zimmerman. We know roughly where to look. After all, how hard can it be?"

"Please," he begged her, "don't leave me behind. I won't run away again, I promise you. I'll do whatever you want."

She shook her head sadly and then wandered from the clearing out of sight. Copely followed.

"Plee . . . eeaase!" Zimmerman screamed wildly. He started to sob.

Chisholm reappeared, so silently it took Zimmerman the better part of a minute to realize through his tears that she had been standing and watching him. She had broken him so easily.

"*Dimittere colligacionis!*"

The noose about Zimmerman's neck dissolved. He wiped his eyes and stood unsteadily.

"Let's go!" she commanded.

Zimmerman stepped over the dead carcass, but as he did so, he spied the chunk of his precious 'Marcusite' protruding from the sand. He stooped to retrieve it.

"Leave it!"

"But I—"

"I said, leave it!"

He hung his head in shame as he traipsed along behind her.

It turned out he hadn't managed to get all that far from them. Distance is deceiving in thick bush; five hundred yards can seem like five miles when there is no horizon, and the ground is constantly undulating.

It took the search party three hours to find their way back to the original campsite. Riegel, who'd been leading the group, stepped out from the bush and was blown sideways into a clump of leafy ferns by an explosion. Those behind him leapt off the path into cover as confused shouts rang around the clearing.

"Cease fire, you idiots!"

"Lay down your weapons!"

"Abayomi! Hendrikx! It's us, dammit!"

Riegel chanced raising his head above the greenery. The men he'd left behind stepped out slowly from behind cover.

Riegel stood and stormed into the middle of the campsite. Some of his uniform was still smoking from the near miss. He tore the staff from the hands of the burly Nigerian and flung it to the ground.

"What's the meaning of this?" He brought his face to within an inch of Abayomi's and screamed the words at him. "You could have killed me!"

"Boss, please . . . we didn't know it was you."

"Didn't know?" Riegel's eyes bulged. He was apoplectic. "What do you mean? Who else would it be out here?"

It was only then that something else registered in the back of his mind. He stopped screaming, and looked around. Something was not right. Something was missing!

"The *Urguts!*"

There was no sign of two of the heavyset animals. The third was tethered beside the fallen log where it munched on succulent vegetation, oblivious to the tension in the middle of the camp.

The rest of the search party filed into the clearing. Chisholm strode forward, leaving Zimmerman with Copely. She had already seen what Riegel had only just realised.

"Would you care to explain, Mr Abayomi?"

Abayomi recognised his precarious position. He glanced towards Hendrikx for help, but the Dutchman had stepped away, putting as much distance between them as he was able.

Abayomi shook his head as if the question were beyond his comprehension.

"I . . . I don't know. This morning, after you left, we noticed one of the beasts had gone. We thought it had broken loose and wandered away, so we secured the other two to the log and went to look for it. We searched for an hour—perhaps two hours—but of this animal, there was no trace. When we returned, another had disappeared. It could not have broken free. Something . . . took both of them away." He glanced fearfully beyond her shoulder at the bush and shuddered. "There are jungle devils everywhere."

Griselda eyed him contemptuously.

"Then you'll be the first one of us that they meet!"

She split the men into groups of three. They carefully checked the ground around the campsite. There were plenty of animal tracks where the animals had been grazing since the previous evening, but away from the camp, there was no spoor to follow. None of them was experienced enough to read anything other than the most obvious signs, and they quickly grew frustrated.

Each of the groups headed into the bush in a different direction. Chisholm, Copely, and Zimmerman remained behind to assess which supplies were left. Almost all the cold weather gear had disappeared, along with many of Zimmerman's geological tools.

By nightfall, all three groups had arrived back empty-handed. It was as if the two animals and all the gear they'd carried had disappeared into thin air. Perhaps Abayomi's jungle devils weren't quite the figments of his imagination after all.

Riegel took particular care to set up a defensive perimeter, designed with the remaining *Urgut* at its centre, and each person conjured a gelatinous bubble for extra protection.

It had been a disastrous twenty-four hours. They resumed their journey the next morning along a different compass bearing. They needed to re-equip the expedition, and the only place they could turn was towards the settlement of Poluostrov.

The remaining gear needed to be redistributed. Griselda Chisholm was only slightly mollified by watching Abayomi, Hendrikx and Zimmerman struggle under the extra weight they'd been assigned.

Not one of the three men dared to complain.

CHAPTER 6

Kate moaned, and the sound of her own voice distantly intruded into the peaceful blackness in which she lay. Her mouth was dry and felt like it was lined with cotton wool. She smacked her lips and rolled her tongue around, searching for moisture. She heard voices, and looked up, and felt herself rushing headlong towards a spinning disk of light.

Blurred images swung into view, the way a station suddenly appears after a lengthy trip through an underground tunnel. She experienced a moment of déjà vu; she'd spun a similar nauseating path into consciousness the moment she'd arrived on Bexus. Snippets of memory began dropping into place as she struggled to work out where she was.

Someone was leaning over her, peering down anxiously at her. As her vision cleared, features became focussed, and she saw with relief that the face was Kareem's. She felt his hand gripping hers tightly, and she anchored herself to his touch and waited for her head to clear.

"Where am I?" she moaned.

"She's awake?" Sigrid's voice sounded anxiously in the background.

Kate closed her eyes and concentrated on breathing slowly and evenly, and the feelings of nausea slowly subsided.

She risked opening her eyes again. She could see a rough, thatched ceiling supported by dark brown beams above Kareem's head. A lantern swung from the rafters, and a dim red glow flickered beyond it as if from a fire.

She tried to sit up and stabbing pain shot through her left shoulder. She cried out and sank back down on to the woven willow bed on which she lay.

"Easy . . . easy," Kareem said softly. He placed his hand on her forehead. It felt cool to the touch. He ran it through her hair, brushing aside the damp strands that had stuck there.

"It's okay," he continued. "We're all safe."

"Where am I?" she asked again.

"We found this hut. It's a musterer's hut, maybe used once a year. It has a barricade of thorns right around it to keep out the nasties. It even has a bed." He smiled. The narrow structure holding Kate was rickety and frail, and only marginally more comfortable than the rammed dirt floor.

"How long have we been here? How long have I been out?"

"This is only the second night. You're doing pretty well, considering . . ."

Kate frowned at him. *Considering what?*

He reached for something, and then held it in front where she could see. It was a large splinter of wood, a foot in length, half an inch wide at its base, and it tapered to a lethal-looking pointed spike.

"This was lodged in your shoulder. We had to get it out. It's a good thing you were out for as long as you were. It was like a little fireworks display back there until we stemmed the bleeding. Mia and Jackson found some Mother's Glove yesterday."

Mia's and Jackson's heads appeared over Kareem's shoulder at the mention of their names.

"Hey there," said Mia.

"You gave us one hell of a fright, girl," laughed Jackson, delighted to see her back in the land of the living once more.

"I thought we'd lost you when you fell off," said Sigrid, rounding out the picture of the group of anxious friends looming over her. "And then again, when I saw what was sticking out of your shoulder. I guess you just can't keep a good girl down."

"Any news of Olivia and Ethan?" Kate asked.

They shook their heads.

"We could fly back and rescue them," she suggested, with more hope than expectation in her voice. She saw Jackson grimace in response.

"A pack of *Abyssi* attacked last night. They couldn't break through the thorns, but their baying spooked the *Galaptagos* inside the barricade. A couple of them ended up in the thorns, and that was when Kareem and I cut the tethers and removed their blindfolds. They took off into the night; we haven't seen them since."

Abyssi were the hellhounds of the planet. Kate glanced at Sigrid; both had survived attacks by these vicious killers.

"It doesn't matter," Kareem added. "We need to pick up Zimmerman's trail again, and we couldn't do that from the air. It's better this way."

Another stab of pain shot through Kate.

"All the time we wait here, he will get further and further away," she sighed. "I can hardly move!"

Kareem smiled.

"What?" she demanded.

"I know you, Kate Gallagher. You're just like your mother—as tough as old boots. We'll be gone from here sooner than you think." He squeezed her hand, and her indignation leaked away.

"I'm tired," she whispered.

—◆◆◆—

Kate opened her eyes. The hut was silent, save for the slow, regular breathing of her sleeping companions. Jackson snorted in his sleep, and the rhythm was interrupted until he rolled onto his side and sank back into slumber.

The lantern had been extinguished; only the red glow of the burning logs in the fireplace lit the room. An empty sack nailed into the window sash covered the sole window in the hut, but a sliver of moonlight crept through the gap between the sack and the wall.

Sparks flew up the chimney, and the firelight flickered from the addition of another log. Kareem was still awake. Kate watched him as he sat by the fire, absently poking at the flames with a stick. He looked to be deep in thought.

He was sitting side on to Kate, and his outline was partially backlit by the fire and heightened by the soft blue glow of his aura. His hair was a mass of tangled, thick black curls long enough to fall in ringlets around his neck. He was sitting on the floor, his elbow crooked against one bent knee, and he rested his head in his hand as he quietly prodded the embers with his stick.

He'd been her constant companion for a few months only, and yet it seemed as if he'd been around forever. Their first meeting had been memorable—he'd tried to kill her; since then, he'd been bent on saving her. Kate was afraid that those kinds of extreme bonds signalled something more intimate.

Kareem turned his head towards her at that instant as if he'd managed to read her mind. She caught the briefest reflection of firelight in his eyes that were otherwise hidden in shadow. They stared at each other across the room.

Kate couldn't see his face; she couldn't read his features. She didn't want to move and break the spell of the moment in the dark and the warmth. She suddenly realised she was holding her breath, waiting. She didn't trust herself to exhale, to risk waking the others, so she bit her lip and closed her eyes and blew out softly through her nose.

She opened her eyes again, slowly. Kareem was keeling beside the bed. She hadn't heard his footfall, but she had sensed a change in the air around her, like something settling and filling the space.

He brought a finger to his lips.

Then he bent forward, and lowered his head, and his lips brushed hers in a tender kiss.

Kate had never been kissed like that before. On Earth, she had been angry, spiteful, and above all, isolated. Boys had leered after her, but none had risked the ridicule and rejection that would have occurred to bother attempting any sort of relationship with her. They'd shunned her and called her names instead.

Kareem had discovered the chink in the wall she'd built to keep others out; in fact, he demolished it every time he'd risked his life for her.

He lifted his head, they drew apart, and she was left with the taste of him on her lips. For a first kiss, he had been far too tentative.

She reached up with her right hand and curved it around his neck and entwined her fingers in the ringlets. She pulled his head towards hers and parted her lips and kissed him once again; not desperately, but with passion and trust, silently acknowledging that she needed him in her life, thereby answering the question that the first kiss had implied.

They parted for the second time, and he gazed down at her. He slid her hand from his neck and held it, then reached out and brushed the hair from her forehead, this time to reveal her eyes framed in her face.

Neither of them had spoken a word, yet so much had passed between them.

Jackson snorted once more and called out something in his sleep. Kate had to cover her mouth to stop herself from giggling, to keep their furtive moment a secret from the others.

Kareem squeezed her hand one final time, and then he crawled to his bedroll a few feet from where Kate lay. He settled on his back and folded one arm behind his head for a pillow. Kate twisted to relieve the dull throb in her shoulder, and lay on her side. The wicker bed creaked beneath her as she shifted.

Both of them wore smug smiles of satisfaction as they drifted back to sleep.

They waited for two days until Kate felt strong enough to continue the chase. Jackson had expected her to be impatient; anxious for the wound to heal and distressed about the fact their quarry was getting away. He was surprised that she needed Kareem to help her move about more than usual, and seemed to be happy to sit without complaint while Kareem made clumsy, lengthy efforts to tend to her dressings.

Jackson mentioned this to Sigrid and Mia when they were all sprawled beneath a shade tree, watching Kareem with his arm about Kate's waist to support her as she walked back and forth in front of the hut outside the barricade.

The girls burst out laughing.

"Men can be so thick, sometimes," Sigrid giggled.

"What—?" Jackson was truly perplexed.

"She's fallen for him," Mia explained. "They've spent nearly every waking minute dreaming up excuses to be near each other, trying not to be too obvious about it. You have to pretend you haven't noticed a thing!" She swore Jackson to secrecy, after which they sat back to enjoy the show.

For Kate, the hiatus gave her time to enjoy the transition from a teenage girl to a young woman. Kareem was just as shy as she, and their first forays in the enclosed public space were little better than clumsy.

"This is embarrassing," muttered Jackson as he watched Kareem straighten Kate's left arm and rested it on his shoulder while he probed the shoulder wound gently. Kate's fingers were caressing his bare shoulder as she occasionally winced in pain.

In the end, it proved too much for Jackson who foreswore his promise and just yelled across the clearing, "Just hold her hand, and we can all stop pretending!"

Kate turned red and glared across at him, but Kareem just grinned at him.

"You're no help!" Kate blurted out and pushed Kareem backwards into the dirt. He rolled and came up with the lop-sided grin still plastered across his face, and she couldn't help but laugh.

He stood and held out his hand. She reached up and took it and together, they strolled back to the others, where the girls were playfully beating up on Jackson.

"Your health has certainly improved over the past minute," Jackson noted wryly.

"He's a very talented nurse—not that it's any business of yours," Kate replied, with the glimmer of a smile.

"Seriously, how is the shoulder?" Sigrid asked.

Kate slipped the shoulder of her shirt down to reveal the wound. The poultice of Mother's Glove had worked its usual magic and the puncture was sealed shut, though puckered in an ugly scar. Kate's aura had disappeared around the entry point. Beyond it, the colour had changed to a dirty purple-blue. From a distance, it resembled a large bruise. Kate's natural golden aura bled through it in places. The wound was healing rapidly, although the sensation of pain would last for many days.

It said much about Kate's character that she had not complained once about the pain since she'd regained consciousness.

"It's time we left this place," Kate replied, readjusting her shirt.

"Are you sure?" Kareem asked. Kate knew the question went beyond his private concerns for her. He wanted reassurance that she wouldn't slow them down any once they began the pursuit again.

"I'll be right behind you," she promised.

After they'd escaped from Streikker, Kareem had made a calculated guess, but a guess nonetheless. He'd directed the *Galaptagos* south, and had continued to be guided by the profile of the land below, following dried out streams, river valleys and natural passes through the hills that the group they were tracking most likely would have used.

It had been a massive gamble. If Zimmerman's true path lay in any other direction, all was lost. They might search for months and never find it again. To predict his prey's behaviour, Kareem had to trust his hunter's natural instinct. He'd also relied on the element of surprise. It was unlikely Zimmerman's party would suspect they were being pursued.

Kate was as good as her word. She stuck like glue behind Kareem for two days while they ventured south, casting ahead for any signs of Zimmerman's passage. There was nothing! There might have been spoor in the next stream across for all they knew; if so, it might just as well be on the other side of Bexus, for all the good it would be.

Kareem decided to call a halt. It was no use pretending, despite the fact that none of the others had complained, or blamed him for leading them on what was, apparently, a wild goose chase. Still, he felt that the responsibility of failure rested on his shoulders. They were going to have to decide on a different strategy.

He could see light ahead of him, where the overgrown stream bed petered out into some sort of clearing. They'd rest there. Maybe they'd even get lucky. Such clearings often signalled a confluence where a number of streams merged into one.

He was right on both counts. Three different dried out streams converged at that point.

And, they got lucky.

Kareem spotted them instantly and froze. Behind him, Kate did the same. She reached behind her back and noiselessly slid Rhyanon from her sheath.

Kareem scoured the area, looking for the trap. There had to be one! He searched out the obvious spots for an ambush, scrutinizing the shadows for concealed foes lying in wait. His practised eyes saw nothing. Still, he waited, motionless, for some careless sign that would confirm the ambush.

There was no one else there, he was sure of it. There was one way to find out.

He crept cautiously into the clearing, all his senses heightened. The ambient chatter of animals fell away as he stepped into view. That was another clue; if someone else were waiting, the bush would be silent.

He signalled the others forward. They were curious as to what had spooked him until they saw them too.

Two uniforms, neatly folded, were lying on top of a rock. Two pairs of boots were placed beneath them, and two helmets rested on top of them. Everything was laid out with military precision.

Kate lifted one of the helmets aside and then unfolded the uniform. It belonged to someone of slight build and was patched in places and streaked dirty with mud. There was no mistaking the faded insignia on the shoulders: the blood red 'V' worn by all of Varak's soldiers.

Kate examined the uniform for any holes, any signs of burning or charring that would suggest how the soldier died. She found none. Did that mean its owner was still alive somewhere nearby? She didn't think so. There had been a thin layer of mould on top, which suggested the piles had been sitting in place for some time. However its owner had died, one thing was for sure: he hadn't been shot at.

Sigrid checked the other uniform while Kareem, Jackson and Mia secured the perimeter of the clearing. She lifted the helmet.

This pile was different.

Hidden beneath the helmet and lying on top of the uniform was a crystal of pink quartz. It appeared as if it had been picked up from one of the stream beds. Kate had noticed lots of quartz lying among the rocks and pebbles as they had trudged upstream. It was weathered around the edges, worn smooth, and it was discoloured too, but that wasn't what made it unusual.

The crystal had been broken in two.

The broken faces were crisp and sharp.

Kate grasped the two halves in the palm of her hand. They felt vaguely familiar.

"Varak's crystal," she whispered. "These are supposed to represent Varak's crystal!" She called the others over.

"Remember that Carruthers told us that Carter had the crystal and that he gave it to Zimmerman. So Zimmerman has the crystal, and someone has Zimmerman, and whoever has him has come from Cherath. These were Varak's uniforms!"

"Could be that Carter is trying to lay the blame on Cherath," Sigrid suggested. "These were left in the open for somebody to find."

"No," Kate said, dismissing the idea. "Carter was as shocked by the ambush as everyone else. Besides, why would he go to the trouble of sabotaging his own expedition? If nothing had happened to them, no one would be any the wiser."

"Kate's right," Kareem added. "It doesn't make sense. Someone else must have found out about his plan beforehand. Someone with the ability to pull enough people together to carry out an ambush and continue on with the quest to locate the source of the crystal. Someone from Cherath."

"Someone sneaky," Jackson grumbled.

His words triggered an image in Kate's mind of a maniac in a black robe challenging her from the top of Cherath's walls: someone whose destiny—like hers—was inextricably linked to the crystal. She saw the black eyes that flashed with hatred, in a face framed by an angry red aura. It seemed to her that the crystal, which had already sought him out once before, had done so again. She knew it, beyond all doubt!

Copely!

The pieces of the puzzle were falling into place. Copely's involvement would explain many things: chief amongst them was the fact that he would have been doubly wary knowing Hawklight was involved, and would have engineered the ambush in such a way so that Hawklight would have suspected nothing.

But Copely had been a pariah among his own people towards the end, shunned by all who'd known him as Varak's puppet. He'd been hauled off the top of the wall by the city's defenders after he'd tossed the broken crystal at Kate's feet.

He'd survived on Bexus as a spy. Information was his currency. He'd obviously learned of Carter's expedition and traded the information—for what? And who would support him? More importantly, who would trust him?

Copely's involvement was the only thing that made sense, and that prospect was frightening. If Copely, or whoever had allied with him ever got their hands on another crystal, Bexus would be plunged back into another period of ruthless dictatorship. Kate understood that, if it came to pass, there would be no future for her—for any of them.

This was fresh motivation to move on. Kareem picked up the spoor at the end of the clearing. There were plenty of boot marks in the sand, and Zimmerman's were amongst them. They'd come up by another path. Kareem's gamble had paid off.

"The tracks are between one and two weeks old," he said as he searched for other signs of activity. Then: "That's odd."

"What's odd?" Kate asked.

Kareem grinned at her. "Tell me what you see," he challenged. This had grown to be a game between them. Kareem was teaching her the skills of tracking, and she had been an astute student—astute and stubborn!

Kate examined the many footprints in the sand. She wondered which were Copely's. If they had met, Kareem would have known. She hoped he would have the opportunity to find out eventually.

She saw how the tracks headed away in single file on the upper side of the clearing. Some of the footprints made deep indentations in the soft sand. Apart from that, she saw nothing odd about—

"There's only one set of animal tracks! Coming in, there were three!"

Kareem beamed at her. "Anything else?"

She pointed. "These, here—someone is carrying a heavy load. And . . . here!" She turned, grim faced. "This will slow them down. We have a chance to close the gap between us!"

"What are we waiting for?" Jackson asked.

Three days after they'd left the safety of the musterer's hut, a group of bedraggled riders limped up to the barricade. The mounts had been pushed hard, and their coats were slick with sweat. The riders were dusty, cold and exhausted, and the barricade was a welcome relief. The mounts could be corralled behind it, safely protected from the night stalkers.

Streikker dismounted and scanned the area. The hut had been used recently. One of the trackers approached him, and led him to where a path fed off into the undergrowth, away from the cabin. There were five sets of footprints, and no sign of *Galaptagos*. Streikker smiled. They were back on foot, and he would hunt them down!

CHAPTER 7

The vegetation had changed. The trees were gnarled with age, their bark greyed and cracked. Their leaves were needle-thin, like a pine variant, but in different shades of yellows and greens. The ground beneath them was familiar: a carpet of dead brown leaves that rustled softly underfoot. The thick undergrowth of the temperate Great Forest was gone. Anything struggling to survive needed a hardy constitution in a land covered by snow for half the year.

The black uniforms were gone, covered by thick coats made from wool or fur. At night, the temperatures plummeted. Campsites were established two to three hours before the daylight disappeared so that enough fuel could be gathered and stacked to supply the campfires that burned throughout the night. The tents trapped some of the heat, but there weren't enough to shelter everyone. A roster was drawn up, and people were rotated to share the prospect of a freezing night, shivering and huddled close to the fires.

Naturally, the roster didn't extend to Chisholm or to Copely. Zimmerman was still out of favour since nobody could explain what had happened to Khushk and Draganov. No one thought Zimmerman could have overpowered them in order to engineer his escape attempt, and since there had been no signs of any struggle, the current theory was that they had simply deserted.

Griselda Chisholm had a long memory, and their names were filed away in it for future reference, just in case they resurfaced. This ability to retain a grudge had been a useful trait in her previous profession under Varak's regime. She'd been an admirer and a close associate of Charlie Hughes, The Magician. Griselda's spy network often uncovered rebels and traitors to the cause, and these would be handed over to Hughes who, true to his nickname, made them disappear for good.

For this reason, she shared with Copely a common hatred of the Gallagher girl who'd turned The Magician's speciality against him. Both she and Copely had made a pact that the girl would bear the brunt of their personal attention once the source of the crystal was safely in their possession. This time, Hogarth would hand her over willingly.

Griselda wriggled on the humped mattress of dried leaves that had been gathered for her earlier that evening. Once she'd created a more comfortable hollow, she pulled the thick blanket around her shoulders and closed her eyes.

She was drifting off to sleep, still preoccupied with planning Kate's demise, when a shout startled her awake. Shadows flashed by, thrown onto the tent by the campfires, and it was evident the whole camp was in some confusion.

She pulled the blanket aside and crawled through the tent flaps, dragging her staff in one hand.

"What is it?" she yelled above the noise.

A number of the runners stopped and glanced anxiously at her. A voice from the darkness beyond the fire answered her.

"The *Urgut* has disappeared!"

Not again!

"Get a search party organised! It can't have wandered far!"

By now, the whole camp had been roused. Men shrugged themselves into warm jackets and grabbed lanterns and makeshift torches.

The animal had been tied to a tree. It must have slipped its bindings since there was no sign of a cut or broken rope. Hoof prints led away from the fire into the darkness. The men tracked them until the disturbed carpet of needles thinned and the hard bedrock broke through the soil.

Riegel found more faint traces of hoof prints for another twenty feet, and then the spoor disappeared altogether.

"Spread out! Form a line. Don't lose sight of each other."

The men moved to either side of Griselda, and she waited until all she could see was a linear series of flickering torches.

"Move forward!" she called.

They managed to keep moving for twenty minutes before the torches began spluttering and some died out. It was hopeless! They would need to regroup and wait until morning.

Chisholm called the halt and the men regrouped. A sudden thought occurred to her, and she did a quick headcount, but no one was missing. She had kept Zimmerman close beside her in case he'd been tempted to make another break for it during all the confusion. He had seemed happy enough to tag along; he didn't want to be left on his own again.

This was another blow to the expedition. The beast had been left saddled with the supplies it carried, which included spare sets of warm clothing, but, more importantly, the chemical analysis lab that the geologist needed. The only remaining geological equipment was the stuff that Zimmerman had lugged in his own pack.

"Is that going to be enough?" she asked him after they'd returned to the camp. He had laid out two hammers, some stone chisels, a loupe eyepiece on a lanyard, a magnetic compass, electrical conducting apparatus and some vials of acid.

Marcus shrugged and nodded. The drills and augurs might be able to be replaced in Poluostrov. The settlement had been a mining outpost before the mines closed down or were abandoned over the years.

By mid-morning of the following day, it was apparent to all that the *Urgut* would never be found. They had lost all three pack animals through carelessness. "Who tied the animal to the tree?" Griselda asked as they were breaking camp.

Riegel answered. "Sedgewick."

"Remove his pack and divide it up among the others," she ordered.

Sedgewick's pack was ripped from his back, and he was pinned against a tree while the contents were strewn on the ground in rough piles for the others to choose. The men despised Sedgewick, not only because he'd been responsible for the loss of the *Urgut*, but also because their own packs were now heavier still.

Sedgewick was stripped of his coat, his uniform and boots, and he was left shivering against the tree, pale with anxiety.

Chisholm addressed the men.

"Mr Sedgewick was remiss in his duties. I hold him accountable." She looked at Sedgewick. "There's plenty of warm clothing with the *Urgut*. All you need to do is find it."

Sedgewick opened his mouth as if to say something, but no sound emerged.

The party headed out. None of the men could meet Sedgewick's pleading eyes. The message had been sent and had been equally clearly received: *don't mess up!*

A cold fog descended as they left, and the shivering Sedgewick was soon lost in the mist.

—⟋∭⟋—

There were no further incidents. The expedition trudged down from the mountains and left the pine-like forests behind.

The route they marched was tedious; heather-like bushy clumps of vegetation covered the ground, which was pitted with hundreds of water-filled potholes large enough and deep enough to swallow a house. The vegetation was springy and thickly distributed, which made the act of walking twice as laborious because each step needed to be knee-high. Grey clouds threatening rain scudded across a heavy sky, and the wind cut through their clothing despite the extra layers they wore.

Riegel led the party, and the others followed, spread out in a ragged line. Abayomi had the keenest eyesight, and Griselda had assigned him to the rear, to check constantly and make sure no one followed. She was paranoid by nature, and she didn't believe in coincidences.

He saw nothing.

Camping in this wilderness proved almost impossible. Tent stays blew out, and the ground was sodden and icy cold. They conjured protective bubbles that kept out the rain, but their clothing was wet and any heat was soon sucked away through the soil. The rain turned to sleet, and tiny needles of ice tore at any exposed skin. They carried no fuel for fires, and their own energy was far too precious to be wasted generating heat for others.

They were greatly relieved to spy on the horizon the dull brown smudge from the sooty peat fires of Poluostrov hanging in the air. The pace of the expedition picked up noticeably and their spirits lifted.

Poluostrov had once been a thriving town, built on the back of the early mining industry. It rose at the edge of a savage environment but was eventually beaten into submission. The miners gave up, and most of the support services disappeared along with them. They left behind the gamblers, the con artists, the crooks and fugitives, and those too stubborn to be forced from the land.

Visitors were a novelty, to be treated with suspicion. Nobody volunteered to visit. This was not one of the top ten vacation hideaways of Bexus. The only two categories of tourists were those looking to find someone, and those looking to hide from someone. Only the latter were welcomed and tolerated.

Hostile eyes followed the sullied travellers as they stumbled along the main street and regrouped beneath the veranda of a two-storey hotel. It was the tallest building in the settlement. There were some tin shacks, but most of the dwellings were constructed of piled slabs of rock or peat bricks stacked on top of one another, sealed with mud and planted with turf. Their windows were small and translucent; inside, they were dark and smoky, but to Chisholm's party who had weathered the inhospitable journey across the flat wetlands they were a welcome sight.

The hotel was the only structure that had a timber frame. Zimmerman wondered where the wood came from, and why anyone would bother to construct such a building here in the first place.

Griselda tugged the door open, and she was engulfed by a wall of hot air that was almost stifling. One by one, the expedition members followed her inside until the entire party was standing and dripping water on the floor of the foyer.

An old woman with one eye glared at them from behind a desk.

"We need rooms," Griselda barked.

The old woman said nothing but gave her a lopsided grin. Griselda wondered if she was crazy.

"Rooms don't come cheap."

Griselda checked out the empty cubbyholes full of room keys. They were dusty from disuse.

"You don't appear to be busy."

The woman shrugged indifferently. "Not much call for travellers this time o' year."

"Then our business will be welcome."

"Prices is prices. If they're not to yer likin', youse can always go elsewhere." Griselda got the lopsided grin again—the woman knew her town; knew the options were limited.

In the good old days, she would have been yanked from behind her desk and hauled away in chains, a gift to The Magician. Things were so much simpler back then. Griselda sighed and turned to Copely.

"What do we have to pay her with?" she whispered. One of the missing *Urguts* had carried more than just mining equipment. When it had disappeared, so had the cash.

"The geologist has been collecting diamonds. Search his bag."

Griselda strode over to where Marcus had slumped to the floor, and was resting against the wall. She snatched his bag from around his shoulders and upended it on the wooden floor. Stones of all sizes, colours and textures scattered across the smooth planks. Griselda was disappointed; they just looked like dull, worthless rocks.

"Which ones are diamonds?" she hissed at him.

Zimmerman hunched forward, and his long fingers danced amongst the pebbles, flicking one, then two, then more at her. By the time he was finished, there was a tidy pile of thirty or more oily looking specimens lying beside her hand. She scooped them up and examined them carefully. As she did so, she noted with satisfaction that the woman had her one eye glued to the proceedings.

"They don't look like much," Griselda muttered.

Zimmerman was pouting like a spoiled brat whose toys had just been confiscated. He shot a withering glance at Copely.

"Perhaps Mr Copely can help you. Ask to see his prized possession."

Chisholm's nostrils flared as she shot Zimmerman a fierce look before turning her gaze on Copely.

"Stuart?"

She was deadly when she was this friendly. Copely felt a bead of perspiration squeeze onto his forehead. The image of a shivering, pleading Sedgewick somehow resurfaced, and Copely knew he was within tripping distance of standing and shivering in his underwear in the snow. He cleared his throat.

"Of course! I forgot!" He reached into his pocket. "Mr Zimmerman asked me if I would keep this safe. For him!" he added unnecessarily since nobody believed him.

He tipped the egg-sized stone into Griselda's outstretched palm. Several of the soldiers licked their lips and their eyes flicked from the stone back to Zimmerman. Their thoughts were almost verbal. *What else is he hiding?*

Griselda's face was an implacable mask, but Copely knew he had blundered by hiding the stone. Zimmerman had succeeded in dropping him in the deep end, but he knew enough to shut up and not make matters worse by trying to explain himself. He'd have to be more careful.

Griselda moved back to the front desk and dumped Copely's diamond on the desk in front of the old woman.

"We can buy half the town for this!" she snapped. "Where are our rooms?"

The old woman cackled as she lifted the stone up to her good eye. Several of her front teeth were missing. She must have had a hard life on Earth for this to be the sum total of her bodily memory.

"Not so fast," she countered. "Let me see the others." After all, she lived in a mining town where most of her customers tried to pay with the finds from their fields.

She pushed the egg-sized stone away. "That ain't no gemstone quality. Wouldn't buy a hot tub 'a water round here. I'll take these five." She palmed the smaller gems as Zimmerman winced. She'd identified the most valuable stones in an instant. "These'll get ya the rooms."

She reached behind her and collected a handful of keys from the cubbyholes and dropped them on the desk. Something in Griselda's manner must have sparked a warning because she slid one of the keys towards her and added, "You'll be wanting the best room, no doubt."

Griselda snatched the key from her fingertips and stormed up the stairs.

"Second on the left!" the old woman yelled after her.

Copely stepped up to the counter and removed another key from the pile. He picked up the large diamond he'd been carrying and examined it in his palm. He turned and slowly sauntered to where Zimmerman sat against the wall, and let the diamond drop and clatter on the floorboards. It rolled and came to a rest against Zimmerman's thigh.

Their eyes met, and Marcus could see the chagrin and humiliation boiling behind the black pupils. He and Copely were never going to be best friends forever, but his subtle subterfuge had backfired and he'd just created another deadly enemy. Copely was letting him know this, should there have been any lingering doubt on his part. He tried to swallow but his mouth was dry.

—⚏—

Zimmerman was called to account. He was seated at a desk in Chisholm's room, which was small, stark, and cold, and nowhere near the price of comfort they'd had to pay. Griselda had been left feeling black-humoured and vengeful. The old woman would be made to pay once another crystal was in her grasp.

Zimmerman's belongings had been searched and his entire collection of stones lay scattered on the desk in front of him.

". . . Anything of value," Chisholm was saying. "I want every diamond, every zircon, ruby, emerald, pearl—"

"A pearl's not a gemstone," he interrupted. He couldn't help himself. He bit his lip at the gaffe the instant the words had left his mouth and wondered if she'd heard. He'd been staring at his collection, and he flicked his eyes up briefly, long enough to note the indignation that burned her face a brighter shade of beetroot, and the tendons in her neck that were like cords. He wished a hole would open in the ground beneath his feet and swallow him. He thought she was enraged enough to kill him.

"... Every ruby, emerald ... *pearl!* ..." she continued slowly, enunciating each word like a threat, "that we can use to trade for clothing and whatever else we lost."

The room fell silent, and Zimmerman kept his eyes focussed on the rocks on the desk.

"Because, Mr Zimmerman, after all that has happened, after all we have been through, if you do not find the source of the crystal after all of this, I will personally guarantee that your last days on Bexus will be so full of pain that you will beg me for release." She leaned forward and cupped her hand beneath his chin and brought his head up so that he was staring into her face.

"Do you believe me?" she asked him.

She'd regained some control; her voice was smooth and even, but it belied an intensity of seething anger that lurked savagely just below the surface. She was even more terrifying than before, if that were possible.

Zimmerman nodded, and his head bobbed in her hand. She released him, and he immediately hunched over the table and continued the sorting process.

Griselda smiled as she watched him work.

Whatever else they thought of Marcus Zimmerman, one thing they had to agree on was that he was a first-rate geologist. The stones he'd collected along the way were welcomed with a sense of unbridled greed among the traders of Poluostrov. Griselda's presence at the negotiations kept the trading relatively honest; she wore menace the way most other women wore makeup, and although the traders were conditioned by most forms of physical hardship, they weren't stupid when it came to recognising a threatening situation.

Zimmerman was able to replace most of the equipment he'd lost. It all took time, and another couple of diamonds exchanged hands at the hotel. The one-eyed woman was a useful mine of information herself when it came to sourcing equipment. The team was even able to replace two of the missing *Urguts* to lug the gear they'd gathered. These beasts, however, were half-starved and ill-tempered creatures that were capable of hauling a fraction of the loads of their predecessors, but it sure beat trekking over difficult terrain, weighed down by overloaded packs.

It took a week to reassemble the expedition. During that time, another two men disappeared, along with some of the precious cold weather gear. This time, they were spotted leaving the town, headed back the way they had come. By the time Griselda heard about it, it was too late to chase them down. Their names were filed alongside those of Khushk and Draganov, meriting special attention once they were caught—and they would be caught, she was sure about that!

They had reached the latitudes low enough for the night skies to the south of Poluostrov to shimmer. The greens and reds of the aurora were created by the bombardment of solar particles which constantly streamed down following the magnetic lines of force at the South Pole of Bexus. They were even more spectacular than the auroras of Earth, perhaps because the magnetic effects of the poles on Bexus were stronger.

Zimmerman was the only member of the group who truly appreciated the sight since he knew the aurora held the clue as to where to search for the source of the crystal. He kept this to himself; his chances of survival were slim to none, and he needed every advantage he could gain if he were to have any sort of future on Bexus beyond the next couple of weeks.

Zimmerman had his eyes peeled on the lights. He was captivated by the way they seemed to flow, drawn towards the horizon the way a leaf gets sucked down the plughole in a basin full of water. He was leaning against the side of a barn, waiting on Riegel and Hendrikx to finish strapping the last of the supplies to the pack animals. Chisholm was planning an early start the following morning, and the three men had been assigned the task of loading and guarding the two scrawny *Urguts*. Zimmerman sighed. His bed at the hotel wasn't up to much, but it was a whole heap warmer and softer than the cold, damp straw stacked inside the barn.

He was startled by a sudden piercing scream. The wall of the barn he was leaning against shuddered once as something heavy crashed against it. Zimmerman heaved the door open and was confronted by a shocking scene of mayhem.

"Grab the rope! Tie it back!" Hendrikx screamed at him.

Hendrikx was holding tight to a rope. He'd taken the strain by curling the rope behind his back, but was being dragged upright across the barn floor by one of the *Urguts*. A second rope trailed in the dirt behind the animal, and this was the rope Hendrikx had meant.

But Zimmerman paled and hesitated. He was sickened by the sight of Riegel, impaled through the hip by one of the horns, clawing at the horn as he was being driven backwards across the dirt bleeding a torrent of sparks from the wound.

"Move, you fool!" Hendrikx railed at him, and it broke the spell. Zimmerman dived across the floor and grabbed the trailing end of the second rope. He was dragged across the floor until he managed to stumble to his feet. He hauled back on the rope with all his strength and felt the wasted bull falter.

"Heave!" cried Hendrikx.

The two men pulled back and halted the bull's forward drive. It sensed the threat from behind and shook its head, and Riegel slipped off the horn and rolled to one side.

Zimmerman was close to one of the posts that supported the expansive barn roof, and he dodged to the side and wrapped the rope around the upright, just as the bull dipped its head and charged Hendrikx.

Hendrikx had anticipated the charge and had skittered backwards as the bull lunged at him. The rope around the post brought the old bull up short. It twisted the bull's head down, and one of the horns rammed into the soft dirt floor. Hendrikx used the opportunity to follow Zimmerman's lead, and before the animal had a chance to react, it was immobilised between the two opposing ropes.

Hendrikx rushed to Riegel's side and used a jacket to try and stem the flow of energy from the wound the size of a fist while Zimmerman ran to the hotel for assistance. By the time he'd returned with the others, Riegel was pale and sweating in obvious pain. Chisholm immediately administered handfuls of Mother's Glove, pressing the goop deep inside the wound to plug it shut. She wrapped Riegel's side tight with bandages until the escaping sparks trickled to nothing. Four of the men carried him back to the hotel and laid him on his bed. There was nothing more they could do for him for the present, and it would be touch and go as to whether or not he'd survive the night.

By the following morning, Riegel had stepped back from the brink of extinction. He was still pale and weak, but he was conscious and lucid. This was more a tribute to his impressive strength and fitness than it was to Griselda's nursing ability.

Griselda was not happy with the latest turn of events. The expedition relied heavily on Riegel's skills; he had managed to lead them all the way to Poluostrov, despite Khushk's defection. Without him, the expedition faltered.

Griselda sat beside him and peeled the dressing back. The poultice of Mother's Glove had hardened into a black, crusty scab. She picked at its edges. Riegel winced, and a small burst of sparks fizzed through the crack in the poultice. Nevertheless, Griselda was impressed with the healing powers of the crushed leaves. Riegel might be left with an ugly, puckered scar the size of a baseball, but he'd be back on his feet within a week. The problem was, it was another week the expedition could ill-afford to lose.

"Hire some of the locals," Riegel grimaced as he whispered. "The old woman will know of some. Pay them what you have to. As soon as I am strong enough, I'll follow you. We can always dispose of them later."

Griselda considered his advice as she watched him carefully. There had already been too many desertions. Was Riegel also lining up his opportunity to leave?

No, she decided. Riegel was smart enough to know that something big would follow. He wanted to be a part of it, a member of the inner circle. There was room for him near the top of the New Order.

"How long?" she asked.

"Four days, at least. No more than a week, I promise." He shifted his weight on the bed and groaned with pain. When he opened his eyes again, she was looking at him, unable to mask the doubt across her face.

He glared at her. "*I promise!*"

She nodded. They had to do something. They were coming to the end of the cache of diamonds that the geologist had collected.

Copely entered with an armful of cold weather clothing that he dumped on the floor at the end of the bed. Griselda stood. There were guides to hire.

"Will you be able to find us?" she asked Riegel.

"Leave a trail I can follow," he replied.

As they left the room, Copely whispered, "Can you trust him?"

"I searched his belongings and didn't find any egg-sized diamonds, so Mr Copely, I think the answer is yes."

Copely felt his ears burn. Chisholm hadn't forgotten his tiny indiscretion. When they eventually did discover the source of Varak's crystal, he knew he was going to have to move fast.

It took the rest of the day to locate the guides and negotiate an agreement. There were three of them: hardened and nut brown, stocky and sullen, and—unsurprisingly—of Innuit origins. They pocketed the last of Zimmerman's gems with toothless relish and slept in the barn and helped pacify the crotchety *Urguts*.

Riegel struggled from his bed and watched from his window as the expedition trudged along the main street in single file, heading south once more. The wound in his side throbbed and made him feel light-headed, and he collapsed back onto the bed and slept.

CHAPTER 8

The lone *Urgut* was tethered to the base of one of the trees. It stood with its head hung low as if it were despondent because there was nothing within reach to munch on. It appeared to be oblivious to the fact that it was bearing a heavy load of supplies. It snorted, and its breath formed a cloud of vapour in the cold air.

The group lay motionless, hidden behind trees no more than forty yards away. Kareem's gaze passed back and forth, searching for one sign that would signal a trap. The animal was the bait, he was certain of it, but after an hour of intense scrutiny, he still could not find what he was seeking: a subtle movement as an attacker shifted his weight, the tell-tale fog of breath, the rustle of dried leaves, the lack of ambient animal noise. This was the second time they'd been presented with a sign, a clue that was too good to be true. Was he becoming too paranoid? No! Rather err on the side of caution.

Jackson stretched his leg, which had grown numb, and the sound of his boot over the carpet of leaves drew a harsh glare from Kareem.

"Sorry," he mouthed by way of an apology as Kareem returned to his vigil of watching and waiting. Kate threw him a warning stare, as well. He shrugged and mouthed, "What?" She shook her head.

Kareem had arrived at a dilemma. Either the ambush was planned to perfection—and he'd yet to encounter one that had—or there was no ambush at all. He decided to risk showing himself once again.

He gestured to the others to remain well hidden and provide covering fire should he need it. He checked the area one final time, then cautiously stood and crept warily into the open space beneath the trees as he approached the *Urgut*.

The animal raised its head, and Kareem could see the white of its eye as it tried to keep him in its line of sight. He kept his weight balanced on the balls of his feet, ready to dive sideways and roll at the first inkling of danger, but the forest remained passive and unthreatening.

He reached the beast, and leaned forward to stroke its neck and placate it. He turned his attention to the load it carried.

The load was bulky and covered by a tough hide, which had been laced down over the load to protect it from the weather. Kareem leaned his staff against the base of the tree, and reached beneath the belly of the *Urgut* to release the ties. He folded the hide back to reveal canvas sacks and boxes slung each side of the animal's broad back. He hefted one of the bags and slipped the drawstring free of the pile.

He withdrew a selection of hooded fur coats and pliable leather boots insulated with a thick layer of wool. His own feet were wet and chilled to near freezing, and it took all his self control not to rip his own boots off and stuff them into the inviting maws of wool in his hands.

This was clearly no ambush. He waved his companions forward, and they emerged through the ground fog like hooded wraiths.

"This has to be from the Zimmerman party!" Sigrid exclaimed.

"Why would they just leave it behind like this? It doesn't make any sense."

Jackson lifted one of the boxes free. Its weight took him by surprise, and it crashed to the ground and broke apart. A glass container smashed, and liquid spilled onto the soil.

"Careful!" he warned. "It smells like some sort of concentrated acid." The liquid hissed as it came into contact with the damp soil, and gave off a faint curtain of yellowish fumes. The remaining contents of the box were strewn over the dead leaves and were clearly a collection of geological tools.

Kareem examined the tether. It had been deliberately wrapped around the base of the tree and tied securely. The animal had been left here on purpose. He moved away from the group and began a thorough examination of the ground for spoor. Kate joined him, careful to stay behind him at his shoulder to avoid contaminating the scene.

"What do you make of it?" she asked.

Kareem bent on one knee. He'd headed south of where the beast was tethered, and pointed to a bare patch of ground, sullied by many footprints.

"They passed by here—you can make out Zimmerman's tread there—and here you can see the marks made by the one *Urgut* in the company. But look, here—the back hoof has been split."

Kate could see the faint line in the mud that traversed the hoof like a crack. She followed Kareem back to where the animal stood. He bent and gripped the creature's left hind leg and lifted it up to reveal the cracked hoof. It was the same animal. Kate frowned. Nothing made sense.

"They lost the animal up ahead," Kareem said. "There's no sign that it came back the same way. What's more, *someone* tied it to the tree. The only explanation I can think of is that one or more of the group deserted, and stole the *Urgut* when they left. They would have been pursued, no doubt, and decided to ditch the beast before they were caught. Nothing else makes sense."

"Well, I say 'Finders keepers'," said Jackson as he slumped against the base of a nearby tree with a pair of thick boots in his hands, and reached to untie his laces. "Strictly speaking, this stuff comes from Hogarth; we're just returning it to its rightful owners."

"Ohmigod!" he sighed as he slipped one cold foot into his new footwear. "Oh, that is so—o warm!"

"He's right," Mia agreed. "Never look a gift horse in the mouth."

They unloaded the stack of supplies, and laid them out into two piles: stuff they could use, and stuff they couldn't. In the 'Stuff They Couldn't' pile, they heaped all the geological equipment, excess tents, and clothing and military equipment that was too large or too bulky. They rummaged through the cold weather clothing for boots, hats, gloves and jackets, and discarded their wet gear on the growing pile of 'Stuff They Couldn't'.

They repacked the supplies they needed, strapped them across the animal, and covered them with the animal hide. The pile was less than half the original size, and included a stash of gemstones, and two bags of Hogarth currency, which had debatable value for trading purposes this far south.

They were well equipped once more. Mia unhitched and led the *Urgut,* which lumbered behind them as they picked up the trail south towards Poluostrov.

The trip was laborious but uneventful. The icy winds that blew all the way from the frozen wastes of the south nipped at their exposed skin, but they kept warm beneath the layers of wool and fur they'd just liberated. Sleet and ice clung to their clothing and caught in matted clumps on the *Urgut's* shaggy hair. Nobody complained, simply because it wasn't worth the effort, so the party trudged along in silence, stepping clear of the sodden mud that lurked beneath the low-clinging wind-resistant scrub.

They passed the point where the Zimmerman party lost the Urgut. Kareem called a halt, and spent the better part of an hour trying to piece together any information from the spoor. He followed the tracks of the lone Urgut, but didn't find any evidence that it had been led away by deserters. Fifty yards from the campsite, the *Urgut's* own hoof-prints had disappeared. Kareem widened his search, and discovered one or two telling signs that had registered the animal's passing, but no more. He returned to the campsite, as mystified as before, except he had a clearer understanding as to why the remaining members of that expedition had failed to track the animal and recapture it.

"Come and see what we've found," Kate said once he'd returned. She led him to a spot beneath one of the pines where a pathetic makeshift bed had been raked together using the dry, dead leaves. Half hidden amongst it was some muddy underwear. Someone had died from exposure here.

Whoever it was, it wasn't Zimmerman. They'd already picked up his unique tread leading down from the shelter of the forest, heading out across the bleak moors, tracking directly south. They were headed for Poluostrov to resupply. No surprises there!

Kate still couldn't get rid of the notion that Copely was behind all of this. The whole plan reeked of his scent, without so much as a scrap of evidence beyond the cryptic placement of the quartz crystals on the dead men's uniforms. She had to succeed, to prevent him—or whoever was protecting him—from wielding the power of another intact crystal. She and her four companions were all that stood in the way of another tyrannical despot.

She glanced behind her at the desolate, windswept horizon, expecting to see a troop of mounted soldiers in pursuit with Streikker at their head. There was no one, but she sensed the danger, and knew they had to press forward with all the strength they could muster.

And then, as if Kareem could read her thoughts, he reappeared at the crest of a low rolling hill and waved them forward urgently.

Very briefly, her heart soared at the sight of him again, and she remembered the warmth and the softness of his kiss.

The eyes of Poluostrov followed them from behind the narrow shutters and darkened glass as they walked wearily along the endless stretch of the main street. They headed towards the single two-storey building five days after the Zimmerman expedition had exited the town along the same road.

The few townspeople they saw bristled with resentment at the appearance of another group of strangers within a week. Some were openly hostile; one man threw rocks at them, but ran away the moment Kareem turned in his direction. After that, they were left alone.

They paused outside the faded peeling sign that drooped from one corner, advertising Rooms To Let. If the Zimmerman party had passed through the town, it would have stopped here to rest and recover. It seemed the obvious place to start asking questions.

They unloaded their supplies under the veranda beside the front door, and then Jackson and Mia led the *Urgut* over to a large barn, looking for some shelter and feed for the animal.

The interior of the hotel was like a welcome sauna compared to the outside temperature. There was no one behind the counter, but an old woman sat snoring in an armchair in the adjacent lounge.

Kate checked the cubbyholes behind the counter as she called out.

"Hello?"

Only one room appeared to be taken. The keys to the other rooms were in place. Kate turned as she heard the old woman stir, then the armchair creaked as she hoisted herself from its embrace. She was not happy to have been woken from her slumber.

"What?" she demanded angrily. Her one eye glared at Kate as she limped around behind the counter.

"We are hoping you can help us," Kate explained. "We're looking for a group of men who must have passed through here, maybe a week ago. We're . . . friends of theirs."

The woman said nothing. She stared at them, sizing up each of them in turn. The door behind them opened, and Jackson and Mia barged in.

"Oh-h, luxury, sheer bloody luxury!" Jackson exclaimed, stamping his feet on the floor, and tugging his woollen hat from his head. The prospect of more customers seemed to set the woman into a darker mood than before. She muttered something under her breath.

Kate tried again. "Our friends—were they here?"

"This is a hotel, Sissy, not a bleedin' information centre. You want to ask something, ask if there are rooms available!"

Kate glanced at her companions. They looked exhausted and in need of rest. She saw her own reflection in a grimy mirror above the cubbyholes, and she was no oil painting either.

"Okay . . . well, I guess we're going to need—"

"They're all singles!" the woman interrupted.

"Very well, fi—"

"They don't come cheap!"

Kate bit her tongue and took a deep breath. She saw that Kareem was grinning at the exchange between her and the woman. She made a renewed effort to remain civil. She asked Jackson for the purse they'd found amongst the supplies strapped to the *Urgut*. He handed it across, and she untied it and spilled some of the coins across the counter.

"*Ppshheww!* That's Hogarth coin! Ain't worth nothin' in these parts!" The woman's voice dripped with disdain, and she waved the back of her hand at the cash in dismissal. Kareem was still grinning. Kate wanted to slap him.

"The other one!" she instructed Jackson. He dug inside his coat for the smaller purse and gave it to her. Kate loosened the drawstring to the pouch, and let a few gems trickle onto the counter top. The old woman wasn't quick enough to mask her surprise; she gave a sharp intake of breath. The power play just switched hands.

Kate began to pick up each of the coloured stones and drop them back into the bag as if she'd just changed her mind about the whole deal. The old woman's right hand immediately clamped hers in a vice-like grip, and this time, the tone of her voice had sweetened.

"Ah-hah, five rooms, you say?" Her left hand appeared from nowhere and the knobbly fingers were stunningly quick in peeling away three rubies, a deep-blue zircon, and a large uncut emerald.

"Hey!" The move caught Kate by surprise, but by then the woman had let go of her wrist and pocketed the gems. She turned her back to Kate and collected five sets of keys while Kate gathered the remaining stones and dropped them back into the purse before the old crone could make a second lunge at them. She wanted to leap over the counter, wrestle the woman to the ground, and retrieve some of the stones; the crone had pocketed gems four to five times the value of the rooms, even if they had planned to stay the month. Kareem's hand on her shoulder steadied her. He was still grinning, but he shook his head gently; this was one battle not worth the fight. He was right, but it didn't keep Kate from seething from the corrupt practice that had robbed her blind. She tossed the purse back to Jackson and snatched the keys from the desktop.

"Ain't no one been by, dearie, in answer to your question," the old woman called to her back. "You're most welcome to wait for your friends here if you want."

That was a lie. Kate had also noticed the dust patterns in the cubbyholes. A large group had stopped by. One room was still occupied. She considered the possibility of a connection.

The urge to throttle the old woman resurfaced after Kate saw the size and the condition of the rooms for rent. They were barely larger than the thin bunks squeezed up against the walls. Each room also had a tiny wicker chair at the foot of the bunk, which doubled as a set of drawers to drop clothing on; otherwise the rooms were bare, streaked with grime and smelled of stale body odour. But they were warm.

The rooms were adjacent to each other on the second floor. The students dropped off their gear in their rooms and reassembled in Kate's room. The three girls were crushed together on the bunk while Kareem sat astride the chair, and Jackson leaned against the wall behind him. Jackson yawned. The warmth was soporific after days camped out in the cold.

"Zimmerman was here! I'd bet my life on it!" Kate said.

"He's not here now," Jackson remarked dryly.

"So, they're ahead of us, but we've caught up some time!" she replied. "We need to be ready to leave tomorrow. Kareem ought to be able to pick up their trail, but we've got to hope the weather holds. A heavy snowfall would obliterate their tracks, right?" she asked.

Kareem nodded. "We'd need a lucky break," he commented.

"Do we know where they're headed?" Mia asked. "This is the last settlement. Beyond Poluostrov, there's . . . nothing."

"So far, they have just been pointing south. We should do the same."

Kareem interrupted. "Well . . . southish."

"Southish?"

"Not true south. There's a deviation of a few degrees west of south."

Kate frowned. She didn't understand. What was west of south that would interest Zimmerman?

Kareem smiled and reached into his pocket. At the same time, he stood and stepped across to the bunk.

"Give me some room," he said. Kate shuffled to one side, and Mia and Sigrid squashed up to the other. Kareem sat between them. He produced a compass in his hand and held it in front of him. He rotated it until the needle aligned itself directly beneath the 'S' marked on the compass.

"That's where they're headed," he said.

Kate was momentarily perplexed. "I don't understand," she said. "I thought you said they weren't heading south."

Kareem smiled and said nothing. A few seconds later, Mia squealed with delight.

"I get it!"

"Get what?" Kate was miffed that the problem had such a simple solution that she still couldn't see.

"They're not going to the South Pole! They're headed for the Magnetic South Pole! There's a difference, right? Something to do with—what's it called—magnetic declination?"

"They've been following a compass," Kareem replied.

A knock at the door startled them.

"Who is it?" Kate called. "What do you want?"

They heard the old woman reply.

"Blankets for the bunks!"

Each bunk had a thin pillow covered by a threadbare pillowslip, but that was all. Kate had wondered about the bedding, and had fumed that this was something else they'd paid for. Jackson unlocked the door and turned the handle.

The woman was standing in front of the door, but she wasn't carrying any blankets. There was a man standing behind her, holding a staff at her throat. The fingers of his free hand were entwined in her hair so that her head was twisted to one side. Jackson caught a brief glimpse of the terror stretched across her face before she was savagely thrust into the room, knocking him aside in the process.

"*Omnes torpor!*"

Kareem tried to dive off the bed, but the girls wedged him in place. Kate tried to reach for Rhyanon, but Kareem's reaction forced her back against the wall at the head of the bunk. A red sphere of light expanded outwards from the tip of the stranger's staff, filling the room before it burst like a bubble and completely paralysed everyone in its path.

CHAPTER 9

Riegel had made a spectacular recovery from the grievous wound that had threatened his life days before. This capacity of the soul to heal was made more remarkable by Riegel's demanding regime as a soldier. He'd begun the road to recovery by pacing back and forth inside his room, frequently collapsing onto the flimsy bunk in pain.

Once the wound had healed over completely, he managed longer stretches, and, by the end of the third day, he had taken to limping the length of the main street of Poluostrov.

He had been preparing for another bout of exercise when he first spotted the weary line of travellers trudging into the town from the north. He watched them from behind net curtains as they approached the hotel, and long before they stopped outside the hotel, he'd recognised the Gallagher girl. He'd witnessed her triumph over Lord Varak, and he'd watched her parade in front of the city walls at Cherath. He knew who she was. What's more, he'd picked up snippets of conversation between Chisholm and the spy, Copely. He knew she'd been marked for special attention, and he sat back on his bed and considered the possibilities and the rewards he'd reap if he could deliver her into their arms.

He had to consider two problems: the state of his health and the fact he was outnumbered. The young, dark-skinned warrior leading the group would be the danger, although Riegel didn't underestimate her other companions. The only way to catch them out would be when they were bunched together, in a situation where he had the element of surprise. He knew almost certainly that they would want to meet up before they settled for the night. He thought about biding his time until they all retired, and then tackling the girl once she was alone in her room, but he discarded that idea almost immediately. Too many things could go wrong: both Varak and The Magician had grossly underestimated her. No—if they were together, they'd be more relaxed, less wary. He lay back on the bed to formulate a plan.

He knew about the lack of blankets in the rooms. The old shrew was miserable in that respect, but the thought of her provided the germ of an idea, which grew because of the utter simplicity it entailed.

His room was out the back on the ground floor, off a short corridor that ran adjacent to the counter. Timing was everything! He crept off his bed and opened his door a crack, just enough to overhear the conversations in the lobby. He heard footsteps echo on the stairs, and decided that ten minutes would be all he would need.

He collected his meagre belongings, then crept out and laid them behind the counter. The old woman had retired to her seat beside the fire, so she was unaware of his presence until she felt a hand stifle her scream. At the same time, a staff was jammed tightly below her jaw.

She was a survivor; she understood what it would take to live beyond the day, and was entirely cooperative. Riegel still didn't trust her, so he kept his fingers tangled in her hair as they crept up the stairs. His side still throbbed, but he barely noticed the pain.

"The girl's room—which is it?" he hissed in the old woman's ear. She pointed to a room in the middle of the hallway, marked by a door with scratched and peeling green paint.

The woman knew what was expected of her. She didn't care what happened to the visitors, but knew that, if she didn't perform flawlessly, she'd become the first casualty. She concentrated on controlling the terror that threatened to choke her words mid-sentence.

The lock clicked, and the door opened. That was Riegel's signal. He shoved the old woman through the door, and her momentum knocked the young man aside and propelled her into the room. Once he'd lost the element of surprise, it became a race to see who would be the quickest to react. The crush of bodies in the tiny room slowed them down and, in the end, it was no contest. By the time the residue of Riegel's charm had dissipated, there were six inert bodies strewn about the bedroom.

—⁂—

Kate knew the curse, although she'd never used it herself. It was a simple, disarming charm; there was a disabling counter-spell, but you had to be active enough to summon it.

Its speed and effects astonished her. The curse had frozen her eyes open; she was still fully conscious and could see everything within the periphery of her vision, but she couldn't move, and unless the spell was broken, wouldn't be able to for countless hours until its effects gradually wore off.

She wanted to scream out her frustration at being so easily ambushed, but of course, she couldn't. Their suspicions ought to have been aroused by the single occupied room when they'd already known a large party had been through the hotel days beforehand. But they'd been tired and the warmth of the hotel had been too seductive—and they'd been careless.

There was movement out to the side, and a shape loomed larger, blocking out some of the weak light from the table lamp. A man peered down at her, his face pulled tight in a leering grin. She didn't recognise him, had never seen him before, but he most certainly knew her. He gripped her by the hair and lifted her head slightly to examine her, and as her head tilted forward, she was able to discern some of the characteristic markings of one of Varak's uniformed guards protruding from beneath his thick insulated jacket.

He let her head fall back against the wooden bed head, and moved to one side to check on the others. He disappeared from view briefly; when he returned, he carried an armful of weather protective clothing.

He dumped the clothing at the foot of the bed and dragged the other bodies from the bed. Kate heard them hit the wooden floor with a thump each time. He then laid Kate flat on the bed, and proceeded to wrestle her into the clothing. Her limbs were stiff and unresponsive, so it took some time before she was fully layered in a hooded jacket, thick skin leggings and fur-lined boots.

"Come on then, my pretty," she heard him say as he pulled her upright into a sitting position before slinging her across his shoulder. "There's someone wants to meet with you, who'll pay a pretty price for the pleasure, I'm thinking."

Kareem's upturned face passed fleetingly before her as the man stepped over his body. His face had been frozen into an angry grimace, but there was a look of absolute helplessness in his eyes that caused Kate to feel fear for the first time. She remembered he had ducked slightly as the door had burst open. Her only hope was that his action had robbed the charm of some of its effects to nail him cold. He was her only hope of rescue. And then he was gone.

She saw the pattern of the stairs coming up to meet her, and felt the man bend to retrieve his gear from behind the counter.

He opened the door of the hotel, and her face caught the chill of the icy wind. He twisted, one side to the other, checking to see if he'd been caught in the act of leaving. Apparently, it was no one's business but his; curtains dropped back into place, and the street remained deserted.

⚬〰⚬

Riegel crossed the street to the barn. He swung the doors open and stepped inside out of the wind. The temperatures had plummeted considerably, and the sky was layered in tumultuous, black storm clouds. Large snowflakes had already fluttered in on the swirling wind, and Riegel knew he was about to step out into a blizzard.

He dropped the girl onto a pile of straw and wandered back to the doors. He glanced up at the sky and drew a deep breath. He debated whether to move back to the relative safety and comfort of the hotel to wait out the storm, but time was a factor. He supposed he should have reduced the risk by applying a final coup de grâce to each of the paralysed people littering the floor, but he sensed it would have created more problems than it solved.

The *Urgut* was tethered to one of the stalls. The hide covering lay draped across the gate enclosing the stall, and the supplies had been stacked beside the stall. There was no sign of whoever looked after the stall, although Riegel imagined he'd been paid to protect the equipment.

He made a thorough search of the barn. He sorted through the supplies and bundled and stowed what he needed. He gathered some leather thongs and some ropes, then flung the girl across the back of the beast and used the thongs to tie her securely in place. He discovered an old compass hanging from a leather lanyard on a nail beside the stall and checked to see if it was working properly. Satisfied, he thrust it into a pocket in the lining of his fur jacket. He threw the hide across the back of the *Urgut*, covering the girl and the equipment, and tied it tightly, placing one loop beneath the animal's tail to keep it secure against the wind. He left the front unattached, then released the animal and led it over to the doors. He swung his leg up and over the animal's broad back, and reached behind to gather the hide about him like a hooded rain cape.

He dug his heels into the animal's ribs and guided it through the doors into the street and pulled up short. Half the townsfolk were assembled in front of the barn, waiting for him, and they were not happy. He could see across to the veranda of the hotel and through the front window. The old woman was seated in her chair, still unconscious while her vital signs were checked. Riegel didn't want to be in the town when she woke up. There was no sign of any of the others from the room. Evidently, the townspeople looked to their own, first and last.

He nudged the beast forward, and was relieved to note the crowd in front of him gave way. The faces were hostile and unforgiving; they might let him depart for now, but he knew he'd not be welcomed back. No one tried to stop him, or pull him from the *Urgut*, nor did they try to prevent him from escaping with the girl. He had no second thoughts about sheltering from the approaching storm; that was no longer an option.

By the time the lumbering beast passed the outskirts of the city heading south, the snow had begun to fall heavily, and the landscape was doused with a white blanket that smothered the horizon and cut visibility to a couple of hundred yards. Riegel corrected the bearing to south on his compass, and bent into the wind, wrapping the hide tightly about him.

Four hours after he'd left Poluostrov behind and had disappeared into the storm, the old lady was revived. She was dopey and uncertain but lapped up the attention. The bodies of the other four people in the bedroom were carried out and dumped into the cellar. Their belongings were collected together and dropped in the broom cupboard by the hall behind the counter. The old lady could decide what to do with them later.

Beyond the city, the snow built up in drifts and blew across the stunted landscape. It covered the tracks of the lonely *Urgut*, completely obliterating all signs of its passage.

Kate lost all track of time. Her face was half buried in the matted fur of the *Urgut*, and it stank of damp musk and stale sweat. Her arms had been stretched above her head and pulled taut with thongs that ran beneath the belly of the animal and were tied to her ankles on the other side.

There was no pain or stiffness, although that was guaranteed to occur once the charm wore off. There was no telling how long she'd be incapacitated; the strength of any charm depended on the skills of the person delivering it. The man had looked like a brute. She hoped he'd only managed to master the basics.

The wind whistled beneath the hide cover and caused it to flap up and down. She was totally helpless. She thought about the fate of her companions. She doubted any of the citizens of Poluostrov would take pity on them and release them from the spell. They'd more than likely rob her friends of every possession, and kill them or imprison them. Her one hope was Kareem. She had to place her trust in him to escape and rescue her, rescue them all.

The diffuse grey light that managed to leak beneath the hide disappeared slowly. The noise of the wind had set up a constant whistling that rose and fell with an almost regular monotony, but she was protected from the worst of the weather's excesses.

The *Urgut* suddenly stopped, and she suspected the man had decided to make camp for the night. She sensed movement and heard the *crunch!* sound his boots made as they dropped into the crusted snow.

He pulled the hide back, and Kate felt the full force of the icy wind briefly before it mercifully fell away again. The beast was moving beneath her, and the man was leading it behind some form of shelter. He bent and released the knots that bound her to the animal and lifted her roughly down from the animal's back. He dumped her in a pile of snow, and she was able to make out a couple of humped shapes in the dimming light. They could have been rock outcrops jutting from the ground; she couldn't tell because they were piled high with snow, but the wind whipped by above and the travellers were protected from the worst of the weather.

Snowflakes drifted down into the hollow in which they sheltered. Away from the wind, the flakes were large and languid, and they settled on her face and clothing. The man busied himself by securing the animal, and then laid out the hide cover to form a crude tent over a frame of supplejack canes he'd found in the barn. Once he had completed the task, he strode across and gripped Kate by the front of her jacket. He dragged her through the fallen snow and dropped her beneath the shelter of the tent.

During the night, the wind grew to a frenzied intensity of shrieking, and the snow was driven, but the storm was far from a full-frontal blizzard. Kate lay on a patch of snow, and she longed to shiver, but she was still captivated by the spell. The man woke once or twice during the night to check on her; once satisfied that she was still immobilised, he rolled over and went back to sleep.

By morning, the wind still hadn't abated. The storm clouds driving the blizzard beneath were south of them, and slowly, inexorably, were moving towards them. Kate lay on her back as the man busied himself with dismantling the crude tent and stowing the canes in a bundle. There was nothing she could do but watch the snowflakes drift down from the burnished pewter skies. One flake fluttered into her eyeball and—she blinked!

She could move! One eyelid—but it was a start. She checked the rest of her body. Another sign: the small finger on her left hand twitched as if she were beating time. The spell was beginning to wear off!

The man returned and bent to examine her closely once again. Some of the snow that had been trapped by the fur lining around his hood had melted, and water droplets fell on her face beside her eye. It took a supreme strength of will to conquer the reflexive blink, and for a brief moment, her eyes welled with tears, but she didn't blink.

He picked her up, slung her across his shoulders, then dropped her onto the back of the *Urgut*. He strapped her wrists to her ankles, and then tugged her body to make certain she wouldn't slip from the animal's back before he secured the hide on top of her and blocked out the light.

Throughout the day, more parts of her body began to respond as the sensation of feeling returned. It started as a faint, tickling before changing to pins and needles—a stabbing, prickling awareness as if she'd planted her limbs in a bed of stinging nettles.

Twice during the journey, she felt the shift in motion as the *Urgut* was hauled to a halt, and the man climbed down and peeled the hide back. He'd grip a hank of hair and jerk her head up, and search suspiciously for any flicker of movement. Sleet tore at her skin, yet she succeeded in keeping her eyes open and unfocussed by concentrating on images of her mother reaching out to comfort her. She shut out the world as the man's grim countenance drifted in and out of focus. She still lacked the strength to resist, to run, or to fight; guile was her only weapon for the time being.

She also gathered confidence because of the interruptions. They suggested the man was unable to gauge the effects of his own charm. He obviously had no idea how long the spell would last, and needed to keep checking for himself. If she could manage to continue to fool him, he'd believe his spell had been highly effective and would relax and not be so vigilant. If she could manage . . .

Now she could feel the bite of the cold beneath her clothing, which had become damp. She longed to stretch and ease the ache that hours of being bound and tossed by the *Urgut's* awkward gait had caused. She shivered involuntarily.

Shivering! Her body shuddered, and she fought to control it. She cleared her mind and tried to relax. She built a mental picture of a walled castle inside her head and retreated behind it, abandoning her limbs and torso to the cold. Behind these walls, she was warm. She waited until she felt her body slacken.

The *Urgut* was reined to a halt, and she prepared herself for another close examination as she felt the man dismount. However, the beast was jerked forward, and Kate could hear the man's heavy boots crunch across ice. Occasionally, a hoof would slip, and the animal would jerk suddenly as it regained its footing. They trudged on relentlessly; the rocking motion was almost hypnotic, and Kate drifted in and out of a restless sleep.

The second day of the journey ended much like the first. The hide was lifted from the animal, and after careful scrutiny, Kate's bindings were untied, and she was dropped into a snowdrift.

Kate kept her head steady but let her eyes take stock of her situation. She appeared to be part way across a field of ice, perhaps a glacier. The man was unhitching the canes, preparing to erect the tent beside a small pile of peat bricks, which had been left exposed as a trail marker. The man was following in the footsteps of the Zimmerman expedition, moving from marker to marker. They were expecting him. They weren't expecting her!

She tried to test her limbs to determine if she had recovered sufficiently to be able to escape. *Possible but doubtful.* She would have to wait and fake paralysis a while longer.

The wind had blown the snow into scattered drifts, piled alongside blocks of ice that would have broken free of the main sheet. The ice itself was riven with deep cracks and crevices, and the shadows they created in the twilight were like long deep black crayon slashes.

This time, the tent was erected in the shape of an italicised 'L' leaning away from the wind to provide some shelter in its lee. The man straightened and stretched before plodding to where Kate lay. He grabbed her by the lapels of her jacket in one hand and dragged her across to the shelter. She lay uncomfortably with a protruding block of ice poking into her back, and waited until he'd turned his back to set about lighting a small fire using the peat pile before she inched sideways to get more comfortable.

Night fell, and the peat fire struggled to throw out pitiful heat. It glowed red with the breeze and smoked, and occasionally, a feeble flame cast long, distorted shadows against the wall of the inclined tent.

Kate lay motionless, waiting for the man to sleep, but he sat prodding at the smoking fire with the end of his staff, trying to coax more flame from the glowing ashes. He occasionally glanced in her direction, but the checks were routine and cursory.

Finally, he'd had enough. He stoked the fire and added fuel, and then settled back on the folded hide and curled into a ball facing Kate. She waited until she'd heard his regular breathing before she dared test her limbs. She bent one up beside her and slowly clenched and unclenched her fist. Her fingers were numb, but Kate couldn't tell whether it was from the residue of the spell or the freezing weather.

She decided to risk moving her head. She needed to be sure he was asleep. Very slowly, she turned her head to the right. His breathing remained rhythmic. She held her breath, twisting slowly until she could see his face. His nose was buried in his blanket, and his fur hat was pulled down over his head. His eyes were shut.

She moved both arms to her side and sat, bracing her body on her elbows. Each new movement brought sharp bursts of pain with it as the numbness of immobility disappeared. She felt weak and unstable, but the time to move was now or never.

She twisted her body away from him and cautiously rose on hands and knees. He snorted, and her foot brushed the stiff hide beneath her boot. She paused, and waited for the return of the sound of regular breathing. It didn't happen. She wanted to bolt from the tent but didn't trust her strength; besides, there was the overwhelming urge to glance behind her at the man.

She turned her head. He was still lying on his side. His eyes were open, and he was staring at her. A hand came up and pulled the blanket from his face, and he was grinning at her.

"*No!*"

She crawled away on her hands and knees, and made it as far as the edge of the hide before he snatched the ankle of her right boot and hauled her violently backwards through the air. She landed on her stomach, twisted onto her backside and lashed out with her other boot. She dislodged his hand, but he was on his knees in an instant and had reached across and pinned her chest with the weight of his other hand.

She tried to twist away, but was forced onto her back with her head a foot away from the red-hot embers of the fire. The man rose above her, and his face was lit like a devil, bathed in the reflected glow of the fire. He tried to sit astride her to stop her from struggling. She lashed out with her knee and caught him in the side of his upraised leg. For a moment, he was off balance, and Kate knew beyond certainty that this would be her final chance to escape.

She reached above her head and thrust her hand into the fire and grabbed a handful of the glowing coals. The pain was immediate and excruciating. She flung them at his face.

He screamed as the glowing embers found their mark. Some fell onto the fur lining of his hood, which immediately caught fire. They lodged beneath his jacket and burned him as he leapt away and struggled blindly to release the jacket bindings. He stumbled backwards and fell against the wall of the tent. It collapsed beneath his weight, and his staff toppled across his fallen body. He raged in pain and anger. Any thought of delivering the girl to Chisholm and Copely had been thrust aside, leaving a murderous lust for revenge in its place.

Kate dived to her left and somersaulted.

"*Caecus!*" she cried, and disappeared, made invisible by the charm only she'd been able to master.

The man blinked and aimed his staff at the point he'd last seen her.

"*Exstinguere!*" he roared. A bolt of white-hot energy flew from the tip of his staff and slammed into the ice, leaving behind a steaming, hissing crater half filled with water. He'd missed the girl completely.

His hair caught on fire, and he dropped his staff, and rolled into a drift of snow. He flung handfuls of snow at his head to smother the flames until he managed to extinguish them. He ripped his jacket open and thrust more snow down his shirt where the coals, trapped by the jacket, had burned and blistered his skin.

Kate cradled her own blistered hand but had the presence of mind to keep to the windswept ice, which was free of drifting snow. The night had closed in around her like a cloak. Her legs were shaking and weak, and she slipped and fell three or four times. She could tell she was leaving a faint trail of footprints to follow, but the wind scudded across the ice and almost immediately swept away the tracks.

She heard a terrible roar like that of a wounded bull, and tried to run. Her legs gave way once more, and she slipped and skidded into an outcrop of broken ice. She crashed into it and cried out against the pain of the collision, having used her burned outstretched palm to break her fall.

She plunged her hand into the snowdrift beside the outcrop and felt almost immediate relief from the burns. She heard the man roar once more and glanced wildly about. She heard the sound of his boots on the ice, and they were running towards her. She hadn't succeeded in masking her escape.

Worse still, the sticky snowflakes had clung to her jacket and her outline reappeared slowly, suffused in a ghostly white. The invisibility charm wasn't so useful in a snowstorm, so she removed it. Spending too much time in an unseen state made her feel dizzy and slightly nauseous anyhow.

A shadow moved across the distant light of the peat fire.

"I'm coming to get you!" his voice echoed above the wind. "I'll find you! And when I do, we'll play with fire again, but you won't be so pretty anymore!"

Kate was helpless without Rhyanon. All she could do was run and hide. She scrambled to her feet to put more distance between herself and her pursuer.

She'd only gone about fifty yards before she realised that she was running along the spine of a ridge of ice because the glacier had cracked into two deep crevasses either side of where she stood, panting. Her footprints in the snow were now clearly marked behind her, disappearing into the murk of the swirling night. The man would spot them and follow them, but that gave her an idea she'd seen once in a movie.

She started by stepping backwards, careful to place each foot in the set of prints behind her. The noise of the wind blasting across the glacier hid the sounds of the man. He would be following her tracks, as well. She needed to make haste before he found her.

She back-stepped for thirty yards until she found the spot she was searching for. Off to her left was a clear platform of ice at the edge of the crevasse. The edge itself was shattered and splintered enough to give her hope.

Kate took a deep breath, then leapt sideways. She landed on the platform, and skidded as her legs slipped out from underneath her. She slid across the platform and dropped off the edge of the crevasse.

Her luck held. Below the lip of the ridge, the top of the crevasse was riddled with cracks, and she was able to grab a handhold before she fell. She squealed as her burned hand sought another handhold, and for a second or two, her legs dangled above the dark, narrow, V-shaped void. She twisted her torso and swung her legs up until one foot found an eroded lump strong enough to bear her weight.

Her chest heaved with the effort of hauling herself into an upright position, clinging precariously to the lower lip of the crevasse. She'd only fallen about five feet, but it was enough to conceal her from sight—just in time!

She heard the crunch of snow from the man's boots, and his ragged, demented breathing, punctuated by moans of fury and agony. He barrelled by without pause, and that was her signal to act. She needed to climb out and backtrack before he discovered the ploy, and she only had seconds in which to succeed.

She reached upwards and grabbed a chunk of ice. It broke away from the wall and dropped into the crevasse, and she very nearly went with it. She hugged the wall with relief for a moment before she forced herself to lean back and search for another handhold.

The wall within easy reach was smooth and slippery. She saw another bulge, another chance, but it was enticingly beyond her reach. She was trapped!

She winced as she let go of the wall and took much of her weight using her damaged hand. Her other arm stretched back, and she swung at the wall. At the same time, she pushed with her feet and pulled upwards using her damaged hand. Her outstretched palm slapped against the ice six inches below the handhold.

She froze as she heard the inhuman wail stab through the night. The man had come to the end of her trail. He'd been outsmarted, and he'd lost her.

She renewed her efforts, swinging back and up in an attempt to grip the tantalisingly close handhold, but each time her efforts fell short. She felt her strength ebb and her legs supporting her weight shook uncontrollably.

The crunch of boots in the snow above startled her, and she froze and clung to the side of the crevasse. She dared not breathe. Her cheek touched the ice wall and her wounded hand shot darts of pain down her outstretched arm.

She waited and listened. The boots had stopped. She closed her eyes. She was determined he would not take her again. She would let go of the crevasse and tumble and crash into the abyss rather than suffer at his hands.

She listened for any sound, afraid to move. The wind whined as it channelled along the length of the crevasse, and it buffeted her clothing and tried to pluck her from the wall.

Without warning, a hand snaked over the edge and gripped her tightly by the wrist. Kate let go and kicked out, hoping to jerk the man over the edge to join her in a headlong plunge, but she lacked the strength and dangled instead like a pendulum above the drop.

She cried out and struggled, and tried to claw at the hand that held her, but she was dragged upwards until she was hauled back over the lip and onto the icy ridge. She lashed out, kicking and punching, her teeth bared, ready to bite, but she was at the end of her tether, weakened and exhausted.

"Kate! It's me!"

The sob of despair caught in her throat, and she blinked to clear her vision. The hulking form above her reached back and pulled the hood of his jacket back. A familiar mop of curling black hair cascaded around his neck and shoulders, and her eyes shot wide as his face caught a faint reflection from the white ice.

She burst into tears and reached upwards. She clasped Hawklight around the neck and buried her face in his jacket as he picked her up off the ice and carried her back towards the dull peat fire.

CHAPTER 10

The blizzard hit them with a vengeance, even before they'd made it as far as the fire. Visibility was almost zero, but Hawklight's sense of direction was unerring. Kate clung to him desperately. She wasn't sure whether she wasn't dreaming or delirious from exhaustion, but she didn't want the moment to end.

"We have to get off the glacier!" Hawklight screamed into her ear. She barely heard him above the wind. "Can you walk?"

She nodded in reply, but when he set her on her feet, she collapsed into the snow. He helped her to her feet again, and he noticed the ugly red puckering on her hand.

She struggled forward once more. The *Urgut* was still tied where the man had secured it. *The man! Where was he?* She thought back to the piercing scream she'd heard while clinging to the wall of the crevasse. At the time, she'd mistaken it for a scream of anger and frustration. She realised it also had sounded like a man being pitched into a crevasse. She searched again for Hawklight, but he was hidden by the swirling clouds of snow.

He reappeared, leading the *Urgut*, piled high with provisions again. He hauled the flap of the protective hide back and rummaged about in a canvas carry bag. He withdrew a large weatherproof coat lined with thick fur and wrapped Kate in it, pulling the hood tight beneath her chin. He lifted her astride the animal and placed her good hand around a hank of hair at the base of the beast's neck. There was nothing he could do for her ruined hand beyond leaving it exposed it to the cold.

He held her head between his hands and gazed into her eyes, searching for the spark of defiance he knew would keep her clinging to the animal's back. He must have been satisfied with what he saw because he gave her a quick 'thumbs-up' and turned into the storm, leading the *Urgut* behind him.

Kate lost track of time. The night turned to dark grey, and she suspected a new day had dawned above the suffocating cloud mass. It was impossible to tell for sure. The hunched figure of Hawklight disappeared and reappeared in front of her, whenever the storm abated to draw a breath before the next onslaught of snow, ice and wind. Kate was drifting in and out of sleep, awakening with a start before the next invitation to close her eyes and drift away proved irresistible. She knew the desire to surrender to sleep could be fatal, but she was unable to resist the temptation and finally pitched forward onto the neck of the *Urgut*.

Kate awoke. She was lying on a thick fur skin on some kind of icy ledge. When she tried to sit up, she banged her head on a ceiling of snow. It was oppressively quiet; any sounds she made seemed to be absorbed rather than reflected.

Stuttering light from a small glass lantern flickered against the walls. She discovered she was lying on a shelf fashioned from packed snow. The cramped room was dome shaped so that any condensation rolled down the ceiling and walls and collected in a well at the bottom, along with the denser cold air. She was sheltering in a snow cave, and a familiar form was hunkered beside her on the shelf. Hawklight lay on his side staring at her.

Kate remembered her blistered hand, and lifted it to her face to examine it in the dim light. She was not surprised to see it had been bound with linen strips, and the tell-tale green poultice of Mother's Glove had leaked out at the sides and hardened into a kind of paper pulp. Most of the throbbing pain had disappeared, so the magical herb had already begun the rapid healing process.

Kate suddenly felt afraid. All of the bitterness and hurt resurfaced from the moment when Hawklight had prevented Kate from interfering with her mother's desperate attempt to save the Hornshurst *Toki Moai*. She'd been spiteful beyond cruel to him. It had signalled the end of their friendship.

Time was the great healer. By the time she'd been able to admit to herself that no one was to blame—least of all, Hawklight—it had been too late. She'd needed to apologise, and then the news of his death had crushed her spirit completely.

"I thought you were dead," she whispered.

Hawklight didn't move, didn't reply. He stared back at her, and the few feet between them in the cramped cave felt like a million miles to Kate.

"At first, I didn't believe it, but I saw your helmet, the burned clothing . . ."

Still nothing.

"Mum's safe inside the *Toki Moai*. I was there when they did it. I . . . thought you might like to know that."

She bit her bottom lip. The words were muffled and muted, and the wall of snow devoured them. Kate dropped her head back onto the pillow of folded fur. She returned Hawklight's gaze; she willed herself not to look away. The silence between them grew.

"I'm sorry . . . I want to apologise to you, but I don't even know how or where to begin," she said softly, and this time, she couldn't face him and turned her eyes aside.

"I knew you'd come." He smiled at her.

His profound belief in her after she'd lost all belief in herself hit her like a brick. She closed her eyes, but tears leaked out.

"I'm so sorry for the way I treated you, Nathaniel," she whimpered, and she crawled across the few feet between them. He sat up, and she laid her head against his shoulder. She felt his arm embrace her and hold her.

"You know, your mother was by far the bravest woman I have ever met, but you do come a close second." She watched his eyes cloud over with the memory at that point. "We talked a lot—when I was carrying her back to Cherath—mostly about you.

She apologised for your behaviour. She begged me to forgive you. And, I guess I was kind of upset too, at that point. I think she was the only one capable of seeing the bigger picture, and of course, she was right.

I'm sorry she was taken from you, I regret the fact that there was no other option, but I would do it all again if I had to. I need you to know that."

"Can you ever forgive me?" Kate asked.

"Can you forgive me?" he replied.

"I came looking for you. But, you said you knew I'd come?" she asked him.

"I was counting on it. By the way, where are the others?"

"That man—took us all by surprise using a paralysis charm. They're back at Poluostrov, but anything could have happened to them since. Nathaniel, we have to go back and find them!"

"Was Kareem with you?"

"Yes, but—"

"Then we have nothing to fear. Poluostrovians are miners, not killers. All they want is to be left alone. They'll have imprisoned them somewhere—maybe a cellar. I even think there's a gaol cell somewhere in the town. Let Kareem worry about that." He smiled. "I'm picking he'll move heaven and earth to find you again."

Kate felt herself blush in the dim light, and she hoped Hawklight wouldn't notice. His grin told her she was wrong. She needed to change the subject. She slid back onto her fur skin and wrapped a blanket around her shoulders.

"We found out about Zimmerman and Carter, and the plan to search for another crystal," she said. "What we didn't understand was why you agreed to lead the expedition in the first place."

"Zimmerman knew where it might be found," Hawklight said. "I needed to tag along to have any chance of destroying it. Carter is a fool who could never be trusted to wield such power. You were right about him all along."

"You were going to destroy it? Wouldn't it have been easier to have zapped Zimmerman?"

Kate's approach to solving life's problems was simple and direct, and it made Hawklight grin again.

"No, there would be other Zimmermans who'd come in his place. None of this is his fault. He's only a pawn in a game with other players. But by destroying the source of the crystal, we can end the game."

"The other player is Copely, isn't it? Was it you who left the broken quartz on the piles of clothing?"

Hawklight nodded. "Copely's one of them. There are others, equally as dangerous, if not more so."

"Well, just Copely on his own is dangerous enough. What I couldn't understand at the time was how he managed to ambush you." She shook her head. "I *should've* known better. I *ought* to have had more faith in you."

"It's a long story," Hawklight replied. "I was suspicious from the start because Carter had handpicked the squad to accompany me. He knew I couldn't be trusted to deliver the crystal to him. The other men were chosen to make sure I wouldn't do anything foolish, but he still needed me to lead the expedition. I'm also pretty sure I wasn't supposed to return.

I couldn't trust any of the troops, but there was one in particular—a corporal named Timmins—whose behaviour was very odd. I watched him grow more nervous the further we went, and the only explanation was that he was playing a game of double cross that involved someone else.

I knew for certain when we reached the clearing. He was really spooked about something, and the place was ideal for an ambush. The whole time, I was expecting a bolt between the shoulder blades, but I gambled on the fact whoever it was wouldn't attack until dusk at the earliest. I chose a spot beneath a tree, which was gloomy enough, removed my helmet and lay down beneath a blanket. I kept the bedroll tied, and when I slid away, I left it behind like a sleeping body.

Whoever hit the bedroll wasn't taking any chances. Luckily for me, it was burned to ash. I watched as Copely and the others took Zimmerman hostage. When I saw that Carruthers and Gonzales had survived the massacre, I knew they'd raise the alarm. *That* was when I knew you'd come. Word would filter back to you, wherever you were. All I had to do until then was to slow Copely down long enough for you to catch up. I stole the *Urguts,* and took a couple of soldiers out of the equation, hoping Zimmerman would escape, but he missed the opportunity."

"There's more bad news, I'm afraid," Kate said after he had finished. "Mirayam is being held for treason because Carter found out we'd slipped away to come look for you. Once the expedition went pear shaped, he didn't want any loose ends. He's sent a team after us, led by a man named Streikker. They caught up with us, but Olivia and Ethan didn't make it."

Hawklight looked shocked by the revelation.

"Killed?"

"We don't know. Captured, for sure. Ethan was badly wounded; he lost an arm, and Olivia stayed behind to care for him. The rest of us managed to escape, but only just. But if what you say is true about Carter . . ." Her voice trailed off as she contemplated the probable fate of her friends at Streikker's hands.

"Streikker!" Hawklight shook his head, and a deep frown creased his forehead. He had to be bad news if Hawklight was worried.

"Streikker's not going to give up, is he?" she asked. Hawklight shook his head.

"Who's left?" he asked.

"You, me, Kareem, Mia, Jackson and Sigrid. Will it be enough?"

"They've already lost six men." Hawklight smiled at the thought. "That would leave nine more, counting Zimmerman. I've counted twelve sets of tracks in the snow since Poluostrov. They've taken on three unknowns. That's six against twelve. Take out Zimmerman and the three guides—they would have to be paid guides, so I'm picking they wouldn't be that keen for a pitched battle—and that's six against eight. Much better odds!" He grinned at her. Clearly, his initial misgivings about Mirayam's student group had long been lost over the intervening year or so since they'd first met him.

They were quiet for a moment. There were still only two of them, despite Hawklight's optimism. Where were the remaining four? But Hawklight was right—Kareem would continue to search for her until her found her. That second thought gave her a secret thrill, something she'd never experienced before.

Something else occurred to her.

"Nathaniel, how did you find me?"

"I was ahead, tracking the party. I wanted to get a fix on their direction before the blizzard hit."

"Magnetic south?" Kate interrupted. Hawklight looked momentarily nonplussed as he always did when Kate outmanoeuvred him on occasion. She got a thrill out of that, as well.

"How did—? Never mind. However, they made a few deviations because of the rough terrain, and at each point, they left markers. They were expecting someone to follow and catch them up. Nine of them entered Poluostrov and only eight left. I was curious who that could be. I decided to head back and see if I could find him first. I wanted to be able to ask him a couple of questions, especially about Copely's newfound partner, the squat, surly woman.

I found the peat fire. There were two sets of tracks leading away from it. I recognised one set immediately, but I needed to follow the other set first. I found him. Turns out, he and I never got the chance to have that conversation after all. Then I came looking for you."

"I used to believe in angels," Kate said. She looked at him. "I still do."

This time it was Hawklight's turn to flush and change the subject.

"How's the hand?"

"Not so sore. But I'm getting to be just about as scarred as you."

He laughed.

"You know, I've never been so consistently wrong about anyone as I have been about you," he replied. "You're stubborn, pig-headed, iron-willed, defiant, rebellious . . ."

"Thanks!"

". . . exceptionally courageous, loyal, honest—although a little less honesty would be refreshing—trustworthy, gentle and loving. I can't figure this mix, nor why it works, but I know what it means. You're a good friend, Kate Gallagher. I'm just pleased that you're on my side!"

They were back together!

CHAPTER 11

Kareem had been too slow to react. They'd relaxed and had lowered their guard in the warm room. He continued to curse himself for that oversight; it was the only thing he could do since nothing else worked. He couldn't even move his eyes.

He concentrated on the movement in the periphery of his vision. A large, hooded man swam in and out of focus. He bent over Kareem briefly, checking for vital signs. He slapped Kareem hard across the face, waiting for a blink reflex that never happened. Satisfied, he moved on to the others.

He began shifting bodies off the bed. First Mia, then Sigrid. The man hovered back into view as he gripped Kareem and slid him off the bed as well. He dropped Kareem's inert body onto the wooden floor, narrowly missing Sigrid's head in the process.

Kareem was aware of his head bouncing as he hit the floor. There would be no pain until the charm wore off, but there would be pain. He thrust the thought aside, and tried to concentrate on the man's features. The black uniform poking out of the top of his unzipped jacket identified him as a soldier of Varak's once mighty army.

The man had stretched Kate out along the bed, and had begun to dress her in cold weather gear while Kareem watched on helplessly. When the man had finished, he hauled her into a sitting position and then tossed her over his shoulder like a sack of sand.

"Come on then, my pretty. There's someone wants to meet with you, will pay a pretty price for the pleasure, I'm thinking."

Kareem heard the words. He knew what they meant. Kate passed by as the man stepped over him, and then all that was left was the sound of his receding boots as they lumbered down the stairs.

Eventually, someone—a cleaning woman—passed down the hall and looked in through the open doorway. She dropped her mop and bucket, screamed and ran. Minutes later, she returned with a group of men—apparently not concerned citizens because they lifted the inert body of the one-eyed woman, and left the others behind where they'd fallen.

Hours later, they returned. The old woman was not with them, but Kareem knew she'd been revived, from the conversations he overheard. She'd been very upset—Kareem had some empathy there—but had concluded that Kate, he, and the others were the ones most responsible for her plight.

He was picked up, none too gently and hoisted down the stairs to the cellar. The two men who'd held him between them dumped him on the cold cobbles, and his head bounced against the floor for the second time that day. This time, he lost consciousness.

When, at last, he came around, he couldn't see. The room was pitch black; it could have been nighttime, it could have been a windowless room. Kareem had no way of knowing the time. He'd developed a splitting headache in the meantime.

Pain had returned! It was the first sign that the charm was wearing off. He tried to call out, to make a noise, but nothing happened. *So, still a way from recovery,* he thought.

He trained his mind to ignore the pain beating a rhythm at the back of his skull. As he concentrated, the pain slowly receded, kept confined from his innermost thoughts. He needed to think!

Kate had been kidnapped. The man who'd kidnapped her had to be one of the Zimmerman party who'd stayed behind, for some reason. Had they been expected? He didn't think so. But they—Kate, in particular—had been recognised. The thought chilled him because he knew instinctively that Copely most likely would kill her the moment he set eyes on her and that thought caused him to curse his predicament once more. Some bodyguard he'd turned out to be!

His elbow tingled, which distracted him. Then one eye blinked. He thought back to the room, to the moment when the man had thrust the door aside to launch the old woman in amongst them. He'd ducked instinctively, and had tried to roll on top of Kate to protect her. But Sigrid, who'd been sitting to his left, had jerked herself upright. She'd been marginally quicker than him to react, and she'd reared up and had tried to shield him, and buy him some time. It hadn't worked—or had it?

At the time, it had felt as though she'd cast a shadow across his path, similar to sheltering from the wind behind a pole: not that effective, but certainly better than nothing. Sigrid had given him a slight advantage.

He tried to speak, and a strangled, gurgling sound escaped his lips. He knew his companions would have heard it, as well. There was nothing to do but wait it out now. The last thing he wanted was to alert anyone on the other side of the cellar door.

He lost all track of time, waiting for his body to recover. A sense of feeling returned to his limbs, creeping upwards through his body inch by agonisingly slow inch. He heard a half snort, half whistle blown from Jackson's nose. Something was happening there as well, but only just.

He managed to sit, but the effort seemed to sap him of all his strength. His arms behaved as if they were controlled by another brain, and his movements were spasmodic and clumsy. He rolled onto his hands and knees, and crawled across to examine each of his companions.

All of them had eye movement. Sigrid was the worst affected; at least Mia's face could twitch, but when she tried to speak, the words folded together in a jumble of noise and Kareem couldn't understand what she was trying to say.

He crawled across to Jackson.

"You can move!" The words were slurred but unmistakable.

Kareem nodded but uttered, "Shhhh!"

"How long have we been here?" Again, slurred and spoken like a man wrestling with his tongue to control a stutter.

"I don't know. A couple of days perhaps."

The sudden sound of a key scratching for the entrance to the keyhole was amplified in the empty cellar. Kareem twisted and crawled as quickly as his strength allowed back to the spot on the floor where he'd awoken.

He heard the sound of boots on the stairs as their hobnails scratched the worn stone. Two men, one carrying a lantern, filed down the stairs and approached the centre of the cellar where the students had been scattered across the floor.

Kareem kept his eyes unfocussed and stared into infinity, past the weaving lantern that hovered above his head. One of the men bent and examined his face for any sign of movement, and waved his hand in front of Kareem's face, trying to tempt his eyes to follow. When he was satisfied, he moved across to Jackson, followed by the other holding the lantern.

Jackson passed the test as well, but Kareem's heart sank when they leaned over Sigrid.

"This one blinked!" he heard one of them say. "The spell's finally wearing off. Another day and she'll be up and about. The others won't be far behind"

The man stood and arched his back.

"Give 'em another dose. That'll keep 'em all quiet for another few days."

"Me?" asked the second, smaller lantern bearer. "I can't. I left my staff upstairs. Where's yours?"

"I don't have it. Come on, the practice'll do ya good!" He turned for the stairs.

"Why always me?" the little lantern bearer grumbled as he scuffled back up the stairs. He left the door at the top slightly ajar as he went off in search of his staff.

Kareem had little time left in which to act. He pushed himself back onto his hands and knees and scuttled behind one of the stone pillars supporting the roof of the cellar.

"Do whatever you can to distract him!" he whispered across the room. *What was he thinking?* The other three were a scant step from being completely comatose. He was on his own.

The door squeaked on its hinges and signalled the return of the lantern bearer with his staff. Kareem pressed his back against the pillar and struggled to his feet, leaning heavily to support his weight. He was weak, and his head was spinning, and he pressed his palms flat against the face of the pillar and shut his eyes tight to try and reorient himself. The spinning sensation faded slowly.

Weak yellow light washed over the cobblestone floor as the man approached. Sigrid had been caught out blinking, so he stopped at her prostrate body first. He didn't appear to notice that one of the bodies had moved.

He stood over her and gazed down.

"Sorry, dahlin'," he said to her, "orders is orders." He tilted his head. "Tell you what," he continued, and bent down onto one knee. He placed his lantern on the floor beside her head. "Since you're gonna be out for some time, let's get your eyes closed."

He reached out a hand and his thumb and finger found her eyelids. He pressed against them and stroked downwards, and Sigrid's eyes slipped shut. While he was doing this, Kareem inched around the pillar on the far side away from the man and risked a peek.

The man was kneeling about six feet from the pillar with his back to it. Kareem's legs felt like rubber and he had to steady himself by gripping the pillar and pressing his back hard against it.

The man stood. Sigrid opened one eye and stared up at him.

"What?" he exclaimed. He shook his head in disapproval. "Tsk-tsk. Have it your own way then," he muttered.

He lifted his staff and pointed the end at Sigrid's face. At that moment, Jackson—whose outstretched arm lay beside the man's boot—opened his hand and gripped the man by the ankle. The man yelped with surprise and tore his foot away from Jackson's weak grasp, and that was when Kareem acted.

He pushed himself away from the pillar and used his few reserves to drive his legs. He launched himself through the air and hit the lantern man with the full force of his flying body. He gathered the man in a bear-grip tackle and hung on as the two of them crashed heavily onto the unforgiving stone floor. The man was trapped beneath him and took the full force of the impact. Kareem continued to grapple with him on the floor until he realised the man was limp and unresponsive. The impact had knocked him unconscious.

Kareem rolled away from him, totally spent, and lay on his back gasping for air. He didn't have time to waste; the man was out for the count but for how long was anyone's guess.

He rolled onto his front and dragged his body across the floor to where the staff had fallen and rolled to a stop beside the pillar he'd hidden behind. He grabbed it, leaned his back against the pillar and pointed the staff at Jackson.

"Abripere torpor!" he whispered.

This time, a green sphere erupted from the staff and engulfed Jackson. Sparks shot across the surface of the sphere and seemed to jolt Jackson like minuscule lightning strikes. His body jumped as if he'd received a halfway decent shock before the sphere exploded and dissipated.

Jackson was able to sit. He looked to be about as weak as Kareem, although he managed to stand unsteadily and tottered over. He took the staff from Kareem's grasp, and applied the same charm to Mia and Sigrid, and last of all, Kareem.

The lantern man groaned from the floor. Jackson zapped him with the same paralysis charm the four of them had endured. When Sigrid had recovered enough to crawl, she hustled across and slipped his eyelids shut.

"Least I could do," she shrugged and smiled apologetically.

The effects of the counter-charm had already begun to work. The fatigue and heaviness of movement bled away, and their strength returned. They sat together huddled around the dim light from the lantern on the floor, waiting out the recovery period while planning their next moves.

Jackson patted his pockets.

"The cash has gone," he said. Someone had rifled the gemstones while he had been paralysed.

"In that case, we'll take what we need," Kareem replied. "We have to figure the *Urgut* is gone, as well as the supplies it carried. We need to locate our staffs, and we'll need some more good cold-weather gear. My guess is our rooms have been ransacked, as well. A compass would be helpful, now that we know where the others are headed. We have to catch up with Kate before Copely finds her."

His face turned grim with the thought. He didn't want to consider any possibility beyond her rescue; he couldn't afford to be distracted by scenarios of what might happen otherwise. He was anxious to get moving, but he knew they had to be fully fit and ready for the ordeal ahead of them.

"What sort of lead does he have?" Mia asked.

"Can't be any more than three days."

Kareem stood and paced back and forth. He was impatient to begin; he couldn't help himself.

"I've got to get moving," he apologised. "We've probably got a couple of hours. After that, someone's going to wonder what happened to him—" he pointed to the overpowered gaoler, "—and someone's going to come looking. We need to be gone by then. I'm sorry."

Mia looked at him. "We won't hold you up!" she promised.

Kareem smiled, and his eyes glinted in the weak light. "Wait here," he instructed. "I'm going to find our things."

Jackson held out the staff, but Kareem raised his hand. "Keep it with you," he said. "If anyone comes down the stairs, make sure they don't go back up. If I'm not back within the hour, then leave. Get away."

"We'll head south," Sigrid said.

Kareem was about to reply, but he paused, and then just nodded.

"I'll see you in an hour," he said.

He melted into the dark, and was little more than a noiseless shadow as he climbed the stairs. The door was slightly open, and it squeaked once more as Kareem's silhouette squeezed beyond it. He pulled it shut behind him.

The hotel lobby was deserted. Kareem figured the old woman was probably stretched out asleep in one of the rooms upstairs. He began a methodical search and easily located their weapons and few belongings stashed inside the broom cupboard.

He crept to the window and glanced outside. The sky was gunmetal blue with heavy storm clouds gathering to the south, piled upon each other, turbulent and roiling with the currents of ice, snow and wind that seeded them. Kareem had never witnessed clouds like them, although he knew they meant trouble.

The wind had picked up ahead of the approaching storm, and litter was cartwheeling along the muddied road outside the hotel. The sly buffeting squealed as it slipped through the crack beneath the door. Opposite, doors had been bolted and windows shuttered, and no one moved about in the street. Snowflakes wafted past the window, joined by sleet. The entire scene was misery personified to Kareem, who preferred the bleak wastes of desert sand to this arctic squalor.

He left the comfort of the hotel via the back door, and slunk down back alleys, heading first for the barn where the *Urgut* had been stabled. It had gone! So had all the equipment it had carried.

He stepped back out into the alley and was blasted by a sheet of cold air. He shivered as he kept to the shadows, moving parallel to the main street, counting the shabby buildings.

His second stop was outside a solid, rough-hewn door. He tested the handle, which was locked, but the door rattled loosely in its frame. There was no time for his usual finesse, so he slammed his shoulder against the door. The door itself was sturdy, but the lock was flimsy and its screws were wrenched from the frame under the impact.

The room was dark, lit only by the shaft of diffuse grey from the open doorway. Kareem found a lantern hanging from a hook beside his head, so he lifted it down and lit it. He was standing in a deserted space lined with crude wooden shelves, piled high with goods. It was the back of the hardware store he'd spied from the hotel window; a storeroom lined with excess stock.

He'd guessed the building would be deserted. No one was out shopping in this weather! The owner would have hightailed it home to the warmth of his own hearth.

Kareem paced up and down the rows of shelves, stopping and grabbing whatever he needed. He made one trip back to the hotel and handed out the armload of insulated clothing he'd collected, along with their stuff from the broom cupboard.

This time, the others joined him for the return journey to the hardware store. They wore as much as they could, and packed extra clothing they thought they might need. There was to be no alternative to finding Kate alive, Kareem promised himself.

He looked at the pile they'd accumulated and stuffed into hide bags. It was more than they could carry; to attempt to do so would slow them down and exhaust their reserves. He instructed them to wait once more while he set off in search of pack animals.

He closed the door behind him and crept along the narrow alley beside the store that spilled out on to the main street. He peeked around the edge of the building, then immediately shuffled backwards into shadow and hugged the wall of the store.

Hans Streikker splashed past the mouth of the alley, head down against the fury of the biting wind, leading a bedraggled *Hon'chai* behind him. His men followed in single file, worn and wet through. Kareem counted twelve, including Streikker. Once the last of them had passed by the alleyway, Kareem shuffled to the entrance again.

They had halted outside the hotel. Two soldiers were gathering the reins of the mounts to lead them across to the barn. Streikker was already out of the sleet on the veranda, stamping the mud from his boots while he surveyed the street.

Kareem figured they had thirty minutes tops before someone let slip to Streikker that there were four hostages lying paralysed in the cellar, and knew that when he went to investigate, he wouldn't find them.

He sprinted back down the alley to warn the others of their predicament. Then he and Sigrid ran back to the barn. They heard the doors slam shut in the wind as they inched along the side of the building, and knew the two soldiers would be inside stripping down the animals and locking them in stalls. Kareem glanced at Sigrid, and she nodded in response, and drew her staff from its scabbard.

Kareem slid one of the doors back, and Sigrid slipped through the gap. Both soldiers were standing together beside one of the stalls, each holding an armload of halters. They turned towards the sound of the whistling wind, caught unawares. They stood rooted to the spot as Kareem quickly entered and slid the door shut again.

One of them opened his mouth as if to speak, but the other's eyes widened as he realised who had entered the barn. He dropped his bundle of metal and leather, although that was as far as he got.

"*Dormite!*" The pulse from Sigrid's staff ricocheted between the two men, who immediately dropped where they stood.

Both Kareem and Sigrid hurried across to check on their vital signs. The soldiers were healthy and dead to the world. One was even dreaming sweet dreams if the smile pasted across his face was any indication. They hauled both soldiers by their boots into one of the vacant stalls and hurriedly covered them in a loose pile of straw. They chose the four strongest *Hon'chai* and re-bridled them from the tangle on the floor. Kareem opened the stalls that housed the other animals and hustled them out into the barn, where they gathered uncertainly.

He cracked open the barn door and checked outside. Across the road, the street was deserted again, and he could see shadows moving across the light from the front windows of the hotel. The afternoon had darkened into a kind of grim twilight. It was time to make their move.

He thrust the double doors aside, and he and Sigrid each led a pair of *Hon'chai* down the alleyway behind the barn. The remaining *Hon'chai* huddled together before one of them tentatively stepped outside, and wandered along the street away from the hotel. Others followed in groups of two or three. Before long, the barn was empty, and snowflakes gathered just inside the door.

Mia and Jackson were ready and waiting with the packed gear. They slung the packs across the four mounts, then gripped the animals at the base of their necks and swung their legs up and over their backs. The fur had grown thicker as the *Hon'chai* had trekked south, although they had lost condition from hard riding throughout the journey.

Kareem felt sorry that they'd not have the opportunity for a well-deserved rest, but there was no other choice. He hoped to put some miles between them and the city before the ruse was discovered. He hoped to gain even more time through Streikker needing to round up the animals that had escaped before he could set off in pursuit once again.

They kept to the back streets, and came out on a pile of loose tailings to the west of the city, then circled to the south. Away from the shelter of the buildings, the snow swirled and fell faster, quickly filling the depressions left by the hooves of the *Hon'chai*.

Kareem took one look at the compass dangling from his neck, tucked just inside his thick outer jacket. He tugged the reins slightly until he was headed on a magnetic south bearing, then drew his jacket up tight across his face until only his eyes were left exposed. The *Hon'chai* beneath his legs snorted and huffed as it plodded along at a steady walk, lifting its legs high to clear the gathering snow.

The three others followed behind in single file, enveloped by the darkening air thick with snow. There was nothing to guide them but the belief that Kate was still alive, and the faith that they would succeed in finding her.

—m—

Streikker noticed the handlers had failed to return twenty minutes after the students had mounted up and left. He strode to the window and peered through the snow to the open barn doors. One remaining, scrawny *Hon'chai* had turned back and was standing pathetically just outside the barn with its head drooped low, hunched against the cold.

Streikker swore and raced for the door. He covered the gap between the hotel and the barn in double-quick time, and stood outside, surveying the empty stalls. He unsheathed his staff and entered warily, searching out the darkened corners for any signs of movement. He passed by one stall, then another—both empty—and stopped outside a third piled with straw along one side.

He poked at the pile with the tip of his staff, dislodging some of it to reveal the sleeping face of one of the handlers. He grimaced with fury, then hurried back outside and began to cast around for spoor on the ground. It took less than thirty seconds to discover the hoof prints and two sets of boot treads leading down the alleyway beside the barn. He followed them around the back and along to where the door to the hardware store swung lazily on its hinges.

The tracks appeared to head west, but Streikker was confident they'd swing back south. He checked the oppressive and threatening sky. The falling snow already would have obliterated the fresh tracks, but that was of no real concern. He'd find them! He'd missed them by minutes! He stalked back to the hotel and reiterated the silent promise to himself. *He would find them!*

CHAPTER 12

O ut of the wind, and wrapped in warm furs, Kate found the snow cave to be pleasantly cosy. The only thing to do while waiting out the cold was to crawl to the entrance tunnel and poke a hole through to the outside to help circulate the air, and also to keep a check on the blizzard's progress.

Kate's guilt had weighed heavily on her, and she continued to punctuate their conversations with abject apologies for the way she had mistreated Hawklight until he'd finally had enough and held up his hand in protest.

"Listen!" he suggested. "Start from the time I restrained you, and talk me through to the present. Cover everything you can think of, leave nothing out. And then, once you're done, no more 'I'm sorry'—ever! Do we have a deal?"

Kate smiled nervously across at him and drew a deep breath. She started slowly at first, reaching back into the memories she'd worked so hard to repress, and stuttered when the lid was blown, and the hurt overflowed. Once she'd started, she couldn't stop. The rawness cut deep, and her tears flowed freely as she described how it felt to lose her mother.

It was as if Siobhan had been trapped in floodwaters, holding on to Kate with one hand. Kate could feel the ceaseless force of

165

the current tugging them apart, and could feel her mother's hand sliding from her wrist, to her palm, to her fingertips. Kate knew what was coming next, and was totally powerless to prevent it. Once the lifeline was severed, all she could do was watch her mother being carried away from the riverbank and drawn beneath the muddied surface. All the while, she'd berated herself for not doing more when nothing more could have been done.

Hawklight listened in silence while she moved, from anger and impotence, to regret at what she'd done, and how she'd retreated behind walls she'd erected and had kept everyone at arm's length, only to realise, once she'd heard of Hawklight's death, she'd never be able to right the wrongs, nor justify the loss of such a friend.

When she finished, she lay on her back and released a huge sigh. A great weight had been lifted from her shoulders, and for the first time in months, she felt a lightness of being. She glanced across at Hawklight and was about to thank him when he cocked an eyebrow and tilted his head.

"We have a deal, remember?" he said.

She laughed at him. "No more apologies, I hereby promise."

When Hawklight poked a hole through the blown snow with his staff, a disk of blue sky was visible. The shrieking wind had been dragged reluctantly along on the coattails of the storm, which had passed by. An eerie silence had replaced it.

Hawklight broke through the crusted covering and crawled out of the cave. The *Urgut* had been tethered by a steel stake driven deep into the ground in the lee of a snowdrift. Its red, shaggy hair was draped in clumps of crusted ice, but it had survived the blizzard comfortably.

Hawklight dug into the snow beside the beast, and uncovered the supplies he'd buried beneath the animal hide just before he'd entered the snow cave. Some of the extra clothing was damp, so he unrolled it and laid it out on top of the hide for the sun to dry it. While they waited, he examined Kate's ruined hand.

"Ouch!" she uttered as he peeled the dried poultice from her hand. Her palm was withered and puckered with lines of scars, and she winced as she remembered the red-hot coals eating away at her hand. Hawklight was unperturbed by the sight and rubbed her palm gently with his thumb.

"Does it still hurt?" he asked.

"Not really. It's not a pretty sight though."

She squeezed her palm. As long as she could hold Rhyanon! She hoped to see her staff again, which was back at Poluostrov with the others. Kate had owned Rhyanon for as long as she'd been on Bexus, and felt naked and lost without her.

Hawklight threw her a pair of gloves; the day was clear, but the air was still bitingly cold, and already her fingertips felt numb.

He grinned at her. "Let's see what Mr Copely has to say, shall we?"

The snow had been left thigh deep from the blizzard. Hawklight forged the way ahead, and Kate followed in his path, leading the *Urgut* on a long rope. Even so, within a couple of miles she stopped and started peeling off layers of clothing and stuffing them in the packs the animal carried. It was plainly hard going: high-stepping a boot out of the snow only to feel it sink back into the soft white powder. Nevertheless, Kate was in high spirits, and she couldn't resist bending to gather a handful of snow to squeeze into a ball and throw at Hawklight's back. He turned and gave her such a look that she burst into laughter, and the sound rippled across the undulating sea of snow ahead of them.

The Zimmerman party had been leaving trail markers for the man to follow. If they'd left more of them, they would now be impossible to find, as they would be covered by a thick blanket of fresh snow. Neither Hawklight nor Kate was worried. They knew where their quarry was headed. All they needed to do was hold the line; sooner or later, they'd encounter them. The trick would be to ensure the encounter was on their terms, not Copely's.

They trekked slowly across the bland landscape for two days. Each afternoon, before the sun had set, they would secure the *Urgut*, then set to with shovels to excavate another snow cave in which to shelter during the freezing nights. It reminded Kate of their quest to find The Magician, during the period before they'd encountered Kareem. Travelling alongside Hawklight made endurance possible: it had transformed the journey into a shared experience in which no one else belonged. It forged their friendship beyond any other factor, and despite the inhospitable environment, she wouldn't have traded it for the world.

Kate spread the fur blanket on the snow shelf she'd helped compact and shape, and nestled in for the night. Hawklight emerged through the narrow tunnel, having checked the *Urgut* and plugged the entrance with snow.

"What are you thinking?" she asked him. "How far away are we?"

"From Copely?"

She nodded.

"Three, four days, I'd guess. I think the blizzard could have hit them hard. We stand a good chance of catching them."

"What about Kareem, Sigrid, Mia and Jackson?"

Hawklight smiled in the dim light of the lantern. "If it was only Jackson, I'd be worried. But the girls have far more sense. And they have Kareem with them. He's an exceptional young man. I have to say I've never met anyone else like him, wouldn't you say?"

He gave her his stupid grin that was guaranteed to make her blush.

"What!" she blustered, but that only made him laugh.

"I've watched the two of you together. Tell me, has he made his move yet?"

"That's none of your business!" she replied curtly, but the smile that traced her lips the moment the words escaped was the only signal that Hawklight required. He lay on his back and cupped his hands behind his head.

"Then they won't be far behind us. You're still kidnapped as far as he's concerned. He's not about to give you up to Copely. My only concern is that he'll see us from a distance, and he'll try to clip me from behind, in a case of mistaken identity."

"Ohmigod!" Kate was horrified at the thought.

"Don't worry," Hawklight said, "I'll try not to let that happen."

They broke through the snow the following morning to a cloud covered sky that stretched to the horizon in one large blanket. Hawklight scanned for hidden storm cloud amongst it, and was relieved not to find any. The wind had returned, but it blew in gusty fits and starts, and caught the surface snow the way a broom pushes dust before it.

The *Urgut* was strangely unsettled. The metal stake to which it had been tethered was bent slightly as if the animal had strained against it during the long, black night. Kate stroked its muzzle, which seemed to mollify it, and when she scratched it behind the ears, it pressed in against her chest and stood quietly, huffing twin clouds of vapour into the cold morning air. Hawklight did a quick search of the area but found nothing unusual in the snow.

They led off in the same manner: Hawklight scouting ahead while Kate and the *Urgut* trudged along behind. Twice during the first hour, the animal stopped in its tracks and refused to move, relenting only when Kate tugged on the rope, and Hawklight came around from behind and gave it a sharp rap across its flank with his staff.

Its behaviour remained a mystery until Hawklight signalled a halt two hours later. Kate waited with the *Urgut* while Hawklight stalked ahead cautiously before bending to examine some imprints in the snow. The *Urgut* shivered and snorted, and constantly tugged at the rope as it attempted to swivel its head from side to side.

"Don't let go of the rope!" Hawklight called over his shoulder. "But come forward and take a look at this!"

Kate's curiosity was piqued. She tugged on the rope, and the animal moved forward reluctantly. As she neared Hawklight, she could make out a separate path of tracks that ran perpendicular to the direction they were headed. At first, she thought they'd come across the imprints left behind by the Zimmerman party, and her hope soared briefly. However, when she drew close, she discovered they were something else entirely.

Hawklight was squatting beside footprints in the snow, easily the diameter of a good-sized bucket. Kate could make out two separate sets of prints. Such a surface area ought to have provided support in the soft snow, serving to spread the load, but these paw prints were set deep in the snow. Whatever left the prints behind was *enormous!* No wonder the *Urgut* was antsy!

"What made them?" Kate asked.

Hawklight stood and slowly scanned the horizon. He didn't answer until he'd turned through a complete circle.

"Only one thing this far south leaves footprints that size," he muttered. "An *Aelouskah*, or Frost Ghoul Bear. Looks like a silver-white polar bear, only twice the size. It's the ultimate predator, the top of the food chain in these parts. It eats anything that moves; anything it can't eat, it'll kill anyway."

He gave her a grave stare. That meant them.

"Have you ever seen one?" she asked.

"No, but I've seen the result of an encounter with one. It was a pack of twenty *Abyssi*, their carcasses disembowelled, half eaten, all lying in the snow. They'd tried to bring just one of these things down. We followed the trail for a piece, then gave up when we came across the remains of another two carcasses it had dragged off."

Kate's eyes strayed to the horizon. She couldn't help herself.

"Normally, they're solitary. You never see them together, unless . . ."

". . . Unless this is a mother and her cub." Kate finished the sentence. Hawklight nodded in agreement.

"How much did we miss them by?" Kate asked.

Hawklight shrugged. "Half a day, possibly. They probably wandered by here sometime early this morning, well before dawn."

"Er . . . shouldn't we get going?"

Hawklight made one last sweep of the terrain. The tracks of the two *Aelouskahs* pointed in an easterly direction, more or less in a straight line until they were lost from sight. He would need to keep an eye out just in case. He'd heard these animals wandered over expansive territories in constant search of food.

Kate was relieved to be moving away, a sentiment she thought she shared with the trailing *Urgut*. It needed no further goading or coaxing to keep up.

The day remained overcast, but thankfully there were no further snowfalls. The wind blew in from the south, picking up the surface snow and turning it into ice crystals, which stung if they hit exposed skin.

They'd taken to wearing goggles with yellowed lenses to cut down on the glare from the snow. They masked their faces with woollen scarves, and lumps of ice formed on the outside of the material where their breath had condensed and frozen with the cold.

They had travelled no more than ten miles when the *Urgut* sank in a pile of soft snow and toppled onto its side. They managed to right it again, but thereafter, it walked with a noticeable limp, and their pace across the snowfield was slowed.

Hawklight called a halt and bent to examine the animal's front leg. He noticed swelling just below the knee. He rummaged around in one of the packs and withdrew a bandage roll. He packed around the joint with snow and strapped it with the bandage to try and reduce the swelling.

He looked at Kate. "Either we set it free and keep going, or we haul up for the day and give the joint a chance to heal. If we keep going like this, it will fall lame."

Kate looked at the animal standing knee deep in the snow with its head slumped. It looked miserable.

"Can we stay?" she asked.

"Sure," he replied. Off to the left he spotted a raised line in the snow as if a low stone wall were buried beneath it. It would afford the *Urgut* some protection. Kate drove the iron stake into the frozen ground once again, and the animal was tethered to it. It appeared to welcome the break since it slumped onto its belly beside the snowdrift.

Kate and Hawklight set about building another snow cave. They began by piling and compacting loose snow into a dome shape, beating it firm with the backs of their shovels. It was hard work, but once the pile was large enough, they took a break to allow the snow to harden and freeze.

There were tent pegs, but no tents in the bundle the *Urgut* had carried. Hawklight inserted a number of these pegs into the walls of the dome. They were about a foot long, a perfect size for a snow cave wall. He then began the laborious task of carving out the interior of the dome, starting with an uphill sloping tunnel entrance. Kate remained outside to clear away the snow he removed, and was on standby to dig him out if the cave collapsed.

Once inside, he completed the pit and carved out one large shelf above it for them to lie upon. He smoothed away the walls, stopping whenever he encountered the tip of one of the tent pegs. Two hours after they'd begun, he was finished, and they were able to feed the waterproof hides and the blankets through the entrance. These would keep them warm and dry throughout the night,

"I thought you'd want to keep going," Kate said after they had settled in.

"This way is smarter," Hawklight replied. "Hopefully the swelling in the *Urgut's* leg will have gone down by morning. Besides, if he's as good as I think he is, Kareem ought to be close to finding us again. This will give them more time to catch us up. I hope he remembers to bring your staff."

The mention of Kareem's name brought a smile to Kate's lips, which didn't go unnoticed by Hawklight.

"You think they're that close?" Kate asked.

"I hope so. I can't imagine the good folk of Poluostrov managing to keep them contained. And, contrary to what I first thought, Mirayam has really done a spectacular job on you and your friends in her training school. She handpicked the lot of you—I still don't know what her criteria are, but so far she's batted a thousand, including Jackson."

Kate wrinkled her nose. "What?" she asked.

"It means perfect scores all round. Her little school could match a hundred soldiers, I'm sure. So, yeah, I don't imagine they're too far behind us. I don't think you could stop them, even if you wanted to. I just hope they found shelter from the blizzard."

"We should leave them a note or something to let them know I'm okay, and that you're okay, as well. I dread to think of Kareem catching you unawares."

Hawklight raised his eyebrows at her, and gave her that smug grin of his that had *As if!* splayed across his face. He was *so sure* of himself! But, where before his manner might have offended Kate, who'd have mistaken it for macho posturing, this time it served to make her feel confident and secure in his company.

"I'd liked to have met you back on Earth," she said.

He shook his head, and his features turned grim as he remembered something of his past.

"I wasn't a very nice person back then," he murmured, and, despite her gently probing, he wouldn't reveal anything further.

Kate yawned. She was exhausted. She had no idea whether there were any residual effects from the paralysis curse, but she hadn't been able to shake the kind of bone weariness that had seemed to linger long after her recovery.

"G'night, Nathaniel," she whispered. She pulled the blankets tight across her shoulder and within a minute or two she was fast asleep.

Hawklight blew out the low-glowing lantern and lay on his back, staring up at the roof of the cave. He hoped he was right about Kareem's determination to find Kate. The two of them couldn't afford to encounter the Zimmerman expedition with just one staff between them. At the same time, if he was wrong—if something had waylaid their friends—they couldn't afford to lie around and wait either. They would need to press on the following morning.

Enough diffuse grey light of dawn leaked past the packed snow at the entrance to the cave so that the interior was suffused with a muted glow. Hawklight's eyes flashed open, but it was not the onset of the dawn that had woken him. Some sixth sense had made him anxious, and he checked that his staff was lying beside him.

Suddenly, the quiet was stabbed by a shrieking, wounded bellow underpinned by sheer terror. Kate sat bolt upright, just as Hawklight reached across and clamped his hand across her mouth. He twisted her head so that she was facing him, and he shook his head in warning.

Don't—make—a—sound!

Another scream that ended in a choking gurgle caused her eyes to swivel sideways. Hawklight kept his hand over her mouth and drew her across to him. He shook his head again, and this time she acknowledged his warning.

He slid her back until she was pressed against the wall of the cave and to one side of the entrance tunnel. He grabbed his staff and held it in a two-handed grip, its tip facing the ceiling. Neither dared to breathe.

The screaming had ended.

Something else was moving about out there!

They heard the crunch of footsteps breaking through the crust of snow that had hardened overnight. It was accompanied by a low growling, deep and menacing, and seemed to come from just outside the cave.

Then—a snuffling sound, like something was testing the air for a scent that was faint but still noticeable. Another growl, wary and full of suspicion!

A primal roar erupted close by, coming from the spot where the *Urgut* had been tethered away from the cave. There was a second beast!

The scratching outside the cave ceased as the footsteps receded. The first animal was moving aside. Kate could hear the wet sounds of licking as the two beasts nuzzled each other, and this was accompanied by low grunts of satisfaction.

The creatures started to feed on the carcass of the dead *Urgut*. Kate could hear its hide tearing as it was ripped apart, and cringed at the wet slop as intestines were tugged from the abdominal cavity and swallowed. Bones cracked between massive jaws like a pistol retort, and the noise of constant chewing was interspersed with short guttural sounds, snorting, licking and swallowing.

Hawklight kept his eyes fixed on the ceiling of the cave. His features were set with a kind of grim determination, and he sat statue-still.

They waited silently while the two animals filled their bellies. The grunting ceased altogether as they snuffled in the snow for loose pieces of flesh and edible offal flicked aside in the feeding frenzy.

They'd finally had their fill. Kate heard a final contented rumble from one of them as if it had overeaten, and they were quiet once more. They explored the area, punching through the snow, stopping occasionally to sniff at the peculiar dome-shaped mound. Kate feared the worst: they had been discovered! Still, Hawklight did not move; he watched and waited.

Footsteps sounded immediately outside where Kate was huddling, and a heavy body brushed against the wall. A clump of snow was dislodged from the inside wall and landed in Kate's lap. Then she heard the footsteps recede. The animal was leaving!

Kate had crossed her fingers. She still held on to silly superstitions from Earth. Was this the luck she'd wished for? She kept them crossed and waited.

There were no sounds coming from outside the cave. She hadn't heard the second animal leave, but she'd been so focussed on the one that had brushed past, she'd not been aware of anything else. She glanced at Hawklight. He hadn't moved.

Ten minutes stretched to fifteen, then to thirty. Kate strained to hear anything, but outside the cave, all was deathly silent. All she could think about was the fate of the unfortunate *Urgut* tied to a steel stake, unable to escape—a stake that she had driven into the ground.

"Nathaniel, I—"

The ceiling of the snow cave collapsed inwards, and she was half buried by chunks of packed snow. She was left staring at a pair of huge, silver-furred paws that had just driven down through the roof of the dome. The huge hole in the roof was suddenly blocked by a gigantic maw still bloodied from the remains of the *Urgut*, lined with dagger-like teeth the length of her fingers.

She screamed at the same time the massive *Aelouskah* roared, and its jaws snapped shut. One of the front paws lifted and swiped sideways, claws extended, and smashed a gap in the wall just above her head. One dark black eye recessed in the shaggy fur glowered at her, and the great head dipped in her direction, its jaws parted again in anticipation.

"*Caecate luce!*"

Hawklight had thrust the tip of his staff directly beneath the angry eye, and a blindingly bright light pierced the remains of the cave. The gargantuan bear roared in pain and rose up on its haunches, slapping at its muzzle with its paws.

Hawklight had shielded his own eyes from the thunder-flash, but Kate caught as much of the brilliant glare as the bear. Her vision was starred with the simultaneous explosions of thousands of camera flashes—painfully so—and she reacted the same as the bear. She squealed and tried to shield her eyes behind her hands. Everything had turned black and she couldn't see.

Hawklight grabbed her by the jacket. He lifted her and flung her roughly out through the demolished gap in the wall. She somersaulted through the air and landed in a thick drift of snow, which broke her fall.

Moments later, she felt Hawklight's body hit the snow beside her. Before she could react, he had rolled to his feet and had grabbed her by the jacket once more. He hefted her to her feet and slung her across his shoulder, then sprinted across the snow.

The blinded *Aelouskah* roared once before dropping back into the cavity of the snow cave, where it lashed out in fury, demolishing the cave with its claws in wild slashing arcs.

"Nathaniel, I can't see!" Kate cried. Her eyes were streaming with tears, but everything remained black.

"It won't last!" Hawklight spat between ragged breaths as he ran. "We've got to get away! The mother could return any minute!"

"That was the *baby?*" Kate was incredulous. She'd never seen a predator as big, or as up close and personal.

He twisted as he ran, looking behind to check on the bear. It had driven its shaggy head into the snow, seeking relief from the burning sensation knifing through its skull. As he watched, it lifted its head. Snow cascaded outwards as it shook itself like a wet dog.

"Uh-oh!"

"What?"

Hawklight had just seen the bear swing its head sideways and fix on the fleeing figures with its good eye. It stretched its neck and raised its head skywards and roared once more—a long venomous blast that shook the air.

"Uh-oh!"

The mother had replied. She was somewhere ahead of them. She had left the cub for some reason and was now headed back towards them. Another glance behind confirmed that the cub had begun to lumber in their direction, stopping often to try and fix their position. He must have been partially blinded in his other eye as well since he quickly gave up trying to peer at them, and resorted to sniffing their trail in the snow.

"This is not good!" Hawklight muttered as he ran.

The continuous explosions of light behind Kate's eyelids abated. She opened her eyes. Everything was white, but her view of Hawklight's legs as he ran was one of dark streaks of blurred movement.

"My eyesight is slowly coming back!" she cried.

Hawklight grunted with satisfaction as he suddenly changed direction. He'd noticed an ice field off to his right. It was broken and humped and rose above the surrounding flat, snowy landscape. From a distance, it looked as if a raging torrent in full flood had been instantly frozen solid. With luck, they could lose themselves amongst the rolling blocks of ice and the pressure cracks and crevices.

The ground beneath his feet turned icy, and Hawklight skidded and slipped. He bounced heavily on the ice, but twisted to cushion Kate, absorbing most of the impact himself. Kate had rolled away and was sitting in a thin carpet of snow covering the ice. Hawklight groaned as he picked himself up. He reached down and helped Kate to stand.

The ice field still looked to be about two hundred yards away, and they appeared to be standing on a frozen lake covered by a thin layer of fresh snow.

"How are your eyes?" he asked.

Kate blinked furiously. She could see forms now, although they were still blurry. Hawklight's features were indistinct, but her vision had begun to clear.

"Not so bad," she replied. "I can see something over there."

"That's where we're headed. Do you think you can run beside me? It's flat all the way there."

She nodded.

They heard another roar coming from the cub. The lake was lower than the surrounding land and he'd been lost from view. If Kate's vision was returning, so was his. They ran with more urgency in their stride.

They were halfway to the ice field when the mother rose above it and stepped out onto the lake in front of them. She was half as large again as her cub, and her vision wasn't impaired. She lowered her head and loped towards them.

They skidded to a halt, and Hawklight stepped in front of Kate. By this time, the cub had crested the brow behind them and was easing himself down onto the lake.

"*Arde!*"

A fireball flew from Hawklight's staff and exploded just in front of the mother. A cloud of snow and steam obscured her briefly before she padded through it. She was tentative, wondering what had happened until she spied the two of them fifty yards away.

"You missed!" cried Kate as another fireball whistled towards the bear. Once again, it exploded just in front of her.

It was unlikely that Hawklight could miss a target that size once: twice was unfathomable.

He'd just made the mother angry. She reared onto her back legs and roared at them. Upright, she was close to twenty feet tall. She was furious!

She fell forward onto her front paws again. Kate heard a sharp retort, like a shot from a rifle. The ice beneath the bear had been weakened, melted by Hawklight's fireballs. Her tremendous weight cracked the ice, and she suddenly disappeared beneath the lake through a hole that had burst around her.

There was no time to lose. The cub behind them bellowed, reminding them that their troubles were far from over. Hawklight gripped Kate by the wrist and started running again, skirting around the enormous hole in the ice where reflected waves still lapped across the water's surface.

They'd almost made the edge of the field when the ice beneath their feet was hit from below. Huge chunks of ice and water were blown upwards, and both of them were tossed through the air as if they'd sprung from a trampoline. Hawklight's staff sailed from his grasp and clattered against the ice behind him, thirty feet from where they'd fallen.

The mother bear had dived beneath the ice and had followed them from below. Her hind legs had touched the muddied lake floor, and she'd pushed off and had careened into the ice cap immediately below them.

Blood poured from a gash in her massive head, staining her fur and turning the water red. Her front paws clawed at the ice to help haul her massive frame from the water. She roared and splashed, and they heard the cub respond.

Kate had rolled to her feet first. Hawklight had landed awkwardly and was struggling to stand. She rushed to his side, and half dragged him up.

"Your staff! Where's your staff?"

He shook his head to clear it and saw his staff lying out on the ice. The cub was bearing down on them quickly. There was no time to retrieve it. He gripped her tightly again.

"This way! Don't let go!"

They bolted for the ice field.

The field marked the boundary between two opposing ice sheets flowing in different directions. The edges where these sheets collided had been fractured, twisted, broken, and forced skywards. Successive seasons had melted and thawed the brittle edges, creating smooth-walled overhangs, crevices and sinkholes where the melt waters had disappeared back below the surface. Down amongst the brutalised terrain, the ice was translucent blue or yellow-green, revealing hollowed out caverns of otherworldly beauty topped with a frosting of snow.

This stark, sculptural beauty was lost to them as they ran, twisting and turning as the route ahead of them fractured into alternative pathways. They dodged: left, left, then right, left again, right again, running on instinct. They had to assume by now both bears were back on their trail.

Kate could see clearly at last. The back of her eyeballs still felt as if they'd been scorched, but everything was back in focus.

They rounded a bend in the ice and came to a dead end. The walls of the crevice down which they'd run were steep and smooth, impossible to climb.

"Quick! Back this way!"

Hawklight kept hold of her hand as they turned back the way they'd come. They backtracked to the first fork and turned left. It was narrower and looked more like a crack in the ice than a route through it. Moreover, the bears were calling to each other; they appeared to have separated in order to trap the two of them.

Kate spotted a dark shadow at the far end of the narrow slit.

"This way!" she said. She let go of Hawklight's hand, and moved along the crack. It was wide enough for her, just wide enough for Hawklight who followed.

The shadow she'd spied was a slit entrance to a hole in the ice, about the size of a small jail cell, but large enough to shelter the two of them. Hawklight had to remove his jacket and turn sideways to squeeze through the narrow gap.

Just as Kate pulled him through, the entrance to the long fissure was overshadowed as the cub pressed his shoulders against it, extended his neck and roared. He butted against the fissure in frustration, but was no match for the tons of ice barring his way. He bellowed again, venting his fury into the slit.

Stalemate!

They were trapped, but they were safe for the moment.

Kate squatted inside the chamber while Hawklight peered through the crack and along the fissure to where the cub was futilely ripping great chunks of ice away from the walls.

"Why didn't you kill the bear when you had the chance?" Kate asked.

Hawklight looked mystified as if he'd not considered that possibility. In the end, he shrugged.

"She was just a mother protecting her cub. I guess I should have . . ."

Kate smiled. Hawklight would always be an enigma to her. She hadn't considered *that* possibility!

Hawklight ducked back inside and put his finger to his lips. They could hear snuffling coming from above, then a low growl. The mother had clambered to the top of the ice formation and had stalked back around. The cub continued to rage as if he was trying to say: *There they are! There they are!*

A muffled thump vibrated through the walls of the chamber, and a large chunk of ice crashed onto the floor of the fissure just outside the chamber's entrance. The mother had located their hiding place and had begun the tedious process of breaking through to reach them.

There was no way out, and without Hawklight's staff, they were helpless.

"If we went back out and you hoisted me up onto your shoulders and gave me a shove, I could scramble over the top and race back and get your staff!" she suggested.

Hawklight smiled at her show of courage but shook his head.

"You wouldn't get five feet before they would rip you apart," he said.

"What if they couldn't see me?"

"They still might be able to smell you."

"It's worth the risk!" she exclaimed. "Sooner or later, she's going to burst on through!"

"You're sure about this?"

Her blue eyes—the colour of the translucent ice—gleamed at him in the semi-darkness.

"*Caecus!*" she commanded, and disappeared.

Hawklight squeezed through the entrance once more and hugged the wall of the fissure. At the far end, the cub eyed him maliciously, and stood watching him as he inched neared. The mother was still preoccupied with busting through to the cavern from above. He didn't want to disturb her.

"Ready?" he whispered.

He braced himself against the wall and felt Kate's weight as she clambered up his back and balanced on his shoulders. She placed her hands against the smooth wall of the fissure and pushed out.

Hawklight bent his arms, palms upward, and Kate stepped into his hands. He extended his arms in a slow and steady manner, while Kate hand-walked up the wall to keep her balance. He straightened his arms above his head, and Kate's head and shoulders poked above the top edge of the fissure. The mother bear was twenty feet from her, continuing to tear away at the ice. She'd already cleared a sizeable hole. This had to work!

Kate leaned in against the wall and reached across to a knob of ice. Its edges were sharp, and she was able to grip it without fear of her hand slipping away. She placed her other arm flat on the top, took a deep breath, and kicked off from Hawklight's outstretched hands. She hauled against the handhold and pulled, her body horizontal and her face pressed against the ice. She kept her legs from flailing, and relied upon her upper body strength to drag herself over the edge and onto the ice.

A fresh breeze ruffled the top of the ice and tugged at her hair where her hood had fallen away. The mother immediately ceased ripping away the ice and raised her head, sniffing the air, testing and tasting the new scent. She uttered a low, mean growl, and dropped her snout to the snow, shuffling towards Kate.

Kate needed to move, and quickly. She twisted in the snow and pushed up in one fluid movement. The mother saw the scuffing patterns in the snow and lunged, just as Kate launched herself across the narrow width of the fissure. She heard the snap of jaws on empty air as she landed on the other side. Her boots skidded beneath her, and she hit the ice on her back once again, rolled off the edge and continued the long slide down the sloping incline of the ice mass, picking up speed as she went.

She spun uncontrollably on her back and crashed into barriers of block ice, which checked her speed but didn't stop it. She was vaguely aware of noise from above, and knew that the mother had crossed the gap in an attempt to follow her. If the bear lost her footing and careened down the same path, Kate would be crushed beneath her.

She managed to contain her spin so that her legs were pointed downhill. An edge rushed to meet her, and before she could react, she slid over it and tumbled through the air. She fell ten feet and hit the snowdrift banked at the foot of the ice wall. It cushioned the impact considerably so that she was left dizzy but uninjured.

She was back on the lake. Far to her left, she spotted the broken hole in the ice where the mother bear had first fallen through. She dragged her body from the snow and started to run in that direction, searching for the second break in the ice where the mother had resurfaced. She heard a loud crash behind her, and knew without looking that the mother had just landed on the lake and would be able to follow the footprints in the snow.

There was no point in staying hidden. At least she could draw the mother further from the ice formation and give Hawklight the chance to escape.

"*Te videri!*"

She materialised as if emerging from a thick fog. The mother caught sight of her and bellowed once more.

Kate's heart sank as the roar was answered. The cub had reappeared ahead of her, and they had her in a pincer movement. She had no idea where Hawklight's staff had landed; even if she had, it was likely to be half buried in the snow and impossible to locate without a thorough search of the area.

She was breathless. The cub was closing, and the mother was less than thirty yards from her. She'd run out of options.

Kate turned to face the mother's charge.

"*Dormite!*"

The voices sounded faint and faraway, but the twin pulses were well aimed and instantly effective. They slammed broadside into the mother. The *Aelouskah* female was unconscious before her head bounced onto the ice. Her immense bulk slid from the momentum of her final charge to within a yard of where Kate stood.

There must have been another command which was carried away in the wind because the cub flopped and rolled to a stop immediately afterwards.

The charging bears had been thunderous, but the ensuing silence was overpowering. Kate had no idea what had just happened. She had no right to be left alive and still standing! She felt the wind tugging at her hair, and remembered how it had treacherously carried her scent to the mother.

She was facing the ice formation. The huge bear lay on its side a pace from her. She glimpsed movement as two figures clambered to join the two still standing on the top of the massive ridge of ice a couple of hundred yards from where she'd slid down.

Her heart skipped a beat as she recognised one of the long, lean silhouettes. Despite the layers of heavy clothing, his posture, his gait, was unmistakable.

He'd been driven relentlessly in his desire to find her, to save her.

She started to laugh, and waved.

Kareem waved back.

CHAPTER 13

opely had never felt more miserable. He'd been punished physically, humiliated, and constantly bullied under Varak. This was worse!

The blizzard had torn the deadman anchors—the tent pegs—from the ground, and the tent's flysheet had been blown away into the night. One of the internal curved rods that kept the tent erect had snapped under the constant pressure of the wind, and the canvas bulged inwards, almost levelling the tent.

Copely had tried to bury himself beneath blankets and skins, but the chill fingers of frost seemed determined to creep beneath the layers to seek him out and expose him to their not-so-tender mercies. The canvas wall continued to batter him each time the wind blew; his teeth chattered and his body shook.

Chisholm had greater control. She was a life force, not a creature of flesh and blood. Those imprinted memories of shaking and shivering were deeply ingrained in the soul, but not impossible to manipulate. The cold here would kill her as easily as on Earth, but she was sheltered; she was uncomfortable, true, but she wouldn't die. She was simply too mean to give in to the temptation. She lay tucked beneath her blankets, and watched Copely with contempt.

ALAN CUMMING

There had been no avoiding the blizzard. They'd seen it coming, and had done their best to seek out whatever shelter they could in this bleak wilderness. It wasn't much. A formation of black rock had shunned the attempts of the climate to whiten everything. It drew the sun's heat, and melted the clinging tufts of snow that lodged in its crevices and cracks. It resisted the force of the wind, which flattened everything else.

Copely and Chisholm shared one of the small tents. They had usurped the most sheltered spot behind the largest of the rocks, and pitched the tent prior to the storm hitting. In the end, it hadn't mattered. The wind swirled in from all sides, battering and hammering them and flinging sleet and snow to try and bury them.

Chisholm turned her thoughts to Riegel. She had an innate sense when it came to judging men. Riegel had been one of the committed few. He was probably smart enough to know there would be considerable gold in the pot at the end of this particular rainbow. There were no doubts in her mind as to where his loyalties lay.

They'd left a series of markers behind them, markers he would recognise and be able to follow. They hadn't counted on the strength of the blizzard. By now it would have obliterated every marker under feet of new snow, and he would have no hope of finding them.

He ought to have caught up with them, despite the debilitating wound. Those things healed quickly on Bexus. He would no doubt be sheltering from the storm. She needed him to return. He was one of the few she'd placed her trust in, and the rest of the company knew it. There had been too many desertions already from the ragtag bunch of mercenaries she had assembled. Besides, there was the matter of the three guides from Poluostrov; their services could be terminated, in the true sense of the word, once Riegel made it back.

188

Marcus Zimmerman shared the tent next to them with Hendrikx, the Dutchman. Hendrikx preferred the cold; he'd turned on his side and was sound asleep. His snoring could still be heard above the shrieking wind.

Zimmerman was fondling the two halves of the broken crystal, rolling them around his palm outside the blanket. He liked to run the tiny compass along the length of each half, delighting in the way the needle swept around and locked in a parallel position. Whatever stellar event had occurred millions of years before had been focussed at the poles of the planet where the lines of magnetic force dove into its depths, directing the rush of energy along with it. The crystal would have been there then, and the tiny iron impurities within it had melted under the attack and realigned, forming microscopic channels that could harness, focus and trap any further energy passing through it.

Zimmerman had never known of any substance capable of transforming energy in this way. He knew it had to have originated at the South Pole, where the inclination of the force lines was ninety degrees. The problem was whether the material had moved since then, either by glacial growth, upthrust and weathering, or even continental drift. Zimmerman didn't know the geology of Bexus, but he was willing to bet he didn't need to go as far as the pole to find its source.

He'd kept one further clue about his precious Zimmermanite hidden from the others. At these latitudes, the crystal glowed. It was only noticeable in very dark conditions—hidden beneath his blanket, for example—but it seemed to pulse with a weak light in pink, green, deep blue and purple hues. Zimmerman had seen those colours before on Earth, and he knew what they represented.

He grunted. There was no way he'd be able to fulfil his task under these atrocious conditions. If he stepped outside, he wouldn't even be able to find the next tent.

The next tent! He knew his fate was sealed inside it. He had no illusions that he would be considered superfluous to requirements once the source of the crystal had been located. He strongly suspected he'd draw his final breath staring at the end of Copely's staff. He needed to keep working on Chisholm. He knew that she thought he was weak—a quisling even—but if she believed he could be useful, she'd protect him.

Whom was he kidding? She'd probably ace him too, in all likelihood, but she was his best shot, and he had to come up with a plan to save himself.

When he finally drifted off to sleep, he was no further ahead with his plan than he'd been when he started.

Kito Yegräyak had lived his life like a weasel hiding in a henhouse, stealing most of what he required without regard to others while running for cover at the first sign of trouble, ever careful to cover his tracks. The more respectable citizens of Poluostrov distrusted him because his alibis withstood scrutiny, despite the fact that he was a compulsive liar. Things went missing when he was in the area. He'd been an upholsterer by trade, but his finished work was so shoddy that no one in the town would use his services. He became a miner through circumstance, and was always on the lookout for other means of income—legal or otherwise.

When the Zimmerman party had advertised for guides, he'd volunteered. The people of Poluostrov were grateful to see the back of him, so they kept their mouths shut and quietly waved their problem goodbye.

Yegräyak's credentials as a guide were, in fact, quite good. He hunted and trapped for pelts throughout the area and was skilled at surviving for weeks at a time in the inhospitable terrain. His two companions from the town bowed to his experience, so he became the leader to whom Chisholm and Copely turned.

Yegräyak had been disappointed initially when he took stock of the inadequately supplied expedition. The two *Urguts* were in such poor condition that they were barely able to carry the load of supplies, and most of what they carried wasn't worth stealing. But the pay was promising. He'd agreed on a 'half-now, half-later' deal once he'd seen the size of the gemstones on offer. He was surprised and suspicious when the negotiations were sealed without too much haggling. He had a sneaking suspicion there wasn't going to be any 'later', but his weasel intuition told him he'd be long gone by that time.

That survival instinct urged him to leave soon, but the rest of him was curious about the goal of the expedition. It had to be worth something spectacular, and he wanted to wait and see if there was any chance he could cut himself in on the deal.

He pulled the tent flap aside, and dug himself through the snowdrift that had accumulated at the entrance. The blizzard had passed them by, finally. The skies were leaden grey, and the wind continued to jostle the clouds, although the air was clear of snow. The landscape was featureless, covered by a clean, fresh blanket of thick snow.

"Everybody out!" he called. "Time to get moving!"

Yegräyak rescued his snowshoes buried in the snow beside his tent, and then went to check on the *Urguts*.

One by one, holes appeared beneath snow-covered hummocks as the rest of the expedition members were roused. They stretched and yawned and slapped their shoulders and stamped their boots in the snow to revive themselves, before beginning the tedious process of digging out their tents and supplies from the heavy covering of snow.

Copely emerged, red-eyed and ill tempered. He'd not slept well; in fact, he'd nearly suffocated when the weight of snow had compressed the tent once the pole had snapped, and he'd been trapped beneath it. Chisholm had pulled him clear. From that point on, he'd been afraid to go back to sleep.

Griselda Chisholm followed him out through the hole.

"You'd better start digging the tent out," she said. Copely looked miserable, which made taunting him all the more fun.

Instead, Copely rounded on Abayomi who, at that moment, seemed to be longing wistfully for the tropically humid streets of Lagos.

"Dig out the tent!" he barked. He broke Abayomi's reverie, and Abayomi muttered obscenities beneath his breath as he knelt and scooped handfuls of snow from the buried tent.

Copely stamped his feet. He'd lost all feeling in his toes.

Yegräyak reappeared from behind the rocks and loped across the snow to Chisholm.

"You'd better come and have a look," he said.

"If they've disappeared again—" Chisholm threatened.

"Oh no, they're both still tied up," Yegräyak replied.

Chisholm indicated to Copely to follow, and they trailed after Yegräyak. Both *Urguts* were staked together in the shelter of the rocks. Only one of them lifted its head to greet them. The other had died during the blizzard and was as stiff as a plank of wood.

Chisholm booted the corpse in frustration and swore.

"Bring me Zimmerman!" she ordered. Yegräyak shrugged, and left to find the geologist.

She fumed silently, banging her gloved fist against the rock. Copely wasn't brave enough to break the silence. He stood to one side, out of her way.

She rounded on Zimmerman as soon as he appeared.

"How much longer?" she demanded. "How much further?"

Zimmerman glanced down at the dead animal at her feet.

"I—I—I'm not certain," he stuttered, fearful of her foul mood.

Chisholm tilted her head and glared at him.

"We're close," he stammered. "It can't be more than a few days now. The magnetic readings are so strong."

She continued to stare at him as if she were trying to make her mind up about something. She had a habit of nibbling on her lower lip, Zimmerman had noticed. It was never a good sign.

Apparently she'd come to a decision over whatever was troubling her.

"Stay here," she ordered. "Sort through this stuff, and identify everything you'll need to get the job done. Ditch the rest!"

She stalked off. Copely followed after firing another contemptuous look Zimmerman's way. He noticed that Yegräyak hovered in the background, waiting to see what Zimmerman was going to chuck away.

Hendrikx appeared moments later, charged with sorting through the other supplies, to determine what they could afford to do away with. He and Zimmerman had to struggle to remove the hide covering, which protected the supplies, as it was trapped beneath the dead body. They managed to untie it and spread it over the snow, and began the chore of sorting through the geological instruments, spare tents, clothing, blankets and fuel carried by both animals.

Half an hour later, they had two piles. They repacked the smaller pile onto the surviving *Urgut*, which bellowed weakly as the load was strapped in place. Yegräyak kicked through the rejected articles, looking for anything of value, conscious of the fact he'd have to carry what he took. In the end, he turned and walked away. It was the first time he'd ever done that.

They broke camp and strung out in a line once more, with Yegräyak at the head.

"Same direction?" he asked, pulling the compass from beneath his jacket.

Chisholm waited for Zimmerman to reply.

"Same direction," he muttered.

He checked the sky. It was still the same slate grey, colourless palette; nothing had changed. He needed the clouds to clear if he stood any hope of finding the source of the crystal. Until then, he had to rely on the vector magnetometer he carried.

Chisholm nodded. It was the signal to move out. She checked the site one final time. They had left enough markers for Riegel to find them. Strips of coloured material cut from a blanket fluttered from the top of the tallest rock. He ought to spot that, provided the weather remained clear.

She shifted her gaze to the horizon and scanned it for any sign of movement, but she saw nothing of interest, beyond a broken ridge of ice to the north and slightly west from where they'd come.

Finally, she turned and followed the rest of the party. Her snowshoes made walking across the snow much easier, and she hurried to catch up. The snow seemed to muffle all sound, and she was surprised at how far ahead the others had gone; she'd hardly heard them leave.

She pulled her hood over her head to ward off the cold. She didn't look behind her again. Had she done so, she might have spotted twin pulses of light coming from the top of the distant ice ridge.

Throughout the course of the day, the cloud cover lifted. Patches of blue sky appeared and grew in size, and for the first time in many days, the sun made a welcome appearance. Zimmerman's spirits lifted. It was the break he had been hoping for.

The ground beneath them had started to undulate. Later that afternoon, they called a halt at the edge of another glacier that cut across their path.

Yegräyak left the party, having suggested it might be the spot to prepare another campsite before night fell, and he headed up onto the ice to try and find a vantage point high enough to chart a passage. The trick was to bypass the hidden crevasses that lurked beneath flimsy bridges of snow. One false step and the whole lot would cave inwards; those trapped on the thin skin would drop anywhere between thirty and two hundred feet, and would be beyond rescue if indeed they survived the fall. Yegräyak already suspected that to sustain an injury would mean being left behind.

The glacier appeared treacherous from this distance. It was as though a psychotic giant had slashed at it with an axe in some murderous frenzy. It was gouged in gaping slits with ragged edges, and those were the ones he could *see*. There were bound to be others.

Once again, he thought seriously about deserting the company and leaving them to their fate. Nothing seemed to be worth the risk, and yet that was what continued to prick his curiosity. The others weren't about to turn back, so what was the value of the ultimate prize they were seeking?

He repressed the urge to save his skin, and this was the second time he'd made a choice which ran contrary to everything he'd ever done before. Feeling uneasy, he spent the remainder of the daylight hours locating the best possible route across the glacier, but he still couldn't shake the sense of foreboding tickling his subconscious.

By the time he'd picked his way carefully back to the campsite, he found it in a state of chaos, and it took no time at all to work out why, since the members of the expedition immediately rounded on him.

"He's back!" he heard someone call, even before he'd stepped into the pool of light thrown up by a ring of lanterns. Someone shoved him from behind, and he stumbled into the tiny clearing defined by the lanterns and the ring of tents they hung from.

"What is this?" he demanded as one of the tent flaps was pulled aside. Chisholm stepped out of the tent, followed by Copely.

"Where've you been?" Her voice was laced with suspicion.

"Where do you think I've been?" he yelled indignantly. "Out on the ice, looking for a way through this—this—" He stumbled for the words. His anger stuttered, replaced by a growing sense of dread. "What's going on?"

"Look around you," Chisholm replied. "Tell me what you see."

He glanced about him. Then it struck him! One tent was missing! Seven faces were staring back at him. Where were the other four?

"Your 'friends' decided to leave us," said Copely from the shadows. "They also helped themselves to some of the gear."

It was true. His two companions from Poluostrov had gone. They'd probably waited until the others had crawled into their tents, and then decided to make a break for it. The prospect of traversing the glacier must have been too much for them. But something had happened. They'd been missed too soon.

Yegräyak checked the sky. It was shimmering under the brilliant aurora, which lit up the landscape like a full moon and bathed it in rainbows. They wouldn't have managed to get very far.

He saw movement out beyond the glow of the lanterns, and then heard the crunch of crusted snow beneath the tread of snowshoes. Everyone turned towards the sound, just as Hendrikx materialised out of the gloom. He was closely followed by Abayomi. Each man wore a pack and carried another.

Hendrikx sought out Chisholm and nodded across at her. *Job done!* She visibly relaxed. Yegräyak immediately knew that somewhere out there on the snow, not too far away, were two crumpled piles of clothing with gaping holes burned through their backs. He held his breath momentarily, grateful to the greed that had prevented him from making the same choice as the unfortunate guides.

He caught Chisholm eyeing him warily.

"Having second thoughts, Mr Yegräyak?"

He shook his head and hoped he was convincing enough.

The excitement had subsided. Yegräyak stumbled to his tent and fell inside. Abayomi joined him moments later, on orders from

Chisholm not to let the guide out of his sight. Yegräyak got the message loud and clear. He'd missed his opportunity to skedaddle. He might as well get some rest instead.

Marcus Zimmerman stood outside his tent, oblivious to the cold. He stared rapturously at the curtain of shimmering lights that seemed so close he felt he could reach out and touch them. They pulsed as if they were alive as billions of ions per second streamed in from space and were distorted downwards by the magnetic pull of the planet.

Hendrikx watched him from just inside the tent. He was confident that Zimmerman wouldn't pull any further stunts, and tossed up whether or not to roll over and go to sleep. The incident with the two guides had totally enraged Chisholm, and her orders to him had been explicit: find them, but don't bother to bring them back! So, while there was an infinitesimal chance that Zimmerman might yet still escape, Hendrikx was unwilling to let it happen on his watch. He yawned, and wondered what was behind Zimmerman's fascination with coloured lights.

Marcus looked at the ragged tails where the lights were closest to the ground. He thought he saw what he was searching for, but he needed to clamber to higher ground to be certain. He started along the path that Yegräyak had followed back to the camp.

"Hey! Where are you going?" Hendrikx's voice quivered with the frustration of having to climb from the warm tent to accompany him.

"I need a higher vantage point!" said Zimmerman. "I'm going up onto the glacier."

Hendrikx grumbled in Dutch as he reached for his fur-lined hood and gloves before zipping his feet into his boots.

By the time he caught up, Zimmerman was standing on the ice holding a lantern and a compass. He could now view the full extent of the aurora, and found his final clue: a streak where the lights seemed to be funnelled downwards, like one of those ethereal crepuscular rays in religious paintings that suggest divine origins.

It signified a point above the ground where the magnetic lines of force were particularly strong—focussed, even—but it was what lay beneath the ground that held special interest for Zimmerman.

He took the bearing and re-checked it for accuracy. He kicked a hole in the snow below where he stood, and then spent ten minutes collecting worn stones, scattered across the surface of the glacier, to mark a stony cairn noting the location. Hendrikx watched in mild amusement, and did not offer to collect the rocks. He privately thought that the geologist was eccentric—a few rocks short of an avalanche, so to speak. He was pleased when Zimmerman had finished, and they headed back down to the campsite again. Zimmerman was humming quietly. He crawled inside the tent and was fast asleep before Hendrikx had removed his boots.

Early the following morning, Zimmerman stood astride the cairn and indicated to Yegräyak the direction they were to proceed. The guide consulted the crude map he'd drawn the day before and made some adjustments, then signalled the party to load up and follow him out onto the glacier.

Zimmerman had been correct. They were still many hundreds of miles from the South Pole of Bexus, but only the source of the crystal could have caused that anomaly in the aurora, and it had apparently moved north with the glacier over the intervening eons of time.

"It's very close," he whispered to Griselda as he stepped ahead of her. He saw her face cloud with avarice, and she inadvertently licked her lips in anticipation. Zimmerman was feeling the same way although for an entirely different reason. He would have his own name up in lights every time another geologist mentioned the word, 'Zimmermanite'.

Copely brought up the rear. He was the last to step out onto the glacier, and he carried an armload of sticks, each about a foot long, cut from the broken tent pole, and some spare ones that the *Urgut* had carried. Each stick had been tied with strips of red cloth. Every thirty or so yards, he poked one of the sticks into the snow, marking the trail along which it was safe to walk. They'd need it to find their own way back across the glacier since Chisholm had other plans for their sole remaining guide.

Yegräyak noticed the markers and reached the same conclusion. Whatever the pot of gold at the end of this rainbow was, he was no longer interested. The irony about being rich was that you needed to be alive to enjoy the experience. He decided to hightail it the moment the first opportunity presented itself; until then, he was in a holding pattern, hoping to survive.

His best chance lay in finding a shallow crevasse—deep enough but not too deep—down which he could tumble and feign injury, ideally out of the line of fire. They'd leave him, especially if he handed over a copy of his map. Once they'd gone, he would hack some steps in the ice and climb out. If he got that far, he promised himself that he would pull up the little red markers and reset them so that they led out into the middle of the glacier where they would end abruptly. If nothing else, that would buy him time.

His luck deserted him. Abayomi was at his shoulder the whole time, and the snow beneath the path he'd chosen sat on solid ice. No gambler would have run with those odds. He'd somehow chosen to stroll through a minefield, and had avoided every carefully laid trap!

Zimmerman was sandwiched in the middle of the straggling line. The needle of his compass had begun to flicker as if it were suddenly unsure in which direction south lay. He watched, fascinated, as the needle turned away from its true bearing, attracted by a greater magnetic force nearby.

He called a halt and signalled the new direction with his arm. Yegräyak turned right, and the rest of the line followed. Marcus handed the compass to Chisholm, and reached into his pack for his vector magnetometer, a hand-held device that tracked the angle at which the magnetic lines of force plunged into the ground. The device read eighty-seven degrees; they were now extremely close.

It took them the rest of the afternoon of careful probing and constantly checking their position before they could make out the other side where the glacier ended. The ice was more broken here where the steady flow of the glacier was countered by the friction against the bedrock through which it moved.

Zimmerman's magnetometer was reading ninety degrees. He'd located the position of the mother lode to within a radius of one hundred yards.

"It's here—somewhere!" He stopped and beamed at Griselda Chisholm, but if he was expecting hearty congratulations and a pat on the back for his troubles, he was sorely disappointed. All Chisholm saw was a broken expanse of ice and snow that extended in all directions. She reached across and gripped him by the lapels of his jacket to be certain he had her full attention.

"You're going to have to be more precise than that, Mr Zimmerman."

"We have to camp here the night," he replied, "maybe over there." He pointed to where the glacier ended, and the sides were flat and covered with snow. "I'll be more precise tomorrow." *At least I hope I will,* he thought.

An aurora is not like a rainbow. A rainbow is an optical illusion. Those who see a rainbow will have the sun behind them and a band of rain ahead of them. The rainbow moves as they move.

Not so with the aurora. It hovers miles above the ground where the magnetic fields bend the solar winds towards the planet.

Zimmermanite was essentially a lens that magnified the magnetic lines of force a thousand-fold. Marcus already knew from his readings that the magnetic fields on Bexus were way stronger than those of Earth, so he was expecting the buried crystal to show itself, provided the weather held.

The night was crystal clear and winked with the eyes of billions of stars. Hundreds of miles above the planet's surface, the solar particles roared, and sped in, and were diverted down along the highways of the magnetic field.

The magnificent lights were ignited, while, above the heads of the Zimmerman expedition members, the air hummed and whispered to them—a kind of *swish* as bursts of energy pulsated. Perhaps it was because they were creatures of pure energy themselves that they felt the affinity with the aurora with an electrical intensity. The hair on Zimmerman's head stood on end as he sat on a lump of ice at the edge of the glacier, and waited.

There was a sharp *crack!* like the sound of a whip cutting the air, and a shaft of blue and green light burst ahead of him out on the glacier and seemed to pierce the ice. Marcus leapt to his feet, and sprinted out between the broken ice cubes to where the light was focussed. It seemed to disappear from view a few feet above the ground, but he marked the position carefully, and trod slowly towards the spot. He carried a can of bright red marker paint. He flipped the lid without taking his eyes from the spot and tossed the paint onto the snow and ice.

Bingo!

He was in his childhood once again, the pirate captain in a spotted bandana, digging for buried treasure in his sandpit, where 'X' marked the spot on the map.

He lay back on the frozen surface of the glacier, tilted his head to the sky and started to laugh. Chisholm and Copely joined Hendrikx at the edge of the glacier, and the three of them stood silently, and wondered about his sanity.

—m—

The sun burst upon the snow in a show of dazzling brilliance. The paint had been chilled and dulled and had formed a plastic skin. It looked like a red wine stain, not the bright red of blood it had been when first poured from the can.

It didn't matter. What did matter was that it was easy to spot.

The wasted *Urgut* had only managed to carry a few tools, so a work detail was drawn up. Yegräyak wasn't the least bit surprised to find himself first in line on the end of a pickaxe. He thought about driving the pointed end through his leg, but gave it up as a bad idea almost immediately. He had outlived his usefulness, but there was no point in hastening along the inevitable. Besides, he continued to be curious as to what lay at the bottom of the hole he was about to dig.

Chisholm and Copely contributed to the labour by blasting away the ice using their staffs. Each blast knocked a crater into the ice about two feet deep. After that, it was up to Yegräyak and the other conscripted labourers to wade ankle deep in the melted ice, and shift the broken blocks of ice out of the hole.

Zimmerman fussed about the edge of the activity, and occasionally got in everyone's way by insisting on clambering down inside the deepening crater to measure the change in electromagnetism.

They were three hours in and eighteen feet below the surface of the ice when Yegräyak—on his third spell behind the pickaxe—slammed into something that sent wicked vibrations up the shaft of the pick. He yelped in surprise, and dropped the tool, and cradled his stinging hands beneath his armpits.

"What happened?" Copely called down to him.

"I hit something, a rock, maybe," he answered.

"Leave it!" Zimmerman ordered. "I'm coming down for a look!"

"I'm coming up first," Yegräyak replied. "There isn't enough room for the two of us down here!"

He climbed the rope ladder that dangled into the hole. Willing hands pulled him onto the ice, and he felt Zimmerman brush past him in a zealous rush. Zimmerman had a geologist's hammer tucked into his belt, and he whipped it out as soon as his boots splashed into the bottom of the hole.

"Send down a bucket on a rope!"

Fifteen minutes later, the base of the hole was practically dry as the final bucketful of water was hauled from the hole.

Zimmerman knelt and examined the hole gouged by the end of the pick. He meticulously tapped at the ice using his hammer to crack it apart and lever it up. He scraped the broken chunks away with his gloved hands, and then repeated the actions until he could make out a solid object covered by a thin layer of ice.

He bent over the object and could feel waves of energy passing through his body as his own force field was disturbed by the magnetism. He felt an odd vibration in his chest, and experienced a mild sense of nausea as he worked, but he couldn't contain the exhilaration once he'd exposed the tip of the crystal lode.

"I've got it!" he cried. "I need to work carefully to extract it. It might only take one stray hammer blow to shatter it."

Chisholm yelled something back to him, but he was too engrossed with his hammering to have heard. It was probably another threat to string him up by his fingernails, he thought absently.

"I said, can we melt it out?" This time her voice was loud and clear and made eminent sense. *Why didn't I think of that?* he thought.

"Send down my staff!"

Abayomi lay on his belly on the ice and passed down Zimmerman's staff, holding it carefully by the handle. The hole was too narrow, and his staff too long to be able to wield it effectively in the hole.

He stepped to one side and aimed the tip at the ice covering of the object.

"Be careful, Mr Zimmerman!"

"Incendere!"

The ice erupted in a hiss of steam and boiling water. Marcus was surprised by the intensity of the charm. He quickly learned to regulate the energy that flowed from him through his staff to the ice so that subsequent blasts were more refined, more focussed, and, therefore, more effective.

The bucket was lowered again, and the bottom of the pit was bailed dry.

The crystal took his breath away. It was about the size of a basketball, and its surface glimmered in a hundred different hues of pinks, blues and greens. He removed one glove and touched it with the palm of his hand. There was an immediate affinity with his energy. It felt as if he had placed his hand over a bathtub plughole to interrupt the circular flow of water down it; the same sucking effect clamped his palm flat against the stone. He was astonished by the force, and tugged his hand clear almost by reflex.

He replaced his glove, and tried to lift the stone, but it wouldn't budge. It must have been compressed as densely as diamond, and, he knew, filled with iron impurities.

"It's too heavy!" he called. "We'll need to slip a net around it and use the *Urgut* to pull it clear!"

Abayomi was the rope man. He peeled apart half a dozen ropes and spliced their ends together to form a crude but effective curved net. He traded places with Zimmerman and fitted the net snugly around the spherical stone, and then spliced the ends together at the end of another length of rope. The resulting knot looked as if a mason bee had crafted a nest at the end of the rope. It may have looked grotesque, but it was exceedingly strong because of the way it had been knitted together.

The free end was tied to a collar looped over the head of the *Urgut*. A girth strap was also attached to take some of the strain from the neck and shoulders of the beast. Hendrikx held the reins, ready to drive the *Urgut* forward. The rest of the soldiers—Yegräyak included—gripped the rope tightly and took up the strain. They looked like an Arctic tug-o-war team.

"*Hi—yaaahhhh!*"

Hendrikx tugged on the reins at the same time that Copely slashed across the *Urgut's* rump with a whip. It lurched forward, and the load inched upward.

Yegräyak slipped on the ice and knocked the legs out from beneath the man in front of him. The stone jolted, and the men on the rope slid towards the hole.

"*Pull, you idiots!*" Chisholm screamed.

Yegräyak scrambled to his feet and gripped the rope. Slowly, the load rose out of the hole. Chisholm gripped Copely's arm so tightly that he had to wrench it free the moment the rock first appeared at the lip of the hole. Zimmerman raced to the edge and laced his fingers through the netting as if he could lift it over the edge by himself. It would have been laughable, except that it worked. Somehow, he must have eased it over a lip in the ice that was the final barrier, and the stone jerked free, and rolled onto the glacier.

They'd done it! Varak's original crystal was nothing but a sliver by comparison. Copely was mesmerised by the sight of the shimmering stone, and he stood transfixed with greed. Zimmerman was already hunched over it protectively, peeling the rope net away, checking for any sign of damage. He was caressing it like a firstborn child, his child—Zimmermanite!

Copely strode across and grabbed the hood of Zimmerman's jacket. He yanked hard, and Zimmerman fell backwards at his feet.

"What do you think you're doing?" hissed Copely. Spittle flew from his lips as all his resentment towards the geologist spilled over in a jealous rage. The time for treating him like a precious, spoiled child was done!

Zimmerman had been rocked back on his haunches. He read the danger signs and bottled his courage. He'd known this day would come.

"Tell me this, Mr Copely," he replied. His voice was steady and even. "How do you plan to transport the stone back home? It took all seven of us, and the *Urgut*, just to lift it out of the hole."

Copely was startled. He didn't expect such a brazen response. He shot a quick glance at Chisholm who was standing to one side, watching the exchange with interest. She'd been willing to clip Zimmerman the moment he'd found the crystal, so why wasn't she stepping in to support him?

"The only way you're going to be able to move it," Zimmerman continued, "is to break it into smaller chunks, and split the load amongst us. But the problem, you see, is that it is a crystal. Hit it in the wrong spot and you'll shatter the whole thing."

He reached behind him, and withdrew the geologist's hammer in his belt, and presented it handle first to Copely.

"Take it Mr Copely. Have a good whack at the stone with it."

The hammer hung in the air between them. Copely didn't move, didn't reach for it. A smile creased Griselda's lips. Zimmerman had also won that round between the two of them. It was time to defuse the situation.

"Thank you, Mr Zimmerman. Your argument was timely indeed. It seems you're still very much a part of this expedition."

Zimmerman picked himself up off the ice, and brushed off the snow that clung to his clothing.

"I mean no disrespect, Miss Chisholm, but you can understand my predicament. I need a safety guarantee more ironclad than just your word. What will happen to me once the stone is split?"

"I'm sorry to disappoint you, Mr Zimmerman, but there are no guarantees, apart from my word. If you don't split the stone for us, we will kill you. If you do split it for us, we might kill you. Then again, we might not. If you split the stone and we kill you, we might find you've destroyed the stone in the process. No one wins.

We want to use the crystal. You want to survive. It's a matter of trust.

The truth is you mean nothing to me, apart from the unique set of skills you possess. I have no interest in you once your work is complete. There is no reason for me to want to see you dead.

Trust, Mr Zimmerman, trust! You have to trust me at my word, I'm afraid. But let me say this. Split the stone for us, and I'll guarantee you my protection for the journey back to Cherath."

Copely tried to interrupt. This was going badly for him. Chisholm silenced him with a glare.

"No one will attempt to harm you. Do I make myself clear?" She directed her promise at Copely. He couldn't meet her gaze.

Zimmerman thought about it. He thought about having them move off the glacier a mile or so while he split the stone. That would give him a clear head start. A little reality check also warned him he'd never survive the wilderness on his own. This was the best he was going to get.

"Deal!" he said.

Yegräyak had slunk away from the limelight when all the focus was on the geologist. It was time to make tracks. Despite Chisholm's reassurances, he knew there was no honour among thieves.

He'd used the pretext of rolling up the rope line used to lift the crystal to the surface, and wandered back to the campsite at the edge of the glacier. They'd dug up a coloured stone that looked to be too heavy and worthless. He had no further interest in it: certainly no interest in lugging a great lump of it out on his back.

He threw the rope inside the small supplies tent, and cast around quickly for anything of value to steal. He realised he needed to be gone before he was missed, but just as he was about to step outside, he spied a pair of soft, supple fur-lined boots made from *Hon'chai* leather. There were still many miles to Poluostrov; he was certainly going to need good footwear to get there.

He quickly unlaced his own tired boots and slipped the new ones on his feet. The thick hair on the inside of the boots caressed his feet with warmth and comfort, and he sighed as he laced them tightly over his trouser legs.

He peered cautiously outside the tent. He could see Zimmerman on his knees through the knot of spectators. The geologist was examining the rock closely, and tapping it with the sharp edge of his hammer. Everyone seemed preoccupied. Good!

He slipped around the back of the tent, checked to see the coast was clear, and then ran hunched over to a wall of broken ice at the edge of the glacier. He smiled. They'd never find him out there.

They wouldn't need to. An explosion at his feet catapulted Yegräyak into the air. He came down hard on the ice and was momentarily winded. He rolled onto his side and watched Abayomi's boots approach.

"Going somewhere?" the Nigerian asked.

Yegräyak was hauled to his feet and was marched back to where the members of the company stood watching Zimmerman at work. Chisholm glanced at him as they approached, but didn't appear to be particularly surprised. She simply nodded at Abayomi, and Yegräyak knew then that she'd anticipated his attempt to escape. His heart sank.

"I believe it can be done," he heard Zimmerman say. "The crystal is flawed, and we can use those lines to split it into good sized chunks light enough to carry."

"How do we even know if it will work?" Copely whined. "I want to test it out first."

Chisholm shrugged. Of them all, Copely had been closest to Varak. He'd seen the Master wield the crystal. He must have known some of the secrets.

"Detach a piece!" she ordered Zimmerman. "Give it to Mr Copely."

Zimmerman identified the piece he could hack away.

"Help me roll it on its side," he said.

It took four of the soldiers to move it, but finally Zimmerman had the corner he desired facing him. He dug out a small stone chisel from his belt and held it at a precise angle to the surface of the crystal. He double-checked the position of the chisel. One wrong move and the corner would shatter, and his credibility would shatter along with it.

He held his breath, and then gave the head of the chisel a sharp, forceful tap with the hammer. To his relief, the corner sheared away cleanly, and a shard of crystal the size of his thumb plopped into the snow. He fished it out and held it up for Copely.

Copely hesitated. He'd waited for this moment forever, it seemed.

He removed his gloves and gripped the crystal fragment in his palm. He felt the tremulous vibrations as his own energy aligned with the microtubules formed when the crystal was first created. Was it the same sense of power that had captivated Varak centuries beforehand? His mouth was dry, and he felt light-headed.

His right hand clamped around his staff, and he turned to face the others. There was one sure way to test the prowess of the crystal.

Yegräyak was standing slightly apart, not making eye contact. Copely gestured for Abayomi, who was standing behind the prisoner, to back away. When Yegräyak saw this, he looked up at Copely, and shook his head, silently pleading with his captor.

The power of the crystal was not to be denied. Copely pointed his staff at Yegräyak.

The command was eerily familiar. Chisholm shivered involuntarily as she heard the chant.

"Dimitte bestias pascere in vita!"

Words uttered by no one but Varak.

A deep red, viscous bubble shot from the end of Copely's staff and enveloped Yegräyak. He tried to push through it, but a sticky substance coating the interior of the bubble stung his hands like an acid burn, and he pulled them away, and wiped them against his jacket.

Small red-black pustules grew out from the walls of the bubble. They grew rapidly in size, and turned translucent so that a dark form could be seen beneath them. Some of the forms wriggled about like fat grubs in a honeycomb.

One of these blisters split apart, dripping fluid. The newly hatched form clung to the wall as it slowly uncoiled. It could have been a butterfly emerging from a chrysalis, but the wings that extended were black and leathery, and tipped with vicious claws at the end of each long digit. Yegräyak thought he was staring at a bat, but its skin was reptilian, and its snout was elongated. It looked like a flying Chihuahua with big teeth.

It flapped its damp wings to dry them off, and sniffed at the air with its tiny snout. More of the pustules hatched in quick succession. Yegräyak decided to act first.

He gripped the animal by the neck and jerked it free of the wall. It squealed in protest and clawed at his hands, then bit him. He recoiled with the intense pain. The bite mark on his hand was already inflamed, and it felt as if he'd thrust his hand into a fire.

He dropped the creature on the ground and stomped on it. His boot crushed its skull, and the wings flapped helplessly before falling still.

He reached for another, but it sensed him coming and took to the air. He tried again, but it was like trying to swat flies using his hand. He just wasn't quick enough.

Two of them flew at him from opposite sides. One hit him in the side of the face and tore a chunk from his cheek. He roared with the pain as the other latched onto his neck and bit down. He tried to rip it away, but it launched itself into the air, and came around and landed on his thigh and bit him through his clothing,

By now, the air was humming with the noise of beating wings. There were too many of them. They ripped his clothing and tore tiny mouthfuls off him. One hit him across the larynx and cut all ability to scream, when screaming was all he had left.

He toppled to the ground beneath the weight of the flying creatures, which swarmed over him like piranhas on a drowned cow's carcass. His clothing collapsed, and the interior of the bubble filled with a red mist that was siphoned back through the umbilical cord linked to Copely's staff.

Copely felt the thrill as Yegräyak was reconstituted into a stream of energy that flowed down his staff and through his hand into the crystal. His whole body felt reinvigorated as it tapped into the passing energy and drank from the flow.

When the mist cleared, everything had dissipated inside the bubble, and it shrank in size until it disappeared completely.

His world stopped spinning, and Copely felt vaguely nauseous. He wondered if he'd blacked out, but he was standing holding his staff. Something was burning in his other hand, and he seemed mildly surprised to discover it was the crystal, which still glowed a dull red colour.

Something had happened. The soldiers had stepped away from him, and he saw the awe and the fear reflected in their faces. The guide, Yegräyak, had gone. His torn clothing lay in a pile on the snow in front of him.

He opened his mouth to say something, but Chisholm interrupted him. She stepped forward, and without breaking his gaze, she quietly and carefully removed the crystal from his grasp. He saw the fear in her eyes, as well.

CHAPTER 14

They slid off the ice and came racing towards Kate, laughing and crowing. She giggled and ran to meet them.

She flew into Kareem's arms, and he swept her off her feet and swirled her in circles while she clung to his neck. He slowed and lowered her to the ground, then held her at arm's length. Apparently, she was none the worse for wear because he broke into the widest grin and embraced her once again.

"What took you so long?" Kate laughed.

"The *Hon'chai* kept breaking down," Jackson replied.

"*Hon'chai*? Where'd you get *Hon'chai* from?"

"Streikker was right behind us. He came in the front door as we went out the back. We 'found' them in the barn and thought we needed them more than he did."

"That's not the only thing we found," said Kareem. He held out a heavy staff intricately carved from a length of dense ebony wood. "It was out in the snow, but I guess you knew that."

"Didn't you recognise it?" asked Sigrid.

"Of course," Kate said. She searched along the wall of ice down which she'd slid. She saw him, sitting on the top, watching them. "It's his."

They turned to see whom she was looking at. Sigrid squealed with delight and waved.

"Ohmigod! It's Hawklight!"

Kareem glanced at Kate. He'd been with her the whole time she had been overtly hostile towards Hawklight, and had witnessed the subsequent sorrow that had stained her heart when she heard he'd been killed.

Kate felt his gaze and flushed briefly in embarrassment.

"We're good again," she whispered.

"General Siobhan will be pleased to hear that," he whispered back.

Hawklight slid down the ice, landed on his feet, and strode towards them. He'd not made thirty yards before Sigrid, Mia and Jackson had pounced on him and half-buried him in a group embrace.

His smile had returned with the Hawklight Kate had come to know and love. They escorted him, their arms linked, all chatting at once.

"I obviously need to go away more often, if this is any indication of the reception I'll get when I return," he laughed. He shook hands with Kareem. "It's good to see you again, my friend."

"And you, Captain."

"I was counting on you." Hawklight nodded towards the two prone bears. "That was good work."

"They're only fast asleep, but I couldn't have managed on my own. Sigrid had to help. One blast wouldn't have stopped either of them." He held out Hawklight's staff. "I believe this is yours," he said. He reached behind his back and withdrew another familiar staff from the sheath slung behind him. "And this is yours," he added.

He handed Rhyanon to Kate.

"We found your campsite and tracked you from there. There's not much left of your *Urgut*, I'm afraid. And then, when I saw the two sets of *Aelouskah* tracks, I was certain we'd be too late to save you."

"You know about them?" Kate asked.

"I've heard about them. I just hoped you'd be lucky enough to escape them, although now I know why," he said, acknowledging Hawklight. "Thank you!"

Kate was miffed. "And I suppose I didn't have anything to do with it."

Kareem grinned. "Well, you might have talked them to death; at least convinced them to see the error of their ways."

She slapped him playfully on the arm.

They trudged back across the snow to the campsite where Hawklight had built the snow cave. Across from the collapsed dome, the snow was smeared with blood, and the ruined, torn remains of the unfortunate *Urgut* were trampled and half-buried.

Hawklight studied the afternoon sky.

"How long will those bears be out?" he asked Kareem.

"Two days . . . three, possibly. We hit them pretty hard."

"In that case, we should stay the night here, then try and pick up the trail again tomorrow."

"Can we at least move further away from that?" Kate asked, pointing at the dead *Urgut*.

"We'll bury it with snow once we've retrieved and repacked whatever supplies we might need."

Kate, Sigrid and Jackson pitched three small tents while Kareem, Mia and Hawklight sorted through the remaining supplies. Once the tents were up, the three of them piled snow to cover the carcass. It could remain buried until another wandering scavenger smelled it and dug it up.

They caught up on events after the sun had set. Kareem had led them away from Poluostrov. They'd made good progress mounted on the *Hon'chai*, and had swung well to the south again. Just before the full force of the blizzard had descended upon them,

Kareem found an abandoned hut, half buried in the ground, supported by low sod walls and a tin roof.

They had sheltered inside, bringing the *Hon'chai* with them. It had been crowded, but the thick fur and the body heat of the animals had kept them warmer than they'd had a right to expect. The shallow hut had been completely buried by the snow, further insulating it from the raging chill factor of the tumultuous, freezing winds.

Kareem had never given up hope of finding Kate again. He believed she'd survive the blizzard; believed that somehow, she'd manage to escape her captor. Yet these thoughts almost drove him crazy with impatience. He was digging the party out from beneath all the accumulated snow before the blizzard had fully abated.

There were no tracks to follow, no spoor of any sort. He gambled on the fact that Kate would be carried south, and pressed onwards in that direction. They would have missed the campsite by a good couple of hundred yards, had Sigrid's sharp eyes not spotted the distant red stain in the snow. The rest was history.

Hawklight spent some time questioning Kareem about Streikker: how many men were with him? How close behind were they? How long before Streikker rounded up the loose *Hon'chai?* How did Streikker know to chase them all the way to Poluostrov? Clearly, he was worried about the pursuit. They would need to keep as many eyes peeled behind them as were ranged ahead seeking their quarry. It was a further complication he could do without.

They checked that the four *Hon'chai* had been secured and were made comfortable before they settled into their tents. The tents were small, two-person affairs, pegged close together, with their tapered ends pointed into the wind to reduce drag.

Jackson and Mia shared one of the tents, and Sigrid removed any further dithering over the sleeping arrangements by throwing her blankets in with Hawklight.

"I hope you don't snore," she said to him as she disappeared behind the tent flaps.

Kate smiled at Kareem as she bent and pushed her blankets ahead of her into the third tent. She kicked off her boots at the entrance, removed her heavy jacket and pulled the blankets up around her shoulders.

Kareem crawled in behind her and zipped the tent shut. Kate felt him remove his outer layer of clothing and tuck it beneath his head for a pillow. He lay on his back and pulled his blanket over himself and stared at the roof of the tent.

She smiled to herself, turned away from him onto her side, and backed her body up against his. There was a moment of uncertainty before he turned towards her, and his arm snaked beneath the blanket to cuddle her.

The brilliance of the sunlight reflecting off the snow cut through the tent to announce the dawning of a new day. Kate's eyes opened with the light. She was still lying on her side, and Kareem's arm was still tight around her waist. It was as though neither of them had moved throughout the night.

She turned onto her back, and Kareem rolled away. He opened his eyes sleepily, grinned at her and then rolled onto his side.

She ran her hand through her hair, scratching at her scalp, then shuffled to the entrance and laced her boots, unzipped the tent, and crawled out into the clear morning air. She stretched to ease the stiffness from her hip and shoulders, and then yawned to clear her head.

There wasn't a cloud in the sky, which was a deep azure blue, rich and colourful. The low angle of the sun glinted off the snow and stung her eyes with its brightness. She squinted into the light, feeling the warmth of the rays on her skin.

One of the *Hon'chai* snorted out to her left. Someone was already up and about and tending to them.

"Jackson?" she called softly, not wishing to intrude on the sleep of the others.

He turned and slipped his hood from his head. Streikker smiled back at her and raised the tip of his staff. He placed one finger over his lips to warn her not to cry out in alarm and then raised his arm.

One by one, his soldiers emerged from the snow. They were dressed in snow camouflage to blend in with the surroundings. They'd done a good job. They'd crept up and encircled the camp, and Kate hadn't spotted any of them.

She tried to think to warn her friends, but to alarm them would be to invite a bloodbath. Streikker's men were poised and ready for battle; they'd been bruised from one encounter already and weren't about to let that happen twice.

Streikker crept up alongside her.

"Call them out," he whispered. "Don't alarm anyone! If they start something, I'll take no prisoners!"

He prodded her with his staff.

"Hey! Everybody up! It's getting late already!" She tried to keep her voice light and playful.

She heard Jackson mumble something like "Go back to sleep!" but it seemed to do the trick. There were various rustling sounds from within all three tents, and lowered voices.

A zip was pulled, and both Mia and Jackson poked their heads out. Whatever they'd planned to say to her died on their lips as two staffs were tucked beneath their chins. Jackson's face clouded with anger when he saw who was standing beside Kate; Ethan was his best friend.

Kareem was next to be cornered. Streikker's staff pointed at Kate's head was all that it took to contain him.

Sigrid backed out of the tent and had stood before she realised they weren't alone. Streikker spoke aloud.

"Go and stand with the others."

Sigrid shuffled over to where the rest of them stood. Jackson put out his arm and pulled her close to his side.

Streikker poked Kate in the back. "You too," he said.

She stood defiantly beside Kareem. None of them showed fear. Streikker was impressed.

"Finally, the 'Famous Five' have been run to ground. You've been charged with treason. It's a capital offence. Whether you're executed now or later is of no importance to me."

"Treason?" Kate exclaimed. "By whose definition? Carter? Do you have any idea what we've been trying to do?"

"I know what I need to know, but I know enough. I know the Council of Hogarth fears you. I know you've sabotaged a peace plan that was crucial to an expedition led by Captain Hawklight. I know that some of these supplies you carry could only have come from the original expedition. I know we can't account for your whereabouts when Hawklight and his party were murdered. It's common knowledge that you and he were no longer on speaking terms because he opposed your intentions to seize power for yourself. He was my friend. I'm here to see that justice is served."

"What—the same justice you served to two of our friends? Since when did the army of Hogarth support arbitrary executions?"

Streikker scowled at Kate.

"Your friends are alive, Miss Gallagher. They've been accompanied back to Hogarth where they will eventually stand trial for treason, as will all of you.' He paused. "Of course, you might also choose to stand and fight, or attempt an escape." He pointed his staff directly at Kate's chest. "Well?"

"Tell me, Hans, how would you go about explaining away the death of my assassin to the Council with me standing by your side?"

Hawklight crawled from the tent.

"Nathaniel! What the—"

Hawklight held up his hand. "First, have your men lower their weapons before somebody gets hurt," he said. He stepped across and embraced the dumbstruck Streikker in a bear hug. "Good to see you again, Hans!"

"My god! Hawklight, you're alive!"

"I see you've met my *friends*," Hawklight replied, emphasising the last word. "Apparently the slight misunderstanding between Kate and me has been blown out of all proportion. I'm curious how you came by that explanation."

"But we have witnesses who saw you killed!"

"They didn't see anything. They were knocked unconscious. They just assumed everyone else was dead, that's all. And Kate had nothing to do with it."

Streikker shook his head as if to clear the clutter of thoughts before beginning again.

"So, Commander Carter—"

"—has been a very naughty boy!" Hawklight finished his sentence for him. "Hans, I'm surprised at you. If Kate had intended to seize absolute rule, why would she throw Varak's crystal away? Maybe you need to ask her this question yourself."

Streikker frowned and turned to Kate. He could feel more clutter building inside his head.

"No one has the right to absolute rule through fear," Kate replied. "Not Varak, not me, and certainly not Carter."

"Carter?"

"Carter found a geologist who knows where to find the source of the crystal Varak used. He wants it for himself. Nathaniel only agreed to lead the expedition because he intended to destroy the source once it had been located. We're here to help him do that. But there are others who want that crystal as badly as Carter, *and* they are ahead of us, *and* they have the geologist. It's up to you, Captain Streikker. What are you going to do about it?"

Streikker pinched the bridge of his nose with his gloved hand as if he'd just developed a searing headache, which, in one sense, he had. Suddenly nothing made sense. Part of him strongly suspected he'd been sold a lie. He stood his men down and gestured to the students to join him and Hawklight.

"Okay," he said, "from the top. Tell me everything. If I think any one of you is lying, we go back to Hogarth. That includes you, Nathaniel."

Streikker learned the truth behind Kate's estrangement with Hawklight, along with the rest of the story. Everything he heard backed up his original misgivings, and his respect for the Gallagher girl grew as each event unfolded.

He'd been in command of one of the units of soldiers pinned between the armies of Hornshurst and Cherath. Carter was nowhere to be seen, but the woman Mirayam, and her ardent troupe of students had been the ones to hold the troops together through sheer strength of will. Calling them traitors under the circumstances that were revealed was nothing short of ludicrous.

He didn't take much convincing.

"We know one member of the party," Kate said. "He's extremely dangerous. He couldn't have put this all together by himself, though. Whoever has helped him is the one to fear. If the crystal falls into their hands, it will be as bad as having Varak back, maybe even worse. And this time, Hogarth won't stand a chance."

"Then it's up to us to stop them," Streikker replied.

"You agree the source of the crystal must be destroyed?" Hawklight asked him. "It cannot be permitted to fall into anyone's hands—theirs, or ours," he added.

Streikker nodded his agreement. "It must be done!"

"Then let's get going," Kate said. "We're wasting time!"

"Fine. Incidentally, where *are* we going?"

"We have to pick up their spoor. In this terrain, we could miss them easily by just a mile or two. We can't afford to let them know we're coming."

Streikker surveyed the snowy flats. "Impossible. The wind would have covered everything with snow."

"Come now, Hans, you're just getting technical. Since when did that ever stop us?" Hawklight grinned at Kareem, who looked like a dog waiting to fetch a ball tossed by its master.

"You take the left, I'll take the right, Hans, the middle. The rest can follow with the *Hon'chai*."

"So you think there's a chance we'll pick up their trail?"

"Look and learn, Hans. Look and learn!"

Kareem spotted the faint indentations out to his left late in the afternoon. To anyone but an expert tracker, the snow would have looked fresh and flat, but both Hawklight and Streikker read the subtle changes with ease.

They conducted a careful examination of the spoor, moving up and down the line, careful not to contaminate the tracks with their own.

The trail continued to point south. The sun, which had really only hovered above the horizon in its path across the sky, was about to set, and they needed daylight to follow the faint spoor.

"Will it still be visible tomorrow?" Streikker asked.

Hawklight checked the sky. It had remained cloudless, and the wind had dropped throughout the day.

"We should be fine," he said. "I think we're getting close. We're going to need to be alert from now on." He glanced at Streikker's white camouflage. "Are there any more of those?"

"I think one of the *Hon'chai* is carrying some. We can check."

They pitched camp about twenty yards from the trail. Streikker had eleven men with him. Ignoring the geologist and guides, it pitted eighteen of them against eight of their foes. Much better odds, Kate thought.

The aurora above their heads shimmered with renewed enthusiasm. Kate had never seen anything more beautiful. It had begun with a faint pinkish glow just on dusk, and then grew in intensity as night fell. It hovered miles above their heads, yet the night was so clear that Kate felt she could reach out and touch it. She lay in Kareem's arms and gave herself over to the splendid light show.

"What do you suppose that is?" she asked Kareem. It looked like a channel down which the exquisite light could travel to caress the featureless snowy plateau.

Kareem frowned. It lay in the direction of the tracks they'd discovered. It was too much of a coincidence. He called Hawklight over.

"I don't know. It could be ten miles away, probably closer to fifteen. I think you're right, though. Anything that can distort the aurora to that degree has to be powerful indeed! We'll know tomorrow, for sure."

Kate suddenly felt uneasy. She had a bad feeling about Hawklight's 'tomorrow'. She knew instinctively that the Zimmerman expedition had already discovered the source.

If they had a working crystal, Kate understood there would be no stopping them. In the battle with Varak, she'd disarmed him by stealing his prized stone, a skill she'd honed on Earth because she'd been an astute pickpocket. Neither Copely nor any of the others would let her get that close to them. Besides, it was a skill that had grown rusty through disuse. Kate believed she had given up that past life for good.

She pulled Kareem's arm tighter about her body as if, in doing so, she could ward off the sense of foreboding.

"What if they have a crystal?" she whispered.

"Then we'll have to stop them from using it."

"I'm scared."

"You'd be foolish not to be."

"Are you scared too?"

"Where you're concerned, I'm afraid I'm just foolish. Don't worry. I'm certain everything will work out in the end," Kareem reassured her.

He kissed her cheek and his lips were warm against her cold skin.

They set off at first light, like ghosts in a mist except for the sharp shadows cast by the sun. Hawklight had been hoping that an overcast day would mask their approach, but the sky was as blue and cloudless as the day before. Anyone keeping watch would spot them two miles away.

They left two soldiers behind to watch over the *Hon'chai*. Their deep red-brown fur stood out markedly against the white canvas of the snow. Hawklight thought they needn't have bothered as he watched his stark, black shadow match him stride for stride across the snow.

He shared the same misgivings as Kate. Copely, armed with a crystal, would be unbeatable, unless they managed to take him out first. His only hope was that their enemy would be too preoccupied and too careless to have posted watchmen. If so, they still retained the element of surprise

Ahead of them, the horizon adopted a jagged profile—another glacier, this one sweeping a broad swathe left to right. The trail they followed didn't deviate.

Two hundred yards out, Hawklight signalled a halt. He could make out a faint line of fluttering red flags that seemed to mark a passage across the glacier. At first, he suspected a trap, but then the voice of reason prevailed. If Copely didn't suspect he was being followed, there'd be no reason to set a trap. The flags simply marked the safe passage.

That would certainly speed things up. Negotiating the glacier would have needed to be a cautious exercise. He waved his group onwards again.

He called a second halt up on the glacier itself. This time, he signalled Kareem to come forward and join him.

Something wasn't right. Kareem sidled over to where Hawklight was squatting, and examined the trail.

"How many?" Hawklight asked.

"I make ten."

"So do I. I counted twelve from Poluostrov. That means two are missing."

"Some guides, maybe?"

"That would be my guess, as well. Trouble is, we should have spotted them if they'd deserted. There's no sign of any tracks heading the other way."

There could be one reason only for that.

They found the point where the tracks of the party deviated from south for the first time. Hawklight pulled the party together

"We're getting closer," he said quietly. "No noise from now on. Hand signals only. Unsheathe your staffs."

Two hours past midday they heard voices. A whip crack snapped the air, and a high-pitched voice screamed, *"Pull, you idiots!"* That wasn't Copely, but it was a voice used to issuing orders!

Hawklight gathered everyone together. Their enemy was no more than a couple of hundred yards away. He split the soldiers into two groups of five and sent them out to each flank in a semi-circular arc. He waited with the students for twenty minutes to allow the men to slip into position unseen.

He spaced the students to his left and right, far enough apart that any blasts wouldn't disable the entire group. It also gave the impression of overwhelming numbers: at least, he hoped so.

They heard a muffled *whuumff!* of an explosion and froze. Hawklight feared one of the soldiers had been spotted, but they heard no further cries of alarm. They began to pick their way quickly across the uneven surface littered with crushed and twisted ice forms.

Kate kept her face pressed close to the ice as she crept forward. She could hear a regular *tap-tap-tapping* from a hammer hitting something solid, although she dared not think what it might signify. She had Hawklight to her left and Kareem to her right. Both moved like stalking panthers across the slippery surface, and she had to hustle to keep up.

Hawklight found cover against a protruding ice block and signalled for the others to do the same. Kate held tightly to Rhyanon and inched forward on her belly to where she'd spotted a depression in the glacier the size of a child's paddling pool.

She released a long, slow breath, and realised that she'd been holding it as she'd crept forward. She glanced about, but there was no sign of the others. She decided to risk a peek and raised her head slowly. As she did so, the words she'd believed she'd never hear again drifted above the ice.

"Dimitte bestias pascere in vita!"

She noticed them standing, grouped together, staring at the unmistakable figure of Copely. A glowing red, gelatinous bubble emanating from the tip of his staff had enveloped another man.

She stared, horrified but transfixed as the scene unfolded. The sounds of the victim's screams as the creatures flew at him and bit and tore him apart were too much to bear. She clamped her gloved hands across her ears and squeezed her eyes shut, but she couldn't prevent the image of Jaime being obliterated by Varak from soaring up out of the depths of her repressed memories. She could still see him writhing as his life force was sucked steadily away while she remained hidden, powerless to prevent it.

A new crystal had been forged, and Copely had fed it for the first time. The spectre of Varak had been resurrected. They were too late!

The sounds of screaming had died away, but the image of Jaime lingered. She saw his smile, the way she'd always remember him, but her guilt—her complicity in his death—snuffed it out.

Kate rose to her feet.

"Nooooooo!" she cried.

CHAPTER 15

Everyone turned towards the sound.

Kate stood shaking uncontrollably, fixated on Copely who appeared to be caught in the last vestiges of a trance.

Copely couldn't believe he was staring at the Gallagher girl—his nemesis. Her hood had fallen from her face, and her long black hair curled around her shoulders. He'd recognised her immediately, and his hatred rose like bile in his throat.

Two others had appeared either side of her. He could have wept. Hawklight stood looking down on him as well. *How?* He'd taken care of him personally. He'd watched as the bolt from his staff had exploded into the sleeping form and had incinerated it. He'd picked up the shattered helmet that had been split in half from the force of the blast. He remembered how delightfully satisfying it had felt despite a nagging doubt at the time that it had all been too easy!

Chisholm was stunned. She'd expected Riegel; she'd scanned the horizon for a sight of him and seen nothing. She'd ordered Abayomi to remain vigilant in case she'd missed him. He'd seen nothing. How did they miss these three—?

One by one, the others stood as if they'd sprung from seeds planted in the snow. White shapes detached themselves from the hewn chunks of ice pushed up as the glacier had squeezed its way north. Chisholm counted six, then another five, then five more. Their staffs were trained in on the tight knot of mercenaries.

Marcus sat off to one side, huddled protectively over the block of Zimmermanite. He knew, for sure, it was about to slip from his grasp forever. He cupped handfuls of snow and started to cover the stone as unobtrusively as possible.

The crystal sliver that Griselda had taken from Copely slipped from her loose grasp and fell into the snow by her feet.

"Stay where you are and drop your weapons!" Hawklight called. He'd noticed the mercenaries shuffling apart. They already knew they were too close together, and that one well-aimed blast could take out half of them.

They hesitated, and then kept shuffling. Two let their staffs fall and raised their hands.

It was the moment Hendrikx had been waiting for—any form of distraction. He let loose a blast and watched it blow one of the white-hooded soldiers into the air before he dived sideways for cover.

The one shot was the signal for mayhem. Another of Streikker's men was hit in the chest. He tottered where he stood, then disappeared, leaving behind a pile of clothing that smouldered before bursting into flame.

One of the mercenaries was flattened by two simultaneous pulses that flung him through the air, twisting him as though he'd been slammed from behind by an out of control vehicle. The remnants of his uniform fluttered onto the snow, laid out in a line that marked the final second of his life.

Kareem launched himself at Kate and caught her just below the knees from behind. She crumpled on top of him as a well aimed pulse flashed past inches from her head. They rolled together back down into the depression out of the line of fire.

Copely dropped to the snow and pawed at it furiously. His hand hit something hard, and he gripped it. The crystal was still vibrating with the residual warmth generated by the remains of Yegräyak's soul as it was being forcibly realigned within.

He twisted to his feet and ran like a jackrabbit, jinking sideways randomly to prevent anyone getting a clear bead on him. Several tried. The glacial ice exploded either side of him, showering him with icy shrapnel that tore through his clothing and cut him superficially, but didn't slow him down. He crested a ridge of ice and dived headfirst over it, propelled by another poorly aimed blast.

Griselda Chisholm moved remarkably quickly for such a stout woman. She rushed sideways, not returning the fire which would have drawn the attention of their attackers. She tripped and rolled in a shallow snowdrift before sliding into a crack in the ice about four feet deep. She kept her head low and followed the line of the crack, which led obliquely away from the fire fight.

She had witnessed another three of her men scattered to the wind along with one of the soldiers in white. Hendrikx and Abayomi had managed to survive, and were drawing fire. From the sounds of the battle, she guessed they were covering each other as they slowly retreated backwards off the glacier.

She paused to catch her breath and consider her options. She could hide, but she knew they would find her; they'd tracked her all the way from Hogarth, so a few miles across the snow would be child's play for them.

Her dream of unlimited power had slipped away, and she had no one to blame but herself. She had surrounded herself unnecessarily with fools. It seemed as if the entire expedition had been jinxed since the day of the ambush, the day Zimmerman had been kidnapped.

Zimmerman! He'd been huddled and isolated at the start of the attack. No one had paid him the slightest attention. It was as if they'd known he wouldn't present a threat to them, so they'd ignored him. He'd been heaping snow over the stone just before she'd dived to safety.

Griselda had witnessed the power of the crystal fragment wielded by Copely. She knew if she could make it safely back to where Zimmerman cowered, she could wield the same power herself.

She listened again for the shouts of men, and the occasional explosions. The battlefield had moved towards the edge of the glacier as soldiers in white uniforms pursued Hendrikx and Abayomi. They were being far more cautious now, unwilling to risk an ambush by their desperate quarry. It was time to make a move.

She rose tentatively and scanned her surroundings for any sign of movement. She had managed to crawl a hundred and fifty feet further towards the middle of the glacier. All the action was to the other side, out of sight.

She could see Zimmerman huddled in the snow. He hadn't moved from the spot. He looked to be rocking back and forth on his haunches, but he was too far away for her to be certain. There was no one else with him.

Time was running out for Griselda, so she had to take a gamble. She leapt from the trench that cut through the ice and sprinted towards Zimmerman. She held her staff ready to blast anyone who stepped into her path, but apparently, they were all chasing the ongoing exchanges of fire.

Zimmerman gave no sign he'd even seen her. He appeared to be in a catatonic state of shock with his arms wrapped tightly around himself.

Chisholm bent and gripped his jacket and shook him roughly. She pushed him and let go, and he toppled backwards into the snow. It did the trick. He gazed up at her as if he'd just awoken.

"Where's the stone?" she hissed at him, and he recoiled in fear. His hand brushed a pile of snow beside him in a gentle caress before he seemed to snap to his senses and dug frantically, revealing the blue-coloured, crystalline lump.

Chisholm spotted the wooden handle of his hammer protruding from the snow. She grabbed it and thrust it at him.

"Break me off a lump, and be quick!" She underscored the threat by pointing her staff at his face.

He blanched and swallowed and nodded his head rapidly. "Now!"

He ran his fingers nimbly across the surface of the stone, feeling the lumps and ridges, searching for the site that would chip away cleanly with one rap of the hammer. His fingers found the spot, a slice about six inches in length, running parallel to the magnetic lines of force.

Marcus was back in his element. He forgot about the threat hanging over him as he appreciated the natural simplicity about the crystalline lines forged during that ancient solar incident. It was a rare thing of great beauty that the geologist in him hungered to exploit. He raised the hammer, and brought it down sharply above the point he'd determined would cause the crystal to fracture cleanly.

The shard of crystal plopped into the snow, gleaming like cut blue glass across its broken face. He reached for it and couldn't suppress the smile of admiration as the crystal caught the sunlight.

"Leave it where it is!"

Hawklight had appeared from nowhere. Zimmerman's hand hovered above the fragment, halted by the curt command.

Griselda was caught completely off guard. Her staff was still tilted towards Zimmerman, and Hawklight was somewhere behind her. She turned her head to face him.

He was no more than twenty feet away from her, and his staff was aimed at her back.

He shook his head.

"It's over. Let it go."

She searched for any sign of compassion in his eyes but saw none. His entire face was devoid of any emotion whatsoever. She thought about surrender—the long trip back, followed by the prospect of a life of imprisonment. Her fall from grace would be complete as she degenerated into early senility brought about by the brutal harshness of prison existence. That had never featured as a part of her grand plan.

Hawklight recognised the subtle change in her eyes.

"Don't do it!" he warned.

His eyes were deep black pits. Griselda was struck by the strange deadness about them.

She smiled sadly at him.

"Don't—"

She pivoted and leaned to one side and brought her staff through a slicing arc towards Hawklight.

"Exstinguere!"

The pulse slammed into her side beneath her outstretched arm. She felt a raging fireball sear a path through her chest. The seat of her soul, the cavity where her heart would have beaten, was obliterated in an instant, and the ties that kept her soul intact unknotted and flew apart.

She was unable to breathe, and felt herself being drawn towards the black holes of Hawklight's eyes. They seemed to expand outwards, and she was on a roller coaster, racing towards them out of control. In no time at all, the blackness was upon her, and she was swept away into the dark void of total nothingness.

Hendrikx had tried to sucker punch the raven-haired girl with a quick blast, and he'd narrowly missed decapitating her. It had been a desperate move, and it had drawn return fire from most of the soldiers. He decided to retreat, taking aim at anything that moved.

Kate risked a glance above the lip of the shallow depression, but Hendrikx had disappeared. Her heart sank. So, too, had Copely.

"Copely's gone!" she exclaimed. "I bet he took the crystal with him. We have to find him!"

Kareem knew better than to try and keep her from harm's way. It would have been a waste of time.

They scrambled out of the depression and headed to the spot where Copely had been standing. Kareem pointed out the tread of his boots in the snow as they disappeared off into the maze of ice formations out on the glacier.

"We should split up," he suggested. "Try and come up from the side. With luck, we'll surprise him."

"Be careful," she warned. "We keep underestimating him."

Kate moved out to the right. She could see how Copely had twisted through a random path, which had saved him from being obliterated. She knew that he would have retrieved the crystal, and was now a force to be reckoned with. It would take some time to harness the true potential of the crystal's power, but already she'd seen enough to know he'd be more than a match in a show down. Their only chance was to ambush him.

She cast around for Hawklight, but he was nowhere to be seen. The only person still visible was the geologist, who was rocking back and forth in the snow. He posed no threat. The real threat was somewhere out amongst the ice formations, gathering the courage to step into battle.

She kept her profile as low to the ground as possible, and flitted through the broken ice, which offered some form of cover. Kareem had gone left and was out of her sight.

She rested her back against an angular pillar of ice and listened for any sound. The explosions near the edge of the glacier were distracting, but she concentrated on filtering them out, focussing instead on any more subtle sounds like footfalls across the crusted snow. The air was still, and the noise of her breathing seemed magnified.

Kate closed her eyes and forced herself to calm down. Her hands tightened around Rhyanon's carved handle, and she felt the faint buzz of anticipation pass back along the wooden shaft.

She gradually worked her way deeper into the belly of the ice maze. Copely could be anywhere; he could have chosen any number of different paths to follow. The telltale tread of his boots had disappeared when the wind blown snow gave way to hard-packed ice, but Kate was relying on a kind of sixth sense to propel her forward. Her destiny on Bexus had been so intertwined with Copely's that she knew she was bound to come face to face with him again sooner or later.

It was sooner than she'd expected.

As she crept forward cautiously from behind a block of ice, Rhyanon was blown from her grip and flung against a translucent ice wall across from her. The staff was driven with such force that it snapped in two, and both pieces clattered onto the ice floor.

Copely stepped out from his hiding place. His staff was pointed at Kate one-handed. He raised his other hand to reveal the blue coloured crystal shard nestled in his palm.

He grinned across at her and said, "You're nicked!" He chuckled at his own joke, which had become a kind of greeting between them.

He glanced at her broken staff, then at the stone held in his outstretched hand. "I'm still getting the hang of this," he confessed. "It's much more powerful than I'd imagined. Once I'm done with you, I'm going to turn it against your precious Captain Hawklight. He won't survive a second time."

"Tell him yourself," Kate said. "He's standing right behind you."

It wasn't much, but it was just enough. Copely faltered, and his head swivelled briefly, driven by fear. Kate flung herself backwards behind the huge block of ice, just as Copely bellowed from the deception and fired.

"Exstinguere!"

Ordinarily, it was a killing blow, but the crystal in his hand intensified its power. The shock wave stunned Kate, and half the enormous block of ice disintegrated. Kate hunched into a ball and covered her head as chunks of ice rained down around her. She was partially deafened by the noise of the blast, but through it all, she could hear the sound of Copely's maniacal laughter.

"Come out, come out, wherever you are," he jeered, and directed another blast at the other end of the crumpled block.

Kate shook her head to try and clear the ringing in her ears. She was trapped, with nowhere to run to.

"Oh, Mama, what am I going to do?" she whispered. Her only hope was to try and stall him long enough for Kareem to come up from behind. He wouldn't fall for the same trick twice, so maybe there was a chance.

She staggered to her feet and stepped out from cover. She wasn't about to die like a trapped rat in a cage.

"Very good, Miss Gallagher. You nearly had me there."

The banter stopped as if Copely realised that there were others hunting him down who might have heard the explosions.

"Goodbye, Miss Gallagher. I'd like to say it's been a pleasure knowing you. Yes, I'd *like* to say it, but . . ." He shrugged and smiled and pointed his staff at her.

Kate raised both hands in front of her face as if to protect herself from the imminent blast. Her final thought was of her mother's smiling face, coupled with the last words she ever spoke to Kate. *"Know that I will always be with you."*

"Dimitte bestias pascere in vita!"

Copely's staff flashed, and a blinding, searing pulse of energy flew at Kate. Kate expected instant oblivion. Instead, she felt a sharp pain in her left hand as a protective aura burst outwards from the ring given to her by her mother, just before Siobhan was confined inside the *Toki-Moai* of Hornshurst.

It appeared as a golden sheen, the colour of her original aura on Bexus, and formed a shield against the lingering string of high-energy plasma trying to penetrate through to Kate. Unimaginable forms inside the plasma battered at the shield, hungrily seeking their prey, but the shield held.

It began to warp and buckle in places, and Kate feared it would be a matter of scant seconds before the shield was disabled, but then the buckling began to assume a form of its own.

The outline of her mother's face appeared. Siobhan's mouth opened, and her voice echoed across the ice.

"Ka—aa—ate!"

It was accompanied by a growling discord, like the collective anger of a mob. More faces appeared, directed outwards at Copely—men and women with the grizzled, stoic features of ancient warriors.

The shield advanced towards Copely. He tried to disengage the charm, but the plasma rope hummed like an open passage down which the shield could travel. His fist gripped the handle of his staff as his energy turned in on itself like an electric shock, locking his fingers in place.

He retreated, but a sheer ice wall blocked his escape. He was trapped. His arm trembled under the strain, and his other hand bled sparks where the sharp, fractured edges of the crystal sliced into his skin.

"Mama!" Kate cried, but her voice was lost in the growing din of outraged voices. The shield was a mass of faces, led by Siobhan, lunging at Copely like Rottweilers straining against their leashes. They snarled and roared at him, driven insatiably by the battle cries from some distant and long-forgotten battle.

Copely tried to summon the killing stroke, but the command caught in his throat and was choked by the fear that gripped his soul. He knew his resolve had weakened beyond revival, and the faces in the shield sensed the weakness and drove forward with renewed intensity. They were inches from the tip of his staff, which suddenly burst into flames where the energy flow had bottlenecked.

The skin of his hand began to peel with the heat, but he couldn't drop the staff. Kate could see his terrorised, contorted face through the shield as he fought for control, knowing it to be a meaningless last measure to survive the onslaught.

Siobhan's voice cut keenly through the wall of noise.

"Nevermore!"

The shield impaled itself on the end of Copely's fiery staff, and the circuit was closed. A shaft of terrible red light lit Copely from within as it coursed through his body and down the arm gripping the crystal. His high-pitched scream reverberated around the ice, and he burst apart in a cascade of showering sparks. The crystal in his grip exploded, and thousands of tiny shards punctured the ice in a wave of shrapnel.

The furore dissipated as, one by one, the faces disappeared from the shield. Siobhan's was the last to leave as the umbrella-like aura slowly vanished.

Kate was left staring at the golden ring around her finger. She didn't understand what had just happened, or why. The sound of Copely's staff fizzing in a pool of melted ice brought her to her senses.

A pile of smouldering ash was all that remained of Copely. She sank to her knees and stared at the black stain on the ice. Tears of relief welled in her eyes with the vivid memory of her mother standing protectively between her and oblivion. Throughout the entire journey, Siobhan had never wavered from her side.

A shout startled her, and she turned to see Kareem skating down the wall of ice. He ran to her, his keen eyes taking in the scene.

"You're okay!"

She nodded.

"Copely?"

Kate shook her head.

Kareem embraced her tightly. He'd heard the explosions and had feared he would be too late to save her. But then, she hadn't needed him. He saw Rhyanon lying shattered in two pieces. There was something else though, something so emotive that it gripped his insides. He was no stranger to its intensity.

"The *Toki-Moai!* What happened here?"

Kate held up the ring, still warm to the touch. Kareem rotated it about her finger.

"Mum appeared. There were others, as well."

"This ring your mother gave you—it's a portal to the *Toki-Moai*. She brought the old warriors, as well. They would have had a score to settle with the bearer of the crystal." He smiled at her and lowered his voice. "Don't let the elders know. They'll want you to give it back."

"She must have known when she gave it to me," Kate mused. "She never told me."

Kareem looked at her strangely, appraising her as if he were seeing her through new lenses.

"What?"

He took her arm and gently pushed back the sleeve of her camouflage coat. He rolled up the thick woollen jersey she wore and exposed her bare skin. It was no longer patchy or mottled. Instead, it was bathed in the pure golden light that had marked her as unique when she'd first arrived on Bexus. It had happened while she was wielding the power of the *Toki-Moai*. Her soul had been cleansed, her transgressions absorbed and shared among the ancient ones.

"I don't understand . . ." she stuttered.

Kareem smiled. "It's their way of thanking you for all the sacrifices you've made. This was never meant to be your war, but then again, no one but you could have fought it and won."

He helped her to her feet and kissed her lightly on the lips. He bent and retrieved her broken staff.

"Here. We'd better go and find the others, but stay close. Rhyanon's not going to be of much use, I'm afraid."

She paused and listened.

"It's gone quiet."

"Let's hope the battle is over."

There had been no quarter shown, no quarter given. Marcus Zimmerman was the only member of the expedition to have survived. Both Hendrikx and Abayomi had continued a fierce running battle and had inflicted a number of casualties before making a last ditch stand against overwhelming odds.

Kareem and Kate were waiting with Hawklight when Streikker's team straggled back. Four soldiers slumped wearily onto the ice and bowed their heads with exhaustion. Kate waited anxiously. None of the other students had returned.

"There they are!" cried Kareem. His sharp eyes had picked them out against the white backdrop of ice and snow. They were moving slowly—too slowly. Something was wrong.

Kate began running towards them. Mia and Jackson were to either side of the tall figure of Hans Streikker, who was carrying someone in his arms.

"No—oo!" Kate hardly recognised her own cry.

Sigrid was unconscious. Her head lolled from side to side as Streikker picked his way across the ice, although he tried to keep it nestled tightly against his chest. Her jacket had been burned by a fireball, and she was bleeding a steady stream of sparks despite the heavy bandaging.

Kate grabbed Sigrid's hand and held it to her cheek. It was cold against her skin, and waxen, like the hand on a shopfront mannequin. Jackson tried to comfort Kate, but she shrugged him away and continued to grip Sigrid's hand until Streikker laid her on a blanket on the snow at Hawklight's feet.

Tears had stained Kate's cheeks. She looked imploringly at Hawklight for assistance. He knelt beside Sigrid and carefully unwound the bandage while Streikker supported her. The movement and the pain caused her eyes to flutter open, and she moaned involuntarily.

The team medic had smashed a bowl full of Mother's Glove into a thick poultice in readiness. When the gaping wound was exposed, a steady stream of Sigrid's soul gushed from the opening. The medic worked feverishly to plug the wound with the thick green goo, and managed to reduce the torrent to a trickle before a fresh binding was applied.

The poultice worked as an anaesthetic, as well as a healing agent, and the pain that had sent Sigrid back into unconsciousness was eventually blocked. Sigrid was wrapped tightly in blankets and covered with a thick fur skin.

"What happened to her?" Kate asked. She hadn't left Sigrid's side throughout and sat stroking her forehead and wiping the sweat of a mild fever.

Jackson shook his head sadly. "I—she—she was hit. She wouldn't stay down! You know what she was like."

Sigrid woke again after dark. The group had camped on the glacier, unwilling to move her. The aurora blazed brightly overhead, and some continued to siphon down through the lump of Zimmermanite that sat exposed on the glacier just outside the campsite. The pulsing curtain of colour brought a smile to Sigrid's pale lips.

A hand drew a dry cloth across her forehead, and she turned her head. Kate sat beside her, stroking her head.

"Welcome back," she whispered.

"It's beautiful. I never thought I'd see them, y'know?"

Kate looked up. The lights made a swishing sound, like distant waves lapping against a shoreline.

"How about next time, we just join a tour group," she replied.

Sigrid smiled at the joke, and then winced as a sharp pain stabbed her side.

"I don't feel so good."

Kate bit her lip. Sigrid had begun to fade. She was pale, and the skin around her hand and wrist was practically translucent.

"You're going to be fine! You've survived *Abyssi* before now—this is nothing compared to that. You need to try and rest, but we'll get you home."

Sigrid searched for meaning in Kate's eyes.

"Please don't lie to me, Katie. I've never felt like this before. I feel—hollow inside."

A tear slipped from Kate's eye, and she wiped it away with her sleeve.

"I'm so scared," Sigrid whispered. "Don't leave me, please." She gripped Kate's hand tightly. Kate lifted the hand to her lips and kissed it.

"We won't leave you," she promised.

Jackson and Mia were sitting the other side of Sigrid. Kate lifted the blanket and crawled in beside Sigrid, and Mia did the same. Kate placed her arm beneath Sigrid's neck, and Mia snuggled against Sigrid's shoulder. Sigrid felt almost weightless, and the translucency had crept to her face. Her skin was glasslike, reflecting back the shimmering lights.

Sigrid slipped back into unconsciousness, and her breathing was steady and even. Kate stroked her hair with her fingertips.

Death on Bexus had always been violent and instantaneous in Kate's experience, apart from Jaime's. A short, sharp blast from the end of a staff was all it usually took to scatter a soul to all corners of the universe. Kate had assumed that's all there was to it.

Back on Earth, she had shared notions of an afterlife, but Bexus was not what she'd imagined. There had been life after death, and who was to say what came next? Her friend was slowly leaking away, and she was powerless to prevent it. Life was a powerful gift, created from crumbs of the universe, providing awareness for a minuscule speck in time. Sigrid was on the platform at the end of that journey, about to embark on a new adventure, or so Kate hoped. The alternative was too bleak to contemplate.

She held tightly to Sigrid, too afraid for her to let go. Eventually, Kate fell into a troubled sleep. When she awoke again just before the dawn, she could look across to Mia. Sigrid had slipped away during the night.

The mood of the camp was subdued. The soldiers were inured to death; it was a constant companion, and though they grew used to it, its cold hand brushed their hearts every time it came calling.

They went through the motions of packing their belongings away. Kate was numbed, and the exercise gave her something to focus on, rather than dwelling on the loss of her dear friend.

Their gear was assembled, and they stood in a circle surrounding the heavy crystalline lump dusted with snow. It looked to Kate like an oversized plum pudding.

Zimmerman was pleading his case.

"Please, you can't just destroy it. It's possibly the rarest crystalline solid in the entire universe. Take it back with us. Lock it away, if you must, but allow me the chance to examine it properly. Who knows what other properties it holds?"

Hawklight shook his head. Temptation and greed were human frailties that could never be ignored.

"Tell me how we get rid of it," he commanded. "That is your ticket back to Hogarth."

Marcus paused. He was being asked to choose: Zimmerman or Zimmermanite?

Eventually, he sighed.

"Let me examine it again," he grumbled.

He took the better part of an hour, feeling the surface of the stone, examining it with a hand lens. He called for men to rotate it, and then upend it. Once he was satisfied, he took his hammer and used the pick end to chisel a dimple at the intersection of two dark streaks running diagonally across the crystal's surface.

"It needs to be superheated, so first, find a rock to rest it on; otherwise it will melt through the glacier. Once it's red hot, one hard tap here—" he pointed to the dimple, "—will shatter it. That's the dangerous bit. It will be brittle, and the internal channels will be blocked, so it'll explode."

"That's my concern," said Hawklight.

"Nathaniel, there must be another way," Kate warned.

Hawklight gave her the same lopsided grin he'd used when he caught her flirting with Kareem. "Let's get busy, shall we?"

They hoisted the Zimmermanite lump and carried it onto a pan of bedrock that had been pushed upwards at the edge of the glacier. It cracked the rock base when they dropped it.

Streikker organised the party in a half-circle while Hawklight went in search of extra clothing and thick hides. Kate held Sigrid's staff carved from bleached hardwood. She could detect the familiar vibrations that were such a part of Sigrid's aura.

"*Incendere!*"

Streikker led off, and the others followed, one by one. They directed the streams of energy at the stone. At first, nothing happened. It was as if the stone were guzzling all of the energy like a thirsty child. But gradually, the intensity of the combined streams backed up as the internal channels were blocked by molten iron impurities, and the stone radiated heat.

Hawklight waddled back to the periphery of the circle. He looked ridiculous, like an overstuffed Michelin Man, and had used belts and rope to strap at least three toughened hides about his torso. He wore a helmet, and his face was masked by scarves and rags, leaving only a slit for his eyes. Kate would have laughed out loud in different circumstances. As it was, she wished he'd found more layers to protect himself.

The stone glowed a dull red. Streikker raised an eyebrow at Zimmerman, who'd been standing to one side.

"More!" he said.

The intense heat had melted all the snow from the surrounding rock, and water ran in tiny rivulets down the cracks in the weathered surface. By now, the crystal was an angry red colour. The dimple could be clearly seen as a dark spot on its surface.

"That should do it!" shouted Zimmerman. "But be quick!"

"Everybody back!" ordered Streikker as the hot plasma streams were extinguished. They backed away at the same time that Hawklight stepped forward, clutching the hammer in his gloved hand.

"Nathaniel, take care!" Kate cried as she retreated onto the glacier searching for a chunk of ice to shelter behind.

Hawklight shuffled into position, then sank to his knees beside the crystal. The rock beneath his legs was hot, and he could smell the fur from the protective outer hide layer as it singed and sizzled.

Already, the Zimmermanite had begun to cool. There was no time to waste. He found the blackened dimple and raised the hammer. He brought the blunt end down with all his strength, turning his head aside at the last possible moment.

The crystal exploded like a grenade, scattering thousands of pieces in every direction. Hawklight was blown backwards by the force of the explosion, and the shrapnel of flying stone shredded the outer layers of protective hide. The air whistled from the flying subsonic particles, which ricocheted off the ice, or landed with muffled puffs into the accumulated snowdrifts.

The last of the flying shards had barely passed before Kate was up and running towards the motionless, smoking form of Hawklight. She slid to a halt beside his body and ripped the layers of smouldering clothing from his torso. She burned her hands on slivers of hot stone trapped between the layers but hardly felt the pain.

She was joined by Streikker, Mia, Jackson and the medic, all frantically tearing and slicing the protective outer layers away.

Hawklight was fizzing from unseen puncture wounds beneath the clothing.

When he was stripped to the skin, he looked as it he'd been peppered with buckshot. Some shards of stone were halfway buried, their tapered ends sticking up above his skin. Kate and the others set about yanking them out while the medic smothered his belly and chest with Mother's Glove poultice.

Hawklight moaned and opened his eyes. A blade of flying stone had sliced a neat gouge about three inches just below his right eye. He blinked to keep out the sparks. Kate reached across and gathered a handful of green goo and plastered it over the wound.

He tried to sit up, but collapsed back onto the ice.

"How'd I do?" he asked groggily.

Kate giggled and threw her arms about his neck and gripped him tightly in an embrace, which lasted to a point where Kareem might have felt jealous. She released him, and shuffled around behind him and eased him into a half-seated position facing the anvil of bedrock.

There was no sign of the Zimmermanite mother lode. Scattered pieces dotted the landscape, glinting in the morning sunlight. Kareem had the hammer in his hand and was searching out any larger slivers that had survived the explosion. Any that he found, he placed on the bedrock and smashed with the hammer.

The superheating had caused the crystal to become extremely brittle. By the time Kareem had finished, what remained of the rock had been rendered useless. The spectre of Varak and his evil legacy—the potential to rule absolutely—had been singularly and spectacularly destroyed.

CHAPTER 16

Two months later, a shout went up around the walls of Hogarth as the first of the riders was spotted emerging from the Great Forest and crossing the grassy slopes on the other side of the ravine.

There were eleven riders in total. They dismounted on the open slope and walked beside their *Hon'chai*, which were shaggy and worn thin by the harsh conditions to the south. A cart carrying a group of handlers trundled across the stone bridge and made its way up the slope to meet them. The *Hon'chai* were turned loose, and left to graze contentedly under the watchful care of the handlers. The remaining meagre supplies were tossed into the back of the cart which then returned to the city.

Kate walked hand in hand with Kareem through the summer meadow. The sun streamed across their shoulders, so gloriously warm that it threatened to impose a laziness of spirit throughout the day, and Kate revelled in the simple pleasure that it brought. She'd had enough of the biting cold, the bleak landscapes, and the dampness and the depression. She was home again, and she couldn't hide the grin.

Hawklight and Hans Streikker led the band across the cobbled bridge, and beneath the towering stone ramparts where the massive iron gates stood ajar. A small crowd had gathered to cheer them through, although most of the citizens of Hogarth were ignorant of the circumstances surrounding their arrival and wondered what all the fuss was about. They shrugged and went about their business, stepping aside to allow the weary travellers to pass by.

The Council of Hogarth was in session, and one of the councillors was bleating tirelessly about the taxes levied against local businesses, in order to continue to fund a large standing army. Elward Carter sat at the head of the table with his eyes closed, bored by the pettiness of local politics, longing for the spotlight as the elder statesman among the city-states once more.

". . . And furthermore, the armies of Hornshurst and Cherath have since been substantially reduced. Gentlemen, there *is* no threat to our security any longer. The longer we continue to pay out for idle soldiers while honest businessmen languish from—"

The doors to the Chamber burst open, halting him in mid-sentence. The councillor looked like a startled fish with his mouth agape as Hawklight strode through.

The sudden din had startled Carter from his daydreams, and he was seized by panic when he saw who was striding across the room towards him.

"Commander Elward Carter, you are hereby under arrest for sedition."

Carter was quick to respond.

"Me?" Carter laughed derisively. He rounded on Hawklight. "You delusional hypocrite! You were the one placed in charge of an entire expedition of men. They lost their lives, and yet, here you are, safe and sound. That group was your responsibility, Captain! This is a case of gross dereliction of duty! I'll have you court-martialled for desertion while under attack." Flecks of spittle flew from his mouth as he screamed an order to the officer of the guard detail.

"Sergeant, arrest that coward!"

The Sergeant-At-Arms was momentarily nonplussed. Captain Hawklight was a decorated war hero. One thing the captain was *not* was a coward, yet he had just been given an order by the Supreme Commander of the army to arrest the officer. He nodded to two aides, and they stepped forward to intercept Hawklight, their staffs held at the ready.

"Stand down, soldier! That is an order!" Hans Streikker stormed into the room and confronted the sergeant.

The Sergeant-At-Arms was totally confused by this stage. His two aides looked to him for guidance, but he was incapable of a decision. All eyes were on him. This kind of incident was well above his pay grade.

"Sergeant!" Carter's voice snapped behind him. "I order you to—"

He never finished. Kate Gallagher stepped through the door, accompanied by Marcus Zimmerman. The words choked in Carter's throat, and he almost passed out with the shock of the sight of her.

He watched as she approached the table. Her eyes never left his. She pushed past the sergeant who made no moves to stop her. She halted at the opposite side of the table between two councillors and put her hand into her pocket.

She withdrew something and slammed it onto the tabletop. When she removed her hand, two halves of a broken crystal rolled to a standstill.

"There is your crystal, Commander. That's all that's left. Take it! We've paid a high enough price for it!"

Carter's legs turned to rubber, and he collapsed back into his seat, shaking.

"*Take it!*" Kate screamed at him. Her eyes were wild, and she was on the verge of losing all control. Carter flinched and gripped the arms of his chair for support.

She gathered the pieces of crystal in her hand in one sweep and flung them at him. They hit him in the chest and bounced back onto the table. One rolled off the edge and dropped onto the floor tiles at his feet.

"Take it!"

Hawklight brushed past the sergeant, who was rooted to the spot, and gently took hold of Kate. The touch of his hands seemed to draw her back from the edge of hysteria, and she stood breathing heavily, glaring at the cowering commander.

One of the senior councillors at the far end of the table stood, knocking his seat backwards.

"Captain Hawklight! Captain Streikker! What is the meaning of this outrage?"

So Hawklight told him.

He introduced Marcus Zimmerman, whose only contribution to the proceedings was to add: "It's called Zimmermanite", apart from nodding in agreement with the events as Hawklight unfolded them. No one spoke, no one interrupted him as, one by one, heads turned in accusation towards Carter. His machinations to recover the crystal for himself were uncovered, and the consequences that had developed from the foiled plot caused gasps of dismay and shouts of outrage. When it was revealed how closely they'd come to falling under the tyrannical rule of another madman from Cherath, the Council members erupted in anger.

Carter found himself hemmed in on all sides. Streikker stepped in to restore order by placing Carter into the protective custody of the Sergeant-At-Arms who was mightily relieved to be following orders he could understand once again.

As Carter was being led away, Kate stepped in front of him. She had retrieved the twin halves of Varak's crystal and thrust them into one of the pockets of Carter's tunic. He couldn't meet her accusing stare and turned his head aside.

Kareem was waiting for her outside the Chamber doors. He gathered Kate in an embrace, and they stood locked together while the Council members filed out. Apparently, the day's proceedings had just been adjourned.

—〰—

The courtyard in the place Kate had known as home was overgrown, and the rooms had gathered a layer of dust that would never have had the chance to settle under Mirayam's stern routine. The house was deserted and echoed of the ghosts of Jaime and Sigrid. There would be ample time to mourn their loss in the coming months; also, to celebrate the time they'd shared together.

Kate was in no mood to sit by idly. The anguish and the heartache caused by Carter's ambitions continued to fuel her anger, and she needed an outlet to vent her feelings. She gathered together some cleaning gear and started in the attic, then worked her way down room-by-room, scrubbing, dusting, wiping and polishing. Kareem found some gardening tools in a small lean-to shed, then stripped to the waist and proceeded to restore some order and serenity to the fragrant gardens in the courtyard. Jackson and Mia had accompanied Hawklight to the city dungeons where the prisoners were housed.

The place had been restored to a semblance of order by the time the gate swung open, and Hawklight entered with Mirayam leaning on his arm for support. Behind them, Mia and Jackson were linked arm-in-arm with Olivia and Ethan.

Mirayam looked even frailer than usual, yet she retained a regal stature suggesting a woman of great presence, which accentuated the angular beauty of her features. Prison had weakened her, not withered her.

Olivia and Ethan hadn't fared much better. Both were pale and skinny. They had been kept apart in separate cells, but they had devised a method of communication that kept their spirits intact through mutual support. The left sleeve on Ethan's jacket had been pinned to its front; he still looked off balance with one arm missing, but if it affected him, he didn't show it. Both he and Olivia were laughing and chatting with Mia and Jackson, catching up on gossip.

Kate came running down the stairs and out through the door that opened onto the courtyard. She squealed with joy and threw her arms around Mirayam, then flung herself at her friends. She danced with delight.

"Welcome home! Oh, it's so good to be back!"

"My god, girlfriend, you look terrible. What have you been doing to yourself? Olivia commented in mock horror, and they all laughed. Prison had taken its toll, but so had the gruelling journey, Kate supposed. She hadn't stopped to look at herself in the mirror.

"I guess we're all going to need a good rest," she said. She turned to Mirayam. "We were worried about you. Your message saved us—" she glanced at Ethan and Olivia,—well, saved most of us. But as it turned out, Hans Streikker—he's okay. And as for him—" she slapped Hawklight playfully on the arm, "—we ought to have had more faith."

Mirayam studied the pure golden glow on Kate's arms and smiled.

"It's you we need to thank, Kate Gallagher." She linked her arm in Kate's, and guided her towards the seat beneath the overhanging tree that smelled so like citrus. "You know, the one thing I've questioned time and time again was the decision to have you brought here in the first place, knowing that I would deprive you of the chance of a life on Earth. I justified the action to myself, but I've never come to terms with it. But you're here now, and what you've managed to achieve to rid this world of evil has been nothing short of miraculous. Frankly, I'm in awe of you, and I count my blessings to number you among my friends."

The Council reconvened the following day, and this time, Mirayam sat at the head of the table. The Council had just passed judgement on Elward Carter, and he was being led away. Many of the councillors still bayed for his blood, wanting him to be imprisoned and the key thrown into the ravine. But Mirayam had pleaded mercy; she had pointed to his long and distinguished career in the service of the city-state as mitigating factors, prior to his downfall brought about by greed and the temptation of the crystal.

In the end, he had been banished, and was about to be escorted to the border and released, together with the promise that he would face a lengthy prison sentence if he ever set foot inside Hogarth again.

His fall from grace was complete, as was Mirayam's rise from the ashes of alleged treason. She had been nominated to fill the vacancy left by Carter, and none of the other councillors dared run against her.

Her students crowded into the cellar to eavesdrop on events as they unfolded. Kate had her ear pressed tight against one of the grilles at floor level to try and catch the muted conversations. When Mirayam's victory was announced, Jackson let out a muted *Yes!* and punched the air. Hawklight, who had taken up his usual position in the Chamber lounging against the far wall beside the cellar, coughed loudly and kicked the grille with the heel of his boot at the same time. The message was clear: *keep quiet down there!*

The students couldn't contain their excitement, and had to creep from the cellar via the storage elevator and out the stall gates enclosed by the outer wall. They hugged each other and leapt about screaming and laughing and hugging each other once again.

Under Mirayam's influence, the triumvirate alliance between the three city-states of Hogarth, Cherath and Hornshurst was reformed, and the process of renegotiating lengthy, intricate treaties was initiated. Ambassadors were dispatched, compromises were agreed upon, and the notion that a long-lasting peace was indeed possible spread throughout the territories.

It wasn't easy. Many were going to have to account for their actions, and feelings of bitterness and resentment towards former enemies were still raw. It was going to take some time, but time was what they had plenty of.

Kate celebrated her eighteenth birthday. She had lost all track of time, so the students picked a date from a hat—the anniversary of the day she arrived on Bexus—which was, in one sense, a birthday in its own right.

They sat around her in a circle, singing 'Happy Birthday' and waiting for her to blow out the candles on a cake she couldn't eat. While they sang, she was struck by how much she had changed over that short course in time.

She had woken, naked and confused, a frightened fifteen-year old girl, welcomed by a stranger and pursued by devil dogs, marked for special attention because of a unique golden aura she couldn't explain until she'd been reunited with her mother.

The qualities of the mother—the courage, the fierce devotion, the warrior, the peacemaker—had been passed down to the child. Yet the child had inherited others—rebellion, stubbornness, and innocence—that had set her apart.

It made her feel uneasy as if her destiny had been preordained somehow. She had created the rift with Hawklight, and it had been the need to redeem herself that had driven her to set out on the quest. Hawklight had needed her, and, without knowing, she had responded. The question remained: who decided how the pieces would fall?

She glanced at Kareem, whose voice was as rich in song as it was gentle with whispered secrets. His features were softened in the glow of eighteen candles—honey coloured and handsome. He grinned at her, and she smiled back at him. Nothing compared to him on Earth, nor on Bexus, for that matter. She had to admit he'd captivated her from the moment she'd set eyes on him, despite the fact he'd been intent on killing her. Hawklight had noticed her behaviour, and he'd been none too subtle about it. She'd tumbled into love and embarked on a new stage in her life.

Later that evening, she whispered to Kareem, "I want to visit Mum again. Can we do that?"

A soft, warm breeze rustled the leaves of the tree overhead. They were sitting on the seat in the courtyard, and she was nestled in his arms. He replied by kissing her lightly against her temple, where the line of her hair met her soft, golden skin.

"Besides, it's time I showed you around my part of the world," he said.

"We'll need to take a detour," she murmured. "There's a group of tiny forest dwellers I want you to meet first. I want to go back and say hello."

"Whatever you wish," he replied.

She stretched out along the seat and rested her head in his lap. He stroked her hair, and they sat together in comfortable silence. She stared up at the stars that blazed across the clear night sky until she drifted into sleep, soothed by the gentle caress of his fingertips.

ACKNOWLEDGEMENTS

Time to put the pen down, but as I do so, I have to reflect on why I picked it up to begin the trilogy in the first place. It came about when I was teaching at the International School of Ahafo in Ghana, and my students had decided that they wanted to investigate and experience the fantasy genre of writing. We made it possible for them to write their own novels, and self published two of them for the school's library. I nurtured a secret passion to do the same one day as the seeds of Kate Gallagher were already floating around my brain.

To say that I was impressed with their efforts is an understatement, and the thought crossed my mind: *If they can do it, why shouldn't I?* So, I did. Thanks, Alejandra and Reno for lighting the path for me. And don't give up the dreams yourselves. Both of you have talents you need to nurture.

To my sister, Jan Sintes, who did such a wonderful job proofing the second book: thanks for the repeated effort here. If any mistakes have crept through, I'd like to say, "Blame her!" although, of course, the ultimate responsibility for publication is mine—so I can't. Jan, when Peter Jackson eventually picks up the movie rights for the books, I'll shout you an all-expenses paid world trip, and will also see what I can do about tickets to the premier.

255

I know there is a hard core of supporters out there, who have done wonders on a local scale in helping to promote the books and encourage others to buy them. It suspiciously echoes the process adhered to by people who flog multi-level marketing products, and who rely on their family and friends to boost sales, but know that I am most grateful for the support you've shown me. You've grown too numerous to name in a few short sentences, but you know who you are, and I'll always be thankful to you for your unremitting support.

Thanks to the team at Trafford—primarily Shelly Edmunds and Sydney Felicio—who have helped in the endeavour to self-publish and promote all three titles. Once again, I would highly recommend this company to anyone who has only gathered rejection slips from publishers and agents, but who is willing to take the risk and pay the price to see their work in print.

I've saved the best till last. I will always be deeply indebted to my amazing wife, Sue Skye. She has an absolute belief in my ability as a writer and has been a constant rock of support throughout. She convinced me that we should buy our first word processor back in the days of floppy disks with 64K RAM. She immediately tossed the clunky Imperial typewriter into the trash, and I've never looked back since. You've been my partner in life, and I love you more than the Universe and all the spaces in between.

Alan Cumming
July 2013

For more information on this book and others in the series, visit online at: www.bexustrilogy.com